Under the Sun

Also by Lottie Moggach

Kiss Me First

Lottie Moggach

Under the Sun

PICADOR

First published 2017 by Picador
an imprint of Pan Macmillan
20 New Wharf Road, London N1 9RR
Associated companies throughout the world
www.panmacmillan.com

ISBN 978-1-5098-1552-4

1 3 5 7 9 8 6 4 2

A CIP catalogue record for this book is available from the British Library.

Printed and bound by CPI Group (UK) Ltd, Croydon, CR0 4YY

For my nieces, Lyra and Meri

Southern Spain, August 2008

From bed, Anna listened to her houseguests next door.

'Fuck, it's hot already,' Farah was saying. 'Did you manage to get online?'

Anna couldn't hear Kurt's reply, only a cough of water as a tap was turned on. She imagined him stooping at the sink in the corner of the guest room, the antique copper basin from Marrakesh that was too small to wash in comfortably.

'I don't know why they bother having a password here,' Farah continued, her patrician voice carrying clearly through the stud wall between the bedrooms. She was a human rights lawyer, used to projecting across international courtrooms. 'Do they think the geckos are going to steal their broadband?'

Again, Kurt's response was inaudible, but whatever he said provoked a gale of mirth so loud and theatrical Anna wondered whether Farah was, in fact, performing to be heard by her hostess. Anna had woken to find Michael's side of the bed empty, as was usual these days.

She hadn't made a sound herself – just lay on her back, hands on her chest, as neat and still as a recumbent effigy.

Farah recovered and Anna heard the guest bedroom latch lift. After a passage across the sitting room, muffled by kilim rugs, there came the heavy slam of the front door. Then, perfect silence.

Was Michael out there, sorting breakfast? Farah and Kurt were very much his friends, after all; mates from Oxford, close for twenty years. Nonetheless, she should get up and go out. But she felt pinned to the bed by the strength of reluctance she hadn't felt since childhood: profound, unequivocal, undiluted by reason. She thought of their neighbour Alfonso's old donkey the month before, being yanked onto a truck headed to the knacker's yard.

Couldn't she just lie here for two days, until Farah and Kurt – 'K', as Farah and Michael called him – returned to London? Or even longer, until this terrible, slow landslide of her life with Michael had finally come to a halt?

No one had opened the shutters in the sitting room. They fitted imperfectly and let in chinks of sunlight, fluorescently bright, as if a nuclear explosion had occurred outside. The smell of Kurt's cigarettes still hung in the air from the night before – there must have been twenty butts in the fireplace, although the couple had only arrived at 9pm – mingling unhappily with the trapped heat and a sour, jammy note from the unfinished glasses of red on the table.

Anna went to the front door. Nothing could be heard from outside: the outer walls of the finca, two hundred years old and two feet deep, were as effective at cancelling noise as the interior ones were feeble. She stalled, reluctant to leave this dim and undemanding place. On the wall beside the door, a collection of Michael's sketches hung from a piece of string, like washing on a line. Love tokens he'd drawn for her over breakfast, each a single image representing what lay ahead for her that day. Most of them dated from London – a book; a theatre curtain; an art opening; the pair of shoes he wanted her to wear when they met that evening. There was a handful from Spain, but they soon stopped. He said the images were getting too repetitive: the sun, a tomato, a glass of wine.

A couple of the sketches had fallen to the floor, and Anna picked them up and carefully re-pegged them. Next to the door was a mirror: she checked the dark shape of her reflection, features indistinguishable in the gloom. Then, finally, she pulled at the oak door and stepped out onto the over-lit, over-heated stage.

When her eyes had adjusted to the brightness, she saw the others breakfasting under the fig tree, as she'd expected. Only no Kurt, just Michael and Farah. They were sitting at opposite ends of the table and had pulled their chairs out of the shade to bask. Michael was sunk low and straight in his seat, arms folded over his chest, like someone dozing at the cricket; Farah's sturdy brown legs were braced against the table. Both had their eyes closed and were smiling, presumably at something one of them had just said.

The sight of Michael looking relaxed and happy was so rare and longed-for that Anna smiled, despite it being nothing to do with her. She walked over, crouched down beside him and stroked his forearm with a finger. He started, eyes flicked open.

'Morning,' she said.

He gave her the same quick smile he gave their builder.

'How are you?' she said.

'Yeah, OK,' he said, closing his eyes again. His good humour disappeared. I shouldn't have surprised him like that, she thought, miserably.

'Hiya,' said Farah, from the other end of the table.

'Where's Kurt?' asked Anna, although she knew the answer: from the bedroom she'd heard him talk about an email from a radio producer.

Farah gestured to behind the house. 'Up the hill, on the phone to *Today*. They want him down the line tomorrow.' She took her feet off the table and leaned forward to take a fig. 'Fuck, it's scorchio,' she said. 'I can't believe you guys don't have a pool. Isn't that the whole point of living here?'

This was, presumably, a rhetorical question, but when Michael said nothing Anna felt compelled to reply. Farah had this effect on her.

'We ran out of money, but we'll get round to it one day,' she said. 'Next summer maybe.' She looked at him. 'Won't we, Michael?'

'Yes,' he replied, eyes still closed.

Feeling marginally comforted, Anna poured herself some tepid coffee from a pink majolica jug. How come Farah was allowed to use a word like 'scorchio'? If she had said that, Michael would have winced.

'What's the difference between a finca and a cortijo, anyway?' Farah went on.

Again, Anna waited for Michael to reply, and when he didn't, she said, 'Well, they're sort of interchangeable, really. Both farmhouses with a bit of land. Cortijos are generally a bit posher.'

Farah didn't respond. Anna's may have been the correct answer, but it was neither funny nor clever.

Michael stirred.

'The people who have moved here from Notting Hill call them cortijos,' he said, 'and the people who moved here from Islington call them fincas.'

'. . . and the ones from Manchester call them haciendas,' said Farah.

Michael sniggered.

'Gideon would call it an ager,' he said.

Farah hooted.

Gideon was someone from their college who Anna had never met. She turned away from them and looked out over the valley. Even in her misery Anna could, abstractly, appreciate the beauty of the scene. The table had been positioned to make the most of the view: framed by fig trees, their glossy palm-shaped leaves straight out of Rousseau, through layers of tufty-bushed mountains to a tiny slash of golden sea. The sun was high and strong, and the light so pellucid that one could make out the details of tractors a dozen kilometres away; the window frames of the houses in the white villages that clung to the mountains like empty barnacles on a rock. There was no sign of movement: the valley seemed stupefied by the heat. The only activity came from the thick hum of bees at the nearby lavender bush.

The breakfast table, too, looked lovely. The ceramics were a mixture of colourful vintage pieces, flecked with indigos and pinks, and austere, peasant earthenware, no two the same. There was not a hint of plastic packaging anywhere; aesthetics were important to them both, and Anna made sure to decant the butter and milk as soon as they were out of the supermarket bag. Three figs sat on a saucer; there was a large plate decorated with slices of *jamón*, already curling in the heat, and thin wedges of sweating manchego. A dragonfly danced around a saucer of apricot jam. The slightly warped, bone-handled bread knife was dug into a huge round loaf that Anna had baked the afternoon before. Kurt's packet of B&H was the only sign of the times.

Sitting in the sun, in front of this view, peeling figs and shooting the breeze with brilliant friends: this was Michael's dream of living out here, she knew. And hers too, she supposed. Only, not like this.

It was just gone 10am. Many hot, unhappy hours lay ahead.

Anna looked over at her boyfriend, his face in profile as he talked to Farah. His head was freshly buzzed – he must have done it this morning, in one of his secret hours without her. Unlike most men with shaved heads, Michael didn't do it to pre-empt baldness, but for practical reasons: it was one less thing to think about so he could concentrate on his painting. An easy gesture to make when you had a face like his. He was half Israeli and his skin was now as rich and evenly brown as the crust on her loaf. When they were out in town he was often mistaken for a Spaniard, until he stood up and his height gave him away. On their trips he'd also been claimed as a local in Italy, Greece, Turkey, even Morocco – brazenly approached by women chatting him up in their mother tongue, pretending to mistake him for Zidane, completely unbothered that Anna was there beside him.

Before Michael, Anna had presumed that people with ravishing partners became inured to their looks over time, but three years down the line, she still didn't take his allure for granted. In fact, she'd become more conscious of it, and it pained her. When they first met, his beauty had seemed almost irrelevant; or rather, a glorious bonus to their extraordinary mental connection. In the fog of early love they'd felt parity on all things. When she'd asked him what it was like to be so attractive, he'd laughed and said, 'You first.'

But now, as that love was draining away – *why?* – his beauty had become a wall between them. She searched under that heavy brow to the dark wells of his eyes for clues; stared at his long nose in profile as he turned away from her. Once, his face was animated and engaged, accessible and responsive to hers; now it was as wary and remote as a celebrity's. Except when he was talking to his old mates, of course.

Just one proper smile, she thought. A squeeze of the knee. An arm casually slung over the back of her chair. A tiny gesture – the kind that, six months ago, was common and unremarkable. Now, just one would change everything. She would forgive him his coldness, his snobbery, his rudeness; she would put aside her hurt and anger at the cruelty of his about-turn. She wouldn't forget, but she would rip this chapter from their life together and never speak of it again, if they could go back to how they were. Because the consequences of this not working – practical, emotional – were too horrific, and, like the boiling frog in a saucepan, she felt incapable of getting out herself.

But there was no smile or squeeze. And of course Farah had noticed, slyly observing behind her shades, as she talked about how she and Kurt were considering an extension at the back of their Stockwell house. Had one of Anna's friends started talking of such a thing – not that many of them had a side return to convert – Michael would have no doubt found the subject suffocatingly bourgeois.

Anna had spent some time analysing Michael's friends and had eventually realized this: by virtue of going to Oxford they had earned an authority in which anything they said was acceptable. It wasn't that some subjects were permissible, and some not, as Anna had thought at the beginning. Rather, that they were allowed to talk inconsequentially or banally because they had already proved their intellectual worth, and everyone knew they were capable of much greater things, like a master pianist playing chopsticks.

Farah was doing her laugh again. Her legs were still braced on the table, giving Anna a good view of the soles of her large, dirty feet. Farah and Michael had had a brief thing at Oxford, before Farah had got together with Kurt, and it had never bothered Anna before, even when she examined photos of them at that time: stylish, mannered pictures that could have been taken in the 1950s rather than mid-nineties. A heavy-fringed Farah curled in an armchair, pulling the sexy bluestocking look in a kilt and brogues. An outrageously beautiful Michael lying back on his forearms on a lawn, looking off to one side, his hair a mess of stiff curls. Photos fit for their biographies; so different from the ill-lit, self-conscious snaps of Anna's lot at Dundee. Michael had said he hadn't really fancied Farah, had briefly mistaken friendship for something more, and Anna could believe it. To her, Farah seemed mannish, with her broad shoulders and defiant grey streaks in her coarse hair, and just generally unsubtle. So different was she from Anna that it seemed impossible anyone could find them both attractive.

Indeed, Anna had always taken it as a given that she, Anna, was better-looking. But now, out here, she wasn't so sure. Farah suited the summer; the sun made her sallow skin glow, and in her denim cut-offs and vest she seemed vivid and definite. Anna was wearing an austere, shapeless, expensive cotton smock that, with her delicate pale limbs, was meant to lend her an appealingly wispy, babe-in-the-woods quality. Instead, next to the strong meat of Farah, Anna felt slight and anaemic; so understated she barely existed.

Michael had once kneaded that slab of thigh braced against the table. Farah's fingers had run through those curls that Anna had never seen.

Anna reached over Michael for the bread knife; he didn't react or attempt to pass it. Suddenly she felt furious; she wanted to scream and upend the table, send the *jamón* flying into the bushes. Why should she be feeling like this, being ignored in her own fucking house by this awful woman and the man who was supposed to love her? Maybe she should do what Michael did when her mother and stepfather, their only other visitors, were here in the spring. Having been entirely silent throughout breakfast, he had, halfway through an admittedly tedious story from Janet about their journey through airline security, suddenly jumped up to announce he was going to look for eggs. Anna started to remind him that all their chickens had been killed by foxes three weeks before, but then realized and stopped herself. He hadn't returned for nearly an hour, by which time Anna and her mum and stepfather were sitting in silence, conversation long exhausted.

Afterwards, when they were alone, Michael explained, with real feeling, that he couldn't bear the provincial way her mother spoke.

'"I went into town for *a* coffee". "I need to pick up some *bits*". She used the word *smellies*, for fuck's sake,' he said, anguished. 'I just can't be around it, Anna. It makes me feel like I'm dying. You understand, don't you?'

And she had understood. But now, she was the one he couldn't bear.

'Oh, hello, he's back,' said Farah.

They all turned to see Kurt emerging from behind the house. The walk up the hill to get a signal had left its mark on him: his nose was pink and sweat darkened his T-shirt. For once, Anna was relieved to see him: at least his lack of interest in her didn't feel so personal.

'All set?' said Farah.

Kurt nodded, and took a cigarette from the pack on the table. 'Except – you'll like this – they wanted to have me up against Elijah House,' he said. 'I told them, "If you actually bother to read his book, you'll realize why that's a shit idea. We're in broad agreement on the salient points."'

'What subject will you be talking about?' said Anna.

'The politics of giving,' replied Kurt.

As Anna was thinking how to respond, Michael jumped up.

'Let's go for a walk,' he said. 'I want to show you two something.'

'Oh, Michael,' said Anna, before she could stop herself. 'Can't we go the other way? The nice walk?'

Michael stared at her with hawkish fury.

'They'll get it,' he said.

Anna and Michael hadn't seen the greenhouses at first; indeed, it was a good two weeks after they had moved into the finca that they spotted them. Anna was sure they hadn't been there when she first saw the place. Admittedly, she couldn't actually remember looking behind that particular hill – it was the least interesting bit of the land and her attention had been drawn towards the view, the almond grove, and the stone shell that was to be their home. But she must have done. She wouldn't have made such a big decision without thoroughly checking out the area, would she?

But the fact remained that during a walk in those early days, she and Michael had climbed a small hill beyond the almond grove and were shocked to discover a clutch of plastic greenhouses. They were some way off, but a blight nonetheless: they covered an area the size of a football pitch, supported by metal frames and the plastic tired and grubby, as if they had been there for years.

They were both stunned. Anna could still recall the sunken look on Michael's face as he gazed out over them, glinting in the sun.

It turned out that their solicitor hadn't picked up on a tiny point in the lease that stated a certain section of the valley had been allocated to plasticulture, intensive crop-growing. Anna had gone over the documentation, being vaguely proficient in Spanish, but had not noticed it either. They had had their first proper argument over it. Michael said she should have picked up on the clause; she ventured that maybe he should learn some Spanish so these sorts of things weren't always down to her.

In any case, there was, apparently, nothing they could do about it. After all, it wasn't their land. Alfonso, their neighbour, said it belonged to some Spanish businessman.

After the initial shock, Anna had tried to be breezy, for Michael's sake. 'Oh well, we don't have to actually see it,' she'd said. 'We'll forget it's there, soon enough.'

'*I* won't,' he had replied.

A week later, he had announced he was making the greenhouses the subject of a series of paintings: turning his gaze from the natural beauty in front of the house to the ugliness behind it. The fact that the sight had inspired him did not, however, detract from the fact that it was Anna's fault that he was having to tackle this subject in the first place.

Michael led the way up the hill, and they stopped at the top. Anna did not join them in gazing out over the view. Instead, she looked at her feet, and closed her ears as Michael explained the thinking behind his latest work, about how he wanted to explore the dichotomy between nature and man's desire for convenience and disregard for beauty.

Kurt started talking about EU subsidies. Anna closed her eyes and felt an intense longing to be back, alone, in her studio flat in London, even with its bi-fold bathroom door and wet rot.

Eventually, Michael said, 'OK, let's go the pretty way now, for Anna.'

He led them back through the almond grove and then into the valley, facing towards that slice of ocean. Michael walked ahead with Kurt, Farah a few metres behind. Just in case Farah felt compelled to hang back to walk with her, Anna pretended that her espadrille had slipped off.

'You go ahead!' she shouted. But of course Farah

was going ahead. She didn't even look round to see where Anna was. Michael did look, but didn't wait. Anna knew which was worse.

Anna watched Michael walking ahead, laughing with his friends. He was wearing a blue-and-red checked cotton shirt which he'd had for years; on one of their early dates, he had teamed it with a diamond-patterned yellow waistcoat, ostentatiously clashing.

Was that shirt the only thing that remained of the old Michael? Maybe he really was a stranger now, every atom of him replaced since three years ago, when they had first come across each other in a gallery in Bethnal Green. But she had been a different person then, too, hadn't she? That day she was wearing a backless top that showed the whole length of her bare spine, even though it was only an ordinary Tuesday afternoon.

Anna had been hired by the gallery to redesign their logo, and was in for a meeting with the owner. Michael was one of the gallery's artists, soon to have a show open there, and that day had been sitting on the floor, crossing things out on a piece of paper. Of course, Anna noticed his beauty, but there were a lot of beautiful men around in East London. What really struck her was his focus on that paper. She later discovered he was rewriting the press release for his show. She admired the fact he took his work so seriously. But back then, she admired everything about him.

The gallery owner was on the phone and showed no signs of hurrying the call. Anna stood by the front desk and watched Michael's profile as he scribbled away, ignoring the deer legs of the twenty-two-year-old gallery girls as they stepped around him, waving away offers of a chair, not realizing or caring that he was in the way.

As she looked at him, Anna thought: I want to be inside your head. In the three years since, she had never stopped yearning for access to what lay inside that narrow, perfectly shaped skull. Even at the beginning, when he was so responsive to and thrilled by her, she was aware that there were whole parts of his mind that were out of bounds to her. That was, of course, a large part of the attraction.

Back then, at the gallery, he had suddenly looked up at her, the only other person in the room who was silent and still, and smiled. And she had smiled back, holding his gaze. It so happened that this moment had come at a good time in her life: after years of house-shares and saving she had recently bought her tiny, lovely flat just within the bounds of Zone 2, she was getting interesting work, it was the start of spring, and she had been cycling around feeling like she had earned her place in this city of progress and opportunity. For the first time in her life, she felt naturally confident. Were it the year before – even the month before – she might have looked away from that direct stare and, when he had come over to talk to her, sabotaged the encounter, feigning indifference, unsure of how to deal with someone like him taking an interest.

At the time, though, it felt utterly inevitable. *Of course* he would smile at her, and of course she would smile back, and of course he would come over and start a conversation (asking her whether she knew the spelling of *verisimilitude*), and of course they would have gone to the dive bar on the corner and sat outside for four hours, barely touching their Leffe Blonde. They couldn't stop talking. That very first night she found herself telling him stuff she had never told a soul, and saying clever, funny things she didn't know she had in her until that moment. They kept bursting into laughter at nothing at all. Just laughing at the wonder of it. He took her hand and turned it over, touching her fingers, and then gazed at her from under that heavy brow, silent for a moment, and her heart turned over.

And he had been in awe of her, this elite man. How extraordinary was that? She was different to everyone he knew: *unspoiled* and *fresh*. He loved that she hadn't gone to Oxford, like his old friends, and that she wasn't part of the East London scene, like his recent ones. He was sick of art girls with their fashionable, borrowed opinions, who played hard to get but weren't worth the chase. He liked the fact she came from the Midlands, and admired her for coming to London to carve a life for herself. She was a self-starter, an autodidact (he didn't seem to count the fact she had degrees from Dundee and the RCA). He would talk for hours about art and abstract ideas and she would absorb it all. She wasn't merely a mute admirer, however: she had just enough knowledge to contribute the odd thought and to ask the right questions, and when she did he seemed genuinely interested in what she had to say. He listened to her – and it made her feel she'd never really been listened to before.

'You're true,' he'd told her, his hand on her cheek. She hadn't liked to ask exactly what he meant.

He had faults, of course, but they didn't seem like faults then – rather, part and parcel of his brilliance. He had very fixed ideas of what was worthy of his time and attention and when she introduced him to her friends and, much later, her family, his high-mindedness was indistinguishable from a complete lack of interest in their small, ordinary existences. Anna had felt awkward on their behalf, but it hadn't dimmed her love for him. After all, hadn't he recognized her specialness? He took her up a level. With other boyfriends, Anna had hidden her true self in order to fit in with them. From the start with Michael, she felt he had unearthed a new, superior self, one she hadn't known existed before.

Now, looking at Michael's long back as he walked ahead of her, Anna started again mentally raking over the past year, trying to pinpoint when and how things had changed. She felt she was searching a room for something lost, even though she had upturned it dozens of times before. How blithely unaware she had been! It couldn't have been before their move to Spain: he was the one who had suggested the move in the first place, who had declared he'd had enough of London and wanted to get back in touch with nature and truth, go somewhere out of reach.

Anna had actually taken some persuading. Despite

a decade in London, she still found the place exhilarating. She felt she had cornered off a little patch for herself in the city and the bulbs she had planted were beginning to blossom. But the life Michael was offering won her over. Moving to Spain, building a house together: it was as good as marriage. Better. She would have him all to herself, them against the world.

Decision made, she'd flown out to Spain alone to view potential properties – Michael had to stay in London to prepare for a show – and found the finca. She'd put in an offer on the spot. Michael had his own flat in Hackney but it couldn't be sold because his mum's company had a stake in it. So, it made sense for him to rent his place out and for Anna to sell hers, and use the money to buy their new home. It didn't really matter who sold what, then.

Did he suspect even then that they wouldn't last? She had to believe that he didn't. It was true that even before the move Michael had had moments of being withdrawn and non-communicative. But he was an artist, and artists were complicated; she had known that all along. So, when he had disappeared into himself, she had always given him the benefit of the doubt and left him be. That was what love was, wasn't it? She was doing everything she possibly could to please and support him, in a laid-back, non-smothering way. Back then, he had recognized her maturity about his moods and been grateful for it: when she excused him from attending her friends' weddings before he'd even asked, he had solemnly thanked her. Occasionally he would announce that he needed to be alone and would disappear for a few days, but then always come back and apologize and tell her he couldn't live without her. The unspoken deal between them, she felt, was that he could be occasionally difficult and she would understand, and he would worship her for it.

Then, Spain. Despite the inevitable cock-ups and frustrations and discomforts – the discovery of the greenhouses; nights spent shivering under piles of clothes in the unheated caravan; wrangling a crew of sardonic, evasive builders; tedious dealings with access rights and JCB licences – Anna had never been happier than during that first six months. The finca was a great act of creation, and she didn't even begrudge the stinging bills. What better use of her money than to pour it, quite literally, into their new home? Michael had seemed thrilled, too, taking endless photos of the finca and her. They would sit out with blankets and wine to watch the sun rise – or, rather, seep, as the light didn't seem to ascend as much as inch across the valley towards them, tinting each mountain it passed before anointing them in their blessed spot, as if the laws of nature had changed just for them.

But between then and now, as Anna's savings were being converted into septic tanks and concrete underlay and eyelet curtains, his feelings towards her had changed. There were no huge rows, nothing to grasp onto; but his disdain could be felt like a drop in temperature. Anna was reminded of her few one-night stands, in which the encounter had an invisible hinge. How, the morning after, everything that had initially aroused and delighted her was suddenly and irreversibly repulsive. This seemed to be an agonizingly drawn-out version.

The confusion and insecurity and anger leached her spirit, and she'd retreated back to her comfort zone of interiors, spending recklessly on unnecessary finishing touches to the house: an armchair covered in Josef Frank fabric that cost more per metre than her weekly London mortgage payment; a heavy oak table with grooves worn from the elbows of generations of almond farmers; a marble worktop for their outdoor kitchen, salvaged from an old pharmacy. If she bought the heirloom, the future might follow.

When he was in his studio she spent hours online, keeping abreast of the news and reading contemporary art websites, so she would have something interesting to say that evening. She knew he shuddered at trivial domestic details, and so spared him all of that, even though such mundanity took up much of her day: changing gas canisters, destroying hornet nests, having to take freezer bags to the supermarket so the milk didn't go off on the twenty-kilometre drive home, chasing up the company who delivered their water by lorry. Still, over dinner, during her carefully prepared takes on world news or humorous observations on their life in Spain, he would often look at her with glassy, unloving eyes, and either not respond or pick her up on something she said. She used to be teasing and glib, but uncertainty had squashed it out of her. She'd never been an intellectual, but she'd had the odd opinion, been capable of some insight, a fresh take on things, but now all that seemed as if it had been written in invisible ink, visible only under the glow of his regard.

Occasionally, after wine, she would confront him, explaining that she had her own issues with him, that he wasn't perfect, but that she compromised and gave him the benefit of the doubt. He'd hear her out, looking at her with that dark, sunken gaze, but offer no comfort. Instead, he'd shake his head, as if there was no point in trying to explain, or smile sadly, as if they both knew that she no longer had any power and her challenge was just a feeble pride exercise. And in the face of his implacability, her fury would again dissolve into confusion and self-doubt. It seemed biologically impossible that his love for her had just evaporated of its own accord. But what the hell had she done to cause it?

The person who knew the answer, but chose not to reveal it, had now reached the top of a ridge, his cabal in tow. Anna lagged behind, the heat and her misery weighing her down like armour. She watched Michael turn and look back at her, and then say something to the others, who also stopped. Anna felt grateful for this crumb of concern from him, and despised herself for it. She picked up pace until she was level with them. They were in mid-conversation.

'. . . It's like the Spanish version of Las Vegas,' Michael was saying. Anna knew he was talking about the vast working-class tourist resort that squatted on the coast, between them and the airport. From where they now stood, its glinting skyscrapers were just visible, surrounded by the seedlings of other buildings in mid-construction. Cranes lined the coastline like storks at a watering hole.

'We went there for a few days last summer, when we arrived,' continued Michael. 'I liked it a lot, actually.'

Anna didn't remember Michael liking it, exactly. He had spent much of the trip taking photos – of the mobility scooters lined up on the sea front; the puce-faced young men with their unholy breakfasts of a pint of Carling and an Oreo milkshake; pensioners sitting with their stout white calves submerged in fish tanks, poor fish nibbling the dead skin on their feet; a sign for 'cultural centre' in front of an abandoned, quarter-built building. Anna, hanging back as he adjusted his zoom, had felt embarrassed about his patronizing attitude to these people and their playground.

They had had a few nice moments, getting drunk on Sambuca and giggling as they watched barrel-shaped eighty-year-olds exercising unselfconsciously on the beach, but Anna didn't remember the jaunt as being fun. But then, the trip had come not long after a conversation between them in which they'd been talking about Michael's niece, whom he adored, and Anna had lightly suggested that maybe they too should have a baby. Michael had taken the comment as a joke – or pretended he thought it was, anyway – and replied, 'Dammit, we forgot to tell the builders to put in a hallway.' It took a moment for Anna to work out that he was referring to Cyril Connolly's 'pram in the hall', and then she'd laughed with him – an in-sync couple whose first priority was their work! – whilst privately resolving to try him again another time.

The thought had been very much on her mind that weekend at the resort, though, and she was painfully aware of how bad an advert for children the place was. They had stayed in a vast, half-empty hotel, with dusty windows and stained walls, and at breakfast had sat in silence, hungover and stricken, whilst overweight kids bellowed around them, squirting artificial cream on their breakfast cereal.

Michael continued, with feeling. 'At least it's honest. I much prefer it to that dump down there,' he said, gesturing down to Marea, a much smaller conurbation a few kilometres along the coast. 'This ghastly little genteel town, stuffed with retirees from the Home Counties. They live this entirely hermetic life, drinking themselves to death, but think they're better than the oiks down the road because they have tapas with their beer once a week. So fucking middle-of-the-road and timid and dreary, full of nobodies measuring out their lives in Irish coffees and the *Daily Mail.* I hate it.'

He looked over at Anna, for the first time that afternoon.

'Anna likes it, though,' he said.

'That's not fair!' cried Anna. 'I don't *like* it. I just said it wasn't so bad. The beach is quite nice, there are orange trees, some cobbled streets. It's not *hideous,* that's what I said.'

The accusation stung, although it wasn't untrue. Marea was OK. And she was more familiar with the place than Michael suspected. Since they arrived she had visited in secret to buy beauty products and get her legs waxed. Then, just the previous month, she had gone there to see a therapist who had advertised in the local paper. *Do you need to talk?* the advert asked, and that was exactly what Anna needed to do. She couldn't bring herself to tell her friends and family that things out here had turned so sour, and she needed one person in the world to know how she really felt. The therapist, a fifty-something woman called Caroline, was entirely silent during their hour together, offering no guidance or thoughts at all as Anna ranted and howled. But Anna didn't need any more: just someone to hold the bowl as she spewed out her hurt and anger and humiliation.

Now, Michael was pointing out the Strait of Gibraltar, and telling his friends about the bird migrations, how the raptors and storks used the rising air currents to soar across the Med at its narrowest point.

'It's meant to be amazing,' said Anna. 'We're going to go to watch it in September, aren't we? Down in Gibraltar.'

Michael didn't respond. Farah glanced at her with a quick, pitying smile.

Kurt started telling them about the ancient and ingenious irrigation system established by the Moors in this particular mountainous region of Spain.

'They revolutionized agriculture,' he said. 'And of course, water is an Islamic symbol of paradise.'

Anna pretended her espadrille had slipped off again as the others moved on.

*

When they arrived back at the house it was 3pm, and the heat was so fierce even Farah was subdued. It was decided not to bother with much lunch, in anticipation of the feast Anna had planned for the evening, and after a few slices of *jamón* straight from the fridge Farah and Kurt headed in for a siesta. Michael announced that he was going to paint and disappeared off to the barn. Anna was left in the outdoor kitchen, and the sheer pleasure of being alone temporarily soothed her misery. Her head empty, she sealed the beef and chopped the chorizo and unearthed the almonds she had harvested earlier that year; a hard-won and scanty haul, just enough for four bowls of soup. Geckos skittered on the wall beside her, catching their dinner. She was washing off the brine when the flow of water thinned. Someone else was using the supply. She turned off the tap and listened. There was the sound of the hose running. Michael was showering behind the barn.

Anna frowned. These alfresco washes had become a habit in the past two months – Michael had even relocated his toothbrush to a tin cup in the barn – and, although a seemingly trivial change in his behaviour, it bothered her hugely. The bathroom was the room in the finca she had worked hardest on, and of which she was most proud. One of the few things she felt confident in was her eye, her ability to make things look beautiful. It was why she went into graphic design and also, she suspected, one of the reasons Michael had fallen for her. When he had first stayed over in her studio, he'd told her it was the loveliest 500 square feet he'd ever slept in.

But the bathroom was more than just organic, understated good taste: it was a love token, inspired by a room in a sultan's palace Michael had admired during a trip to Istanbul, early in their relationship. More than anything else in the finca, she had created the space just for him.

The room itself wasn't large, just big enough for the vital furniture: a freestanding bath, wall-hanging cistern and sink, all vintage 1920s, plus a small armchair. There was a shuttered window and floating stone shelf holding a couple of paperbacks, an etching and a cup of wild flowers. The antique loo seat was a thing of austere beauty: square, treacle-coloured mahogany, like one in a medieval monastery.

So far, so lovely. But what made the space extraordinary was the tiling behind the bath – a five foot square panel of antique tiles, some Arabic in design, others majolica and Delft, all various vivid shades of blue. They didn't match, but that was the point: some were even broken, the grouting thick and obvious. The effect was glorious and unstudied, as if a sultan's courier had accidentally smashed a section of priceless tiling in his master's quarters and had quickly replaced it with whatever other blue tiles he could find to hand.

In Istanbul, Michael had said, 'that is my perfect room', and she had recreated it for him. Yet there he was outside, with his hose.

Keenly aware of how much he loathed domestic talk, she hadn't mentioned his new habit for a while.

Eventually she couldn't help it – carefully framed, of course, in a jokey tone.

'I drove all the way to Barcelona for that loo seat!' she had said, sliding her hand under his T-shirt to feel his ribs (even after three years, she found it impossible to be near him without touching). 'And had to endure a half-hour monologue from the guy in the antiques shop, about the *anciana* whose house it came from.'

She was seriously downplaying the effort involved. The seat had actually come from Madrid – and that was the least of it. There were the *World of Interiors* back issues. The Internet research into how to make antique seats fit modern pans. The hours – dozens of hours – on eBay, waiting to pounce on exactly the right tiles. Even collecting the tiles took some effort: remote houses in the valley such as theirs had their post delivered only as far as a service station on the main road, nearly ten uncomfortable kilometres away. They were not alerted when post was waiting for them, so she would drive there every day on the off-chance of a delivery. She had told Michael that she had come across a box of tiles abandoned by the roadside – half driven over, to explain the smashed ones. What an amazing find!

She also left out how much it all ended up costing: an eye-watering amount that she justified because Michael would love it so much, and they would appreciate it every day. Or so she had thought.

'You must use it, Michael!' she had said, in what she judged was the right tone: playful and archly overdramatic.

But she had got it wrong. Or he had taken it wrong. He jerked away, so her hand slipped from his shirt, and raised his eyebrows.

'I *must* use the bathroom?' he said, wilfully misinterpreting her. Surely he knew that she was using the imperative because that was how bold, assertive, exciting people spoke, and being emphatic was a sign of intimacy. She had spoken to him in a similar way in the past, she was sure: he *must* read *The Old Man and the Sea*; he *must* try the pesto from that deli in Farringdon.

But now he had twisted the whole thing to become ridiculous and strangely prurient, and made her out to be the kind of person he knew she was not, who had nothing better to do than notice how many times he visited the bathroom. A small-minded, controlling woman.

The memory of the incident, which was never mentioned again, made her insides clench. She put down the almonds and walked over to the barn. Michael was holding the hose above his head, eyes shut, wearing just his shorts. Not wanting to shock him she waited, watching him lasciviously, observing the muscles shifting under his skin as his hands moved the hose over his shoulders. How was it possible that Michael was almost forty – the same age as Kurt, with his widow's peak and podgy, tapering fingers?

Sensing another presence, Michael opened his eyes. He didn't look too surprised to see her. She smiled broadly, to make clear her intentions weren't hostile, and went over to him.

'Let me,' she said, taking the hose. Such was the

heat, his shoulders were already almost dry. Anna aimed the plume of water at his chest, and traced its passage with her finger, running from the hollow at his neck down to his concave stomach. Inching closer, so the water caught her dress, instantly drenching the thin cotton, she raised her right foot and slid her bare toes up and down his damp calf. The heat from the sun seemed to intensify and the sound of the insects grew louder. She looked up at him and he returned her gaze, unreadable. As always with Michael, her desire welled up: if he had touched her, she would have come in seconds. She would have fucked him right there, on the ground, in view of the house.

But instead he reached for the hose, turning it away from them, and gently disengaged himself from her grasp.

'It's OK,' he said, not unkindly. 'I have the right angle when I do it.'

But rather than continue with his wash, he walked over to turn off the tap. Anna remained standing where she was, looking down at the water pooling on the parched, resistant earth. Although the rejection wasn't unexpected, she still felt unable to absorb it. After a moment she looked up. Michael was standing ten feet away, still, his back to her. He could have walked back into the barn, but instead he turned.

'Why can't you speak?' he said, suddenly. 'Can't you say anything?'

'What do you mean?' Anna replied. 'I have been.' She lowered her voice, mindful of their guests in their room nearby. 'You know what it's like with those two.'

They had talked before about Farah's fondness for the sound of her own voice. It was accepted that that was how she was, loud and opinionated, and had bound them together in the past. But, it seemed, that observation could no longer be made.

'Farah's a good friend,' he said.

'I know!' cried Anna. 'I know she is. But you know what she's like.'

'You're scared of her because she's strong,' said Michael. Though shocked, Anna was grateful that he was finally engaging with her, even in this way.

'That's not fair!' said Anna. 'We're just different. We've always been different.'

When did he start wanting her to be more like Farah? Surely, the point of her was that she was *not* like Farah.

Michael shook his head and turned away.

'I've got to do some work,' he said.

Anna watched as he headed back towards the barn, and paused for a moment before ducking into the dark interior. As if he had briefly considered just carrying on walking, past the barn, through the almond grove and into the mountains, never to be seen again.

Finally, it was the evening, and they could start drinking. Although it was still warm and light Anna lit the fire, a pit over which they had placed an antique iron gate to act as a grate. Farah positioned herself at the edge of the table beside the rosemary bush, snapping off branches and throwing them onto the flames, the smell of the roasting herb filling the air. Anna, having refused Farah's offer of help, was in the kitchen, making more fuss than was needed over the food. They were having soup, stew, salad and a tart: she had already done all the hard work. She watched Michael's shoulder blades move under his T-shirt as he uncorked the red, that body that was no longer hers, and closed her eyes in shame at the thought of the moment with the hose.

Kurt was telling Michael about Twitter, a new social networking service.

'I can't see it rivalling Facebook,' he said. 'But it's not uninteresting in its potential as a self-promotional tool and news disseminator.'

'You must use it, Michael,' said Farah, with what was obviously the right sort of airy, emphatic tone for the phrase. She had changed into a white salwar kameez, as if to atone for her too-brief shorts during the day. Not, of course, that Farah would ever feel the need to atone for anything. 'For your work. Build the Michael Mizrahi brand.'

Anna, safe behind the kitchen counter, laughed at the joke. Michael, the least commercially minded person they knew!

But Michael appeared to be taking the proposition seriously.

'Yeah, maybe,' he said, nodding. 'I'll look into it.'

Anna sighed, and retreated back to the almond soup, as the others talked.

Michael and Farah had now moved on to something to do with economics. Northern Rock being returned to the private sector. Dow Jones industrial index. Indy Mac Bancorp going down. She didn't have a clue what they were on about.

After checking the seasoning, she poured the creamy, oil-flecked liquid into an earthenware bowl, and added some ice cubes and apple wafers. *Ajo blanco,* the speciality of the region. The almond grove was where she went each day to deposit her Pill, secretly dropped from her palm as she checked on their crop. The soil must be full of hormones – maybe the soup would be, too. Then, in her reverie, she heard her name, and looked up.

'What about you, Anna?'

From the table, Farah was smiling at her.

'Sorry?'

'Getting any work done?'

Now she asked? In all the evenings Anna had spent with Michael's friends in London, rarely had anyone shown interest in her work or treated her as if she was anything more than Michael's plus one. Back then it rankled, because she had something to say. Now, she didn't. Although the plan had been to establish a freelance graphic design business, and she'd had images of herself designing a new typeface whilst sitting underneath a wisteria-carpeted pergola, the truth was that the finca – and Michael – had been her full-time occupation, and she hadn't even begun to think about other work.

She opened her mouth to say something but the

words withered, and instead she just shook her head. Farah turned back to the table, and Anna looked down at the soup. She had a sudden, disquieting sense that all her past achievements no longer existed; if she opened the cupboard in which she'd stored them, she would find them turned to dust.

She brought the bowl over to the table and, although it was still not yet dark, decided to light the candles. Kurt was telling them how he was now refusing media invitations to opinionate on various topics of the day; although it was easy money, he didn't want to be seen as a hack. He started telling a story about an old university friend of theirs who wanted to be a novelist and had asked Kurt to read her manuscript. He didn't let the arrival of his bowl of soup interrupt his flow.

'I had a spare hour so I read the thing and of course it was dreadful, meretricious and middlebrow. A few weeks later we met at a launch and she asked, had I had a chance to read her novel? And I said yes, I had. And that was that, I went off to get a drink. Then, the next day, came this long email saying how upset she was that I hadn't said anything about her book, that I could have just lied and said that I liked it or found something nice to say about it, or lied and said I hadn't read it. Anything rather than making it so clear that I didn't think much of it.'

He put down his spoon, his voice rising.

'I had to explain to her: look, I didn't tell you what I thought because I didn't want to upset you but I am not going to lie to you, I am not going to say your book has merit when it's not true. I can't do that. My opinion *means* something, it's how I earn my living, you must understand that? Ask your mother if you want to be flattered.'

Farah had already finished her soup and now resumed snapping off bits of the rosemary bush and chucking them onto the fire. Couldn't she stop doing that?

'I can't believe Meredith ever got into Oxford,' Farah said. 'She was so dreary and third-rate. The kind of person who clings to the fact she's "nice" and "kind", and a good listener and loyal friend, as evidence that she's worthwhile. Always remembering birthdays, sends thank-you cards for dinner before you've even had time to clear up the dishes.'

'God, yes,' said Michael, 'those grand gestures of thoughtfulness. Something to hide behind because they either don't have the balls to say what they really think, or aren't capable of formulating anything original at all.'

He was looking at Farah as he spoke, but the words hit Anna hard. She had his family's birthdays marked in her diary. She sent handmade thank-you cards. But he was talking about this Meredith, right? Her boyfriend and his friends, sitting in the house she had built, eating the soup she had made, from almonds she had picked – of course they couldn't be talking about her?

The fact she had had a few glasses of wine emboldened her to speak.

'But maybe she doesn't have an opinion,' she said.

'You don't have to have an opinion on everything. What about doubt? An underated virtue. I think it should be celebrated.'

Anna was pleased with this: it felt like the kind of conversation the others would have: counterintuitive, abstract, provocative. But it fell flat. All Kurt said was, 'The most important thing is that people do their own thinking.'

'Niceness is often a front for having nothing to contribute,' Farah added, as if this was the last word on the subject.

God, she loathed these people. Michael cleared the empty bowls. No one had commented on the soup: all those almonds, grown and picked with such effort. Anna stood up and walked over to the kitchen with him, but Michael said nothing, keeping his attention trained on Farah and Kurt. He fetched another bottle of wine and sat back down. Anna dished up the beef and chorizo stew. Over the valley, the sun was finally sinking, staining the mountains peach. The air was still sultry but a cooler breeze blew. The tree frogs had begun their non-stop evening chatter; no worry about one of *them* being left out.

As they ate Farah talked about the dissident's case she was working on and then, as was her habit, abruptly changed the subject.

'Listen, I can't come to Spain and not swim. Can't we go down to the coast tomorrow?'

'I have to work,' said Michael. 'I can drive you at tea time, but not before.'

'Why doesn't Anna take us?' said Farah.

Anna shuddered at the prospect of those bumpy hours in the car with them before remembering that it wouldn't be possible at all. She opened her mouth to make an excuse as to why she couldn't take them: but Michael got there first.

'Well, Anna can't, you see, because . . .'

'Michael!' said Anna, cutting him off, aghast.

Michael looked at her, challengingly, but didn't continue.

For the rest of dinner Anna didn't speak, and didn't care if her silence was noticed. As soon as she had finished her stew, Farah started breaking off the rosemary bush again, and Anna felt the anger growing until she opened her mouth to stop her. Just in time, Michael suggested that they take their tart indoors, so they could listen to some music. He put on some of his ghastly, alienating jazz and sat on the Josef Frank chair; the other two took a sofa each. Anna lit an unnecessary fire and then positioned herself on the floor between Michael's legs, leaning on his thighs, which had as much emotional connection as a cushion, and less comfort.

She closed her eyes and half-listened as the old friends talked – about books and American politics and Kurt's work and old friends – and her absence from the conversation remained unremarked-upon. Once or twice she thought of saying something but simply didn't have the energy and sat there, slumped.

Eventually, she miserably raised her head, flushed by the fire, heavy with wine, and announced she was turning in. She got to her feet, leaned over to kiss

Michael, and went into the bedroom, where she lay fully clothed on the bed. She heard the burr of their conversation, Farah's laughter passing easily through the paper-thin walls. It went over her head, as she drifted in and out of sleep. The cistern groaned once or twice.

Then she heard Farah say, quite clearly, 'She's sweet, but I can't pretend I'm interested in anything she has to say.'

Immediately, Anna was alert, senses tingling. They weren't talking about her, surely? It was Meredith again?

Someone – Michael? – said something, at length. Anna couldn't quite make it out.

Farah again. 'I'm not sure what she brings to the table.'

Anna closed her eyes. And then, with some effort, she sat up in bed and shouted at the wall, as loud as she could muster:

'I bought the fucking table!'

1

Southern Spain, December 2009

Not everyone in Marea went home for Christmas. Of Anna's customers from the bar, Mattie had no ties left in the UK. Richard went back only to buy used mobility scooters which he shipped over and resold at the big resorts down the coast. Graeme vowed, publicly and repeatedly, he would only leave Spain in a box.

And there was the modest legion of old troupers who clung on year-round, couples who had been together so long they had morphed into the same size and who spent their days circuiting the promenade, holding hands as if plugged into a power source. When David and Rose, who lived in the building along from Anna, heard that she would be alone they timidly asked if she'd like to join them for Christmas lunch.

'We're sure you've got something far better to do,' said Rose, looking at David as she spoke, 'but we thought, just in case . . .'

'You're very kind,' said Anna, meaning it, 'but I've got plans.' She didn't add that these involved a box set of *Lost,* some fresh sardines and, her present to herself, two bottles of good verdejo. Eight euros a bottle was an extravagance, but she justified it: decent wine was necessary to soften the experience of spending three days in her apartment. A former holiday let above the bar that had been included in the sale by the tearfully grateful vendor, it was a desultory space, even by the standards of its previous existence. No one, Anna felt certain, had ever walked in and said anything more fulsome than 'Well, looks clean enough.' The living room was three metres wide and meanly furnished, with a dining table for four and a faux-leather sofa for two. The walls were stucco and the floor tiled in the bloodied peach colour that was the Spanish builders' equivalent of magnolia. On one wall was a small window overlooking the square, grilled despite being a storey above the ground; on the other a *Breakfast at Tiffany's* poster, which seemed to be de rigueur in Spanish holiday lets. Anna imagined a warehouse somewhere full of surplus stock: thousands of Holly Golightlys twinkling in the gloom.

Anna had done little to make the place personal or homely, but there were now a couple of Christmas cards propped up on the table, both from customers at the bar advertising their small businesses. One was from Mattie, a handmade effort: a photocopied picture of herself in a sexy Santa outfit, brandishing a duster, with the strapline *Keep it clean this Christmas!* The other was from Karen and Tommy, who ran both a local estate agency and a minicab business. The image was an awkward amalgamation of these two services: a drawing of a villa, with a reindeer relaxing on a lilo in the pool whilst a cab waited for him outside. Karen had signed the card from both of them, in girlish, barely joined-up writing, and added a note: 'Thank you, Anna, we value your custom.' Anna imagined Tommy beside his wife at the kitchen table, wincing inwardly as she wrote.

Tommy and Karen were spending Christmas with their daughter in Hampshire. He had texted Anna that morning to say Happy Christmas, accompanied by three exclamation marks and a dozen kisses. She imagined him excusing himself from the family festivities and sloping off to the loo to send it.

The sole object of beauty in the apartment was the Josef Frank armchair that Anna had squeezed into the taxi, along with a few bags of clothes, on that final journey down from the mountains. When she wasn't downstairs at the bar she was curled into the chair; she'd even taken to sleeping in it, rather than the hard, small double bed in the back.

Mid-morning on the 25th, Anna was getting into viewing position, laptop balanced on the arm of the chair, when she heard the ping of a text. Her friend Jess. *Merry Christmas doll! So jealous of you in the sun. Look what we've been reduced to . . .* The text appeared to refer to a photo attachment that, mercifully, hadn't come through. It would, Anna was sure, show Jess and Tim and their son Jack in an ironic novelty festive pose: all wearing matching woolly hats and pretending to shiver. Maybe even some tinsel tied around the bump of number two.

She and Jess had been so tight, once, back in London. Then Anna had met Michael and been subsumed into him, and Jess had started seeing Tim, that guy she wasn't entirely sure about, and the rails their lives had been running along, once so close they were touching, started veering apart. Jess had put an end to her ambivalence by accidentally getting pregnant. Then Michael had left, and Tim had turned out to be Superdad. Even if Anna was still in London, she felt, she and Jess would be living in different countries.

Jess was the only person Anna had told anything near the full story of what happened up at the finca. Anna had gone back to the UK for Christmas the previous year and visited Jess at her and Tim's new place in Walthamstow. Jess had expressed her shock and disbelief and said the right kind of things – Michael had taken leave of his senses; Anna was the best thing that had happened to him; he'd come crawling back. But her response had an impersonal, stock quality to it. When Anna had asked Jess about her life, Jess had dismissively claimed she had nothing to say, she was so boring these days, but her actions betrayed her. As her friend spoke, Anna watched her steal glances at Jack flicking through a book on the floor, and smile when he crawled over to place a proprietorial little hand on her leg. Ultimately, Jess couldn't conceal the fact that now she was the one distracted by a love affair too intense and extraordinary for words.

And now, all those years of intimacy and connection had reduced to fortnightly texts, postcards of little lies that were never challenged. Or, rather, one big lie: that

325 days of sunshine a year were a substitute for meaningful relationships.

Feliz Navidad! Anna texted back. *Gorgeous here. Give Jack a tickle from me xxx*

It was nearly 1pm UK time. Anna thought, vaguely, of those back home gearing up to lunch – a millions-strong army of strained Brits, sluicing the potatoes in their tray of goose fat, frowning at the still-pale mound of turkey, suppressing annoyance at their relations. This time last year, she'd been one of them, spending the day with her mother and stepfather, and it had been awful. It wasn't long after Michael had left and, as they laid the table, Anna had asked her mother for a loan so that she could get back to London before selling the finca. Before she'd even finished her proposal, her stepfather Bill had barrelled in from the conservatory and told Anna how they couldn't possibly spare anything. As buy-to-let landlords, they were up shit creek, too. Didn't Anna know what was going on?

Yes, Anna knew. A week after Michael bailed out, she'd sat in a bar in town and stared at the muted TV footage of the Lehman Brothers employees with their boxes. Through her film of misery, the news had come as no surprise. The world was falling apart? Of course it was. And she'd felt it herself, in Spain, when the estate agent told her that she had little chance of selling in the foreseeable future. But she was still put out that this incomprehensible, faraway event had so quickly sealed off her only escape route – and that her mother offered no resistance to Bill, even though that had always been her way.

Point made, Bill had pressed it home by spending the entire lunch talking about interest rates and negative equity. Whenever Anna started to say something, her mother had nervily interrupted to remark on what the dog was doing.

When they were alone again, over the washing up, Janet had apologized to Anna for not being able to help. 'Maybe you could use the money Grandma left you?' she'd added, and Anna had said nothing, too upset to admit that that quite substantial inheritance had been ploughed into the finca, too.

Wasn't Anna lucky to be spared all that now? She fired up the DVD of *Lost*, watched one episode, cooked her sardines, and then ploughed through another two. She was down to the last heel of a bottle and picking the soft fish bones out of her teeth, when the Skype icon started hopping on her laptop screen. Marie-Anne.

Anna was minded to ignore it, but knew her half-sister would keep calling and calling, unable to countenance the fact that Anna was at her computer but not answering. She pressed pause on the DVD and fixed on a smile to accept the call. Marie-Anne, her husband and their two daughters appeared on the screen, squashed together on a sofa. Anna angled the laptop so that the camera picked up the fabric of the chair rather than the porridge-coloured wall behind it.

'Happy Christmas!' they shouted.

Marie-Anne was wearing a red velour slanket. Despite – or because of – her very grown-up job as a headhunter, Marie-Anne felt strongly about the importance of relaxing at home. Marie-Anne and Steve had a relationship unfathomable to Anna, in which mystique and sex appeal didn't seem to feature at all. They openly discussed bowel movements; plucked each other's grey hairs; bickered over the pick and mix at cinemas.

'We've got a present for you, Auntie,' said her oldest niece, with a sly smile. She waved to someone off-camera.

A figure loomed into the screen, at first too close to identify: just a reddened neck and a chain. Then, it stepped back and a head of greasy grey curls came into focus.

'Surprise!' said Marie-Anne. 'Derek, sit back here.'

She reached up to pull the man back onto the sofa, sandwiched between her and Steve.

'Dad!' said Anna. 'I didn't know you'd be there.'

'Neither did we,' said Marie-Anne, tartly. 'Did we, Dad?'

'Where's Elsbeth?' asked Anna.

'Back in Copenhagen, I believe,' said her father. 'Eating open sandwiches and telling her friends why they must never marry an Englishman.'

'She's left?'

'Yep,' said Derek. 'Yesterday. Opened the last door of her advent calendar and it said, "dump the useless bastard".'

'Oh God, really? For good?' said Anna, but couldn't muster surprise, either that her dad's third wife had finally tired of him or that he had already converted it into a glib anecdote. Or that he'd turned up at Marie-Anne's, unannounced; he'd pulled a similar trick when his previous relationship ended, knocking on Anna's door with a bag, disguising his need for shelter as an act of spontaneous fatherly love. Surprise!

'She'd already talked to lawyers about money and everything,' said Derek. He started detailing the proposed financial settlement, his offence at Elsbeth offering him a studio flat in Manchester. From Marie-Anne's expression, Anna guessed that he had already discussed this subject at length. Her half-sister found it impossible to dissemble, nor would it ever cross her mind that she should do so.

Anna noticed that Derek's feet were squashed into too-small towelling slippers, rather than the pointy-toed boots he saw as his trademark, and imagined his grimace as his daughter asked him to take off his shoes at the front door.

'You and me both, eh,' Derek said.

'What?' said Anna, who had tuned out.

'Ditched! By that horrible fella. All for the best, eh?'

'Er, yeah,' said Anna. She hadn't spoken to Derek since the break-up; he'd never even met Michael. Marie-Anne must have filled him in. Her half-sister had been unbeguiled by Michael, from his conversation to his clothes; 'That stupid big scarf, like a boa constrictor.'

'How was lunch?' Anna said, to change the subject.

'Grand,' he said. 'Big old bird and some sort of fishy thing . . .'

'Mackerel pâté,' interrupted Marie-Anne. 'We usually have salmon, but this year we had to cut back, what with everything . . .'

'. . . And Steve took admirable charge of the

decanter,' said Derek. Anna noticed his knee jiggling. 'Made sure we didn't get squiffy.'

He winked and nudged his son-in-law, too hard. Steve smiled thinly.

'So, how's the *vida loca*?' Derek continued.

'Oh, wonderful,' said Anna, going onto autopilot. 'As ever. I love it here.'

'Cheap, is it?'

'Yeah, really cheap. You can have a great quality of life.'

'Had your grapes yet?'

'What?' Was this an uncharacteristically coy reference to wine?

'No, that's at New Year, isn't it,' he went on. 'You eat grapes as the clock chimes, stuffing them in, no time to swallow. I did it once in Ibiza, with Julia. She looked like a hamster come midnight.'

'Yeah, grapes are for New Year. Today I'm having dinner with a bunch of friends,' said Anna, then added, gratuitously, 'down on the beach.'

Marie-Anne frowned.

'In December?'

'It's boiling,' said Anna. 'Well, not *boiling* but, you know, T-shirt weather. There's a guy here, Paco, who lives on the beach all year round . . .'

'Oh yes, the old boy who discovered the shipwreck when he was a lad and makes paella,' said Marie-Anne, annoyed. 'You've told us.'

'Christmas dinner on the beach!' said Derek, closing his eyes in mock ecstasy. 'Stop it! You're making me want to go back to Bali!'

Anna saw Marie-Anne twitch with disgust. Derek had spent the first two decades of his daughters' lives AWOL in Bali, dropping unapologetically back on the scene when his luck ran out there.

'Go back there, then,' Marie-Anne said.

'You'll be in the bar, will you? For New Year's?' continued Derek, oblivious.

'Course,' said Anna. 'Biggest night of the year.'

By the time they hung up, Anna wished she'd ignored the call. She felt grateful Derek was there to deflect Marie-Anne's more penetrating questions about what the hell Anna was doing with her life, but the news of his break-up had lowered her, flattening a section of the fencing she had erected around herself, and unwanted thoughts began to seep in.

This was especially dangerous on the one day of the year when she could confidently picture what Michael was doing. She had spent the first Christmas Day of their relationship with him at his mother's house in Highgate, a free-form, afternoon-long lunch in their basement kitchen with his imperious mother, actress sister and writer brother, and various stylish cousins and grand family friends up from Dorset. Michael claimed they loved her, although Anna hadn't got that impression. They all had high, uncompromising conversational standards, and although they gave her a chance, asking her questions and inviting her opinion, by the time the goose came out Anna felt keenly aware that she had failed the audition to be a person of interest to them. She felt gauche, as if she kept on breaking invisible rules and being too eager to please, asking his mother for the recipe of her spinach and burrata tart and trying to engage the insouciant sister in a conversation about the themes of the Royal Court play she was appearing in ('Hey, do you mind if we don't? It's my day off'). Still, her failure to crack their code hadn't mattered, because Michael hadn't seemed to notice, and, under the table, his hand had barely left the top of her thigh.

Was there a new Anna there now beside him – fetching, flushed, near mute, thrilled to be the audience for this gilded, glamorous clan? Destined for the same fate, another three-year cycle? Or, far worse, had the new one been accepted? *That's her,* the mother would be saying to him, sotto voce, as she ground cardamom seeds for the coffee. *It took you a while, Bobo, but you got there.*

Anna fetched another bottle from the windowless galley kitchen, which now reeked of sardines. It was the hinge of the afternoon; the light had shifted, and the ridges of the textured paint cast tiny shadows on the walls. In the square, church bells rang three times. As usual at these moments, Anna's anger with Michael was quickly subsumed by mourning for the life that didn't happen, and self-pity for the one she appeared to be inhabiting. She curled herself up tight in the chair, hiding her face in the arm, like a Pompeii victim, wincing as she heard the laptop slip off the chair arm onto the tiled floor. The muted chattering from the square outside seemed to increase in volume, until it was so loud that people might as well be promenading around her own sitting room.

In a sudden movement, she straightened up. She'd been here before, and knew what she had to do.

Come on. Up. Out.

She drained her glass, stood up unsteadily, and set about finding her shoes.

Anna lived on Marea's old square, which abutted a promenade overlooking one of the town's several photogenic coves, and within thirty seconds of locking her door she was facing the Med.

She'd never really understood the spiritual allure of the ocean, especially the stretch that bordered Marea. In contrast to the coursing, mutable Thames, throwing up fragments of human history with every tide, the water here seemed to her just a vast, placid pond, every interesting creature within it long since fished out. But the salty air had its uses. Reaching the handrail of the promenade, she leaned forward towards the sea, its steel blue surface like a hurriedly ironed sheet, and breathed deeply, drawing in the minerals and expelling the booze from her system. After a few minutes of dizziness she felt – not sober, no, but revived. Back on track.

Anna wasn't the only one out; the square and promenade milled with Brits and locals on postprandial turns. She hadn't been exaggerating to people back home about the warmth. There was a slight breeze but it was definitely clement, and the unclouded sky and egg-yolk sun seemed to be preparing themselves for the high season. Amongst the Brits, jumpers had been tied around waists; sunglasses put on. Above her head, planes cut through the blue, descending towards the airport; even on Christmas Day, there was regular traffic. The palm trees lining the promenade welcomed the new arrivals, their balled fronds outstretched like stilled cheerleaders. Muzak Christmas carols issued from a speaker somewhere in the square, joined by a tinkly tune from the coin-operated train ride stationed on the promenade; the train was dutifully rocking back and forth, a local child onboard, having a Christmas treat.

A man strolling past with his wife bellowed 'Happy Christmas, lass!' to Anna, and she smiled and waved back. Someone from the urbanization; she couldn't remember his name. They blurred together, these British male retirees, with their ice-white hair and pink, amiable faces. The difference between the Brits and locals was most pronounced on high days like this, she thought: the expat couples in their fleeces, near silent, long past the need to impress, and the Spanish families in Sunday best, their fast chatter bouncing off the tiled surfaces of the square. And of course, with the Spanish came kids. Practically all the expats left were over fifty; the young families, dependent on work, were the first to flee back to the UK when the economy crashed. Out here, Anna was considered young; a babe.

Amongst the Spanish, Anna spotted the woman who worked at the You Chic gift shop opposite the bar. The woman was now wearing a suit and a little hat, like someone from the 1940s, and laughing with an older man – barely recognizable from the beleaguered-looking person who emerged from the shop each morning to hang up dusty novelty T-shirts and watermelon-shaped handbags, and who rarely responded to Anna's greeting.

A quartet of pensioners sat around the fountain in the centre of the square – more a sculpture now, really, as water hadn't flowed from it for a year, since drought was officially declared and the council banned unnecessary water use. A flock of tiny birds permanently hopped around its base, ever hopeful it might restart. Anna watched as one man crumbled a biscuit to feed to them. Then, the birds scattered and a flurry of barking heralded the arrival of half a dozen mongrels straining on their leads, and, dragged behind them, a middle-aged English woman. The woman had harshly henna-ed hair and was wearing a poncho that was too warm for the weather. This, Anna knew, was Caz, an eccentric who rescued dogs abandoned by expat owners who had fled back to the UK. Caz and the dogs took a daily turn around the square, and occasionally she'd stop by Anna's bar, sipping a red wine and lemonade in silence, resolutely unclubbable and resistant to the laboured jocularity of the other expats around her, as if engagement with humans would somehow detract from her mission.

Now, Anna watched Caz step onto the terrace of her rival bar, Sweeney's, and sit at a table, the dogs sinking to the ground at her feet. Most of the establishments in the square were shuttered up today, including Anna's, but Sweeney was joylessly hardworking. She watched him now bring out meals to a couple on his terrace, holding the plates with a dishcloth and depositing them with the briefest of smiles, before dropping a laminated menu on Caz's table.

Maybe Anna should have opened today: she'd have sold a few Irish coffees to this crowd. She supposed it wasn't too late – it was simply a matter of walking across to her bar, lifting the shutters, warming up the coffee machine. But she remained where she was, leaning against the railings, looking around.

Down on the beach below her, a small band of metal detectorists were combing the sand. Anna identified one of the figures as Graeme, a regular, who had a stiff knee. The men reminded Anna of a pack of ageing wild animals on a hunt – sticking together for efficiency and safety, but essentially, each working for himself. Whoever happened upon that hoard of Armada gold would not be sharing it out. Along from Anna, an elderly couple had also stopped at the railings to watch. The woman glanced over at Anna and smiled guilelessly, as if to say, 'Well, how about this, then!' as if they had happened upon a shoot for the new Bond film, rather than four pensioners inching along the sand.

Often, Marea's perpetual Sunday atmosphere made Anna feel as if she was at a dead stop, trapped in resin that was slowly hardening around her, sealing her off from the things that made existence worthwhile: history, progress, culture, wit, conversation, nuance. But on occasion, out of nowhere, she was ambushed by a strong, exhilarating sense of inhabiting the present. She smiled back at the woman, then closed her eyes and lifted her face to let the sun's weak heat soak through her lids. Maybe Jess wasn't being sincere when she said she wished she were here, but lots of others did yearn for exactly this. Look at all those planes. All those series of *A Place in the Sun*.

She knew by now that this feeling shouldn't be trusted: after all, it was a similar state of mind that had led to her buying the bar. She had stood close to this spot, intoxicated, feeling not unpleasantly marooned, and had noticed a *Se Vende* sign on the little bar across the square, citing an extremely modest figure that was almost exactly what she had left in her savings. The sun and booze fuzzed her discernment, and masked her other reasons for staying in Marea.

She wasn't going to think about all that. The verdejo had now settled in a sweet spot: she felt energized and invulnerable. She looked towards the ocean. The spume lapped the sand as gently as champagne froth. Maybe she should go for a swim. That would be a stylish thing to do, wouldn't it, to jump into the sea on Christmas Day? She didn't have her stuff with her, of course, but she could go in in her underwear. Give the promenaders something to look at.

Yes, she thought, that's exactly what she'd do. Plunge into the bracing, briny ocean. Commune with the elements. Maybe she'd start swimming every day. To her shame, she'd only been in the sea once since moving to the town.

Buoyed by the plan, she started down the beach steps, taking them two at a time. The African hawkers were stationed halfway down as ever, their Louis Vuitton knock-offs laid out on blankets, ready to be scooped up if the police came along, but they seemed to be taking the day off from the hard sell and didn't call out to her as she passed. Further down was a trio of Spanish youths, smoking; she was hit by the smell of weed as she passed.

Down on the beach, Anna pulled off her shoes and headed for the water, but by the time she got there, her enthusiasm had waned. Undressing, getting in, the chilly water clamping her legs, then her waist . . . getting out, getting dry . . . it all suddenly seemed far too much effort. She stalled by the water's edge, her toes scratching at the damp sand. What now?

She looked around, at the neat pile of banana boats and the ranks of thatched beach umbrellas, patiently waiting for the season to start. The jumble of apartments and hotels behind the beach, like a load of boxes in a shoe shop's storeroom. The scene had barely changed in thirty years, she knew; she'd seen pictures. Even the typeface on the signs was the same. Marea didn't update for the sake of it.

The detectorists had moved on, and she was now the only one on the beach. No, wait. By the rocks at the far end, by the blue wooden fishing boat, was a man tending something on a fire. Paco! The famous Paco, who lived on the beach, crouched over his paella, even on Christmas Day.

She realized she had never actually talked to Paco, the celebrity of Marea, the old man of the sea whose image adorned postcards. How could this be? Now was the time to make his acquaintance. She started off down the beach towards him, breaking into a run in her eagerness, enjoying the unexpected exercise. As she neared him, she saw that the receptacle Paco was tending was not the vast, thirty-tourist paella dish he used in the summer – of course it wouldn't be – but a modest grill, on which he was roasting sardines. The old man had paused in his cooking and was watching Anna run towards him, his expression unreadable. She came to a halt and beamed at him.

He must have been pushing seventy but was a good advert for a life on the sand: grizzled but barely withered, with a shiny, speckled bald head and an upper body dense with muscle. His white vest was luminous against his brown-black skin, the grey hairs on his chest exposed.

'*Feliz Navidad!*' she said. After a moment he nodded and returned the greeting, his voice raspy.

'I had sardines too,' she continued, in Spanish, pointing at the fire.

He squinted at her. '*Que?*'

Anna started to repeat herself but, suddenly, felt foolish. Giving him a quick smile, she raised a hand in farewell, and turned back up the beach.

Paco said something else that she didn't catch. She turned back and he repeated it, this time pointing to the fish on the grill, and she understood that he was asking her to join him. She shook her head and smiled and talked fast, using English words he probably couldn't understand, to try and cover up her lack of real excuse.

'*Muchas gracias, señor,*' she said finally, putting her

hands in a prayer position, before turning and heading back.

Imagine, Anna thought, as she made her way to the steps, if that was the sole triumph of your life. One swim as a thirteen-year-old and the chance discovery of a wreck that became your town's tourist attraction. It was the only notable thing Paco had ever done – well, so she imagined – and he had capitalized on it, buying his paella dish and getting into the guidebooks and managing to eke a lifetime's living out of it. A modest, unassuming life, but probably no less fulfilled than that of a movie star or an explorer.

Nearing the top of the steps, she had an idea. Why not? It was Christmas, after all. She sprang up the last few steps and back across the square to the bar and, keeping up the pace, up to her apartment, where she grabbed a screwed-up bunch of notes that she had left on the kitchen counter. Around thirty euros in total, change from a cash-and-carry trip. Then she hurried back down to the beach. This time, the Africans and Spanish youths watched her as she flew down the stairs and hit the sand, speeding back towards Paco. Breathing heavily, she reached the old man. He now had the sardines on a plate, ready to eat, holding a bottle of hot sauce as he stared at her.

'Here, for you,' she said, thrusting the pebble of cash into his hands.

Paco looked at the money, and then back up at her, dark eyes narrowed. Then he took her hand with one of his and placed it over his heart. Her fingers pressed against his bed of chest hair, as stiff as nylon.

'*Gracias,*' he said, with deep solemnity. '*Muchas gracias.*'

'No problem,' she said. He released her hand and she smiled, embarrassed, before turning to head back up the beach towards home.

As she reached her apartment, Anna remembered the verdejo had run out, and ducked into the bar for more supplies. The place was a sight. She hadn't cleaned up since the last time she'd had customers in, three days before Christmas, when the expats had gathered to watch the Spanish national lottery on TV. They'd all entered as a group, with a single ticket, and expectations were high. This, they were sure, would be the thing that saved them, that would wipe out the problem of their houses being worthless and the effects of the rotten euro on their pensions. The floor was littered with the plastic shells of party poppers and their sodden innards, like squashed worms; there was a discarded Santa hat and a pair of glittery novelty sunglasses. The air smelled sour from sticky pools of spilled drinks on the tables. The aftermath might have led an observer to think that the group had won, but of course they hadn't. When the final ball had been pulled from the spinning gilded cage and its number atonally sung by the schoolchild chosen to deliver the bad news, Anna, fuelled by several coffees with brandy and unable to bear her customers' collective naked disappointment, had insisted they all pop their poppers anyway.

Back upstairs, she glanced at her phone, and saw that her mother had called. After listening to the voicemail – an overly detailed description of the dog-shaped charm that her husband had bought her for her bracelet, and an unfunny joke about Anna having tapas for lunch – Anna sent a bland text in return, before turning off the phone and climbing back into the chair. When *Lost* ended she went straight onto *24*. The hours passed seamlessly, stupefied, one episode and *copita* bleeding into another, slivers of manchego every so often. Her unwashed hair grew stiff and her scalp itched. Her laptop was only for watching the TV; she hadn't any desire to go online and read the news or, worse, look on Facebook. No, the only way through was to keep her old life at bay. Far from home, starved of details, anaesthetized by wine, she could endure. From the wall Holly Golightly in her tiara, cigarette holder aloft, gazed down at her, bemused at how different women could be.

At some point on the 28th or 29th, the doorbell rang. Anna was dozing and jolted awake, unfolding herself stiffly and moving across to the window. The hair below was unfamiliar; male, dark and glossy as a seal's. Spanish.

A rep for a soft drinks brand? Last month, she'd had an inspection visit from the company who had loaned her a display fridge, checking that she was using it only for their products, as their contract stipulated.

Before Anna could retreat, the man tilted his head and looked straight up at her. He smiled, apparently unsurprised to see her there at the window, and with a single wave summoned her downstairs.

There was something about his manner – as if he was expected – that made her follow his command and go to the door. When she opened it he addressed her by name and added, in English, 'I hope this isn't inconvenient.'

It didn't sound like a sincere concern. The physical authority she'd glimpsed from above had been an illusion: the man was short and slight, no bigger than her. Anna shook his hand, conscious of the contrast between her sweatshirt sleeve and his cufflinks. He had the kind of blandly handsome, symmetrical face used to advertise dating sites. He didn't look as if he wanted to jet-wash her terrace.

'I knew this place when it was a bakery,' he said in English, indicating the bar. 'When I was a boy. I used to come down here to get the bread, I was always first in the queue in the morning. Once the bread was so hot, by the time I got home my chest was burnt pink, this perfect oval.'

He mimed hugging a loaf of bread to his chest.

'Ah,' said Anna, smiling. So he was a local boy made good; a businessman now living in Madrid or somewhere who had come home to visit his parents and succumbed to nostalgia as he passed his old haunts.

'You own it now?' he said.

She shrugged yes, embarrassed, as if she was personally responsible for the English invasion of his town and the replacement of hot loaves with cheap pints.

'I was going to make it into a little cafe,' she explained, apologetically. 'Or anyway, that was the idea.'

It seemed a long time ago now, that plan to bring down some of the furniture from the finca; paint the beams; put in bookshelves; source really good coffee.

'Not much profit in tea,' said the man, in the tone of someone who knew.

'No,' she said. 'Not that much in beer, either, it turns out.'

'But you like it here? In Marea?'

'Oh yeah, it's great,' she said, not wanting to insult his hometown.

'Really?' he said, with genuine curiosity. 'You like it?'

She nodded, smiling. She couldn't gauge his tone.

'I like to be by the coast. I swim, you see,' she said. By now she was almost believing her own hype, that she was a frequent, enthusiastic swimmer. She wanted him to think she was different from the other expats, sealed off in their sterile urban developments. 'And I like the people here. The local people. I talked to Paco on Christmas Day. You know Paco? The guy on the beach?'

'Of course,' he said, holding his palms to the sky. '*El Tio*.'

Anna had heard the word before, but couldn't recall exactly what it meant. An endearment of some kind.

'Anyway,' he said. 'Forgive my sentimentality. The business I am here for – that is your property up at Yalo?'

Anna stared at him, thrown by the change of tack. 'What?'

'The finca. Your phone number is on the sign outside. I have called you several times since Christmas.'

She said nothing, suddenly wary. He must be an official. She'd forgotten to pay some bill on the finca, or another arcane tax had been quietly introduced. She tilted her head and smiled noncommittally, the way she did in the bar when the talk turned to immigration.

'The sign outside says your house is for sale,' he said, 'but is it also available to rent? I would like to rent it.'

'*Perdón?*' Anna frowned. She repeated his question in Spanish, to make sure he was saying what he meant to.

'*Sí, sí,*' said the man impatiently, '*alquilar.*' Then, switching back to English, he explained that he wanted to rent the house for three months, possibly longer, and could pay 600 euros a month.

'I wish I could afford more,' he said, with an exaggerated sigh. 'But times are tough, are they not?'

He was looking at her steadily. Anna broke from his gaze, looking at a desiccated bougainvillea gripping the wall of the building opposite. Her brain felt locked, unable to process this turn of events. Was this a scam? A mistake?

'Starting on the first of January,' he pressed on. 'We can pick up the keys on Friday. New Year's Eve. You will be here?'

Anna saw he was flicking his fingers against his thumb; beneath his suave exterior, the man had the energy of a street hustler. She nodded, to break the tension, telling herself *I'm just agreeing that I'll be here on New Year's Eve,* but knowing that she was really consenting to the whole bewildering thing. She was rewarded with a full-beam smile.

'Fantastic!' he said, leaning to touch the top of her arm, like a politician. 'I am very happy.'

Then, with the hint of a frown, as if he'd just remembered something, he added, 'I suppose you'll want a contract?'

'Oh no, no,' she heard herself saying. 'We don't need to bother with that.' She didn't want to displease him, or interrupt the momentum of the deal.

He nodded to signal his approval of her lack of dreariness, of not needing to do things by the book. She smiled back, and the man held out his tiny, fine-boned hand.

'Well, we will see you on Friday then,' he said. She shook his hand and he held it for a brief moment before turning to walk away, towards a large BMW parked up a few yards up.

'Hey,' called Anna, 'what's your name?'

'Oh, yes,' he said, turning back. 'I am Simón.'

See-mon. A business card appeared from his pocket, and he passed it to her with a magician's speed before walking briskly back to the car.

Belatedly, thoughts and questions crowded into her head. She called after him, 'I haven't been up there for a while, you know. I think it's not that clean?'

'That doesn't matter,' he said, glancing back, as if, again, such concerns were for other people.

'You know there's no pool?'

'Fine,' said Simón, over his shoulder, as he reached down for the door handle. 'We don't need that.'

Anna watched him climb into the driver's seat, too big for him. He had left his engine running and the car's wing mirrors folded in protectively as he reversed down the narrow street. She looked at his business card – *Simón Ruiz* and a number, nothing else – and thought of all the things she hadn't asked him, and all the things he hadn't asked her.

But 600 euros. The same amount she had once spent on curtains for the finca's guest room, or two nights in a so-so boutique hotel. Now, it was enough to ease the constant, low-level unease that emanated from that foot-long wedge of unopened mail under the bar counter. A thin cushion for her life.

It had been months since she had been up to the finca. Almost a year. Cleanliness was one thing, but what if it had been ransacked or invaded? She imagined rats' nests, insect swarms, vines breaking through broken roof tiles. Blood stains on the windows, from confused birds flying into the glass.

Back upstairs, she plugged in her phone and texted Tommy, asking for a lift when he got back to Marea the next day. And then, finally, she started to think about what it might feel like to go up to the finca again.

2

The following afternoon, Tommy pulled up outside the bar in his Rover. The insignia sticker on the side read *Marea Minicabs.* Tommy's insistence on running his business above-board was affectionately mocked by the others; every other expat with a car had a sideline in unofficial airport runs.

He jumped out and opened the rear door for Anna, like a chauffeur, his hand brushing her hip as she climbed in. He was wearing a brand new checked shirt, still with the creases in.

'Why are you so happy?' asked Anna from the back seat, as they pulled away.

'I'm seeing you!' he replied, exuberantly. It was their standard exchange when they saw each other; a little in-joke. Anna's question was ironic – Tommy always seemed happy, jolliness was his default setting – and his answer earnest and adoring.

Tommy turned left onto the coast road, and Anna realized that he was heading towards the Plaza del Sol, the abandoned development off the coast road where they occasionally went to have sex. Of course he would be; she hadn't told him otherwise.

'Actually, can we go up to Yalo? To my house?' she said, leaning forward between the seats. 'I need to do something there.'

'Oh!' said Tommy, and she saw disappointment shadow his face, before his smile returned. 'Okey doke.' He executed a U-turn and headed along the narrow coast road, towards the mountain turn-off.

'So finally, I get to see the famous finca!' he said. 'It looks lovely in the photos.'

He was being polite. When Anna had put the house on the market, she'd taken the pictures for the website herself, close-ups of the architectural details and windowsills, in an attempt to appeal to the arty mountain crowd. In thumbnail form, however, the pictures looked almost wilfully bad alongside the perfect finishes, bland expanses of marble and cobalt blue swimming pools the other properties had to offer. Tommy's initial blurb on the Marea Moves website had stated that the place 'needed updating'; Anna had insisted he change it.

Anna felt a wave of apprehension at what they were doing, going up there.

'So how was your Christmas?' she said, deflecting. 'The twins sweet?'

'Oh, gorgeous!' he sighed. 'They got these mountains of presents, but then sat there playing with the wrapping paper!'

Anna smiled indulgently. 'I still can't get over the fact you're a grandfather.'

'Actually, I read the other day that the average age

of first-time grandparents is forty-nine,' said Tommy. 'So I'm bang on!'

'How obedient of you!'

'As I keep telling you, I'm entirely average,' said Tommy. Anna reached through between the seats and squeezed his shoulder. One of the things she liked about Tommy was his good-natured self-effacement.

Her affection for him diminished, however, as he started to tell her about his trip to Hampshire. For an unshowy man Tommy was, usually, a good storyteller. It was one of the things that had made her give in to him, during the succession of liquid afternoons the previous spring, when he had come to the bar by himself and patiently wooed her. Nursing a half, he'd told her wry stories about his neighbours at the urbanization, painting a *Twilight Zone*-like scene where families would come round for dinner, normal as ever, but then vanish overnight, flitting back to the UK under cover of darkness and leaving the keys to their worthless villas in the door. One man, whose house had been repossessed but had nowhere to go back to in the UK, apparently now lived in limbo at the airport, looking like a respectable traveller but then bedding down on plastic chairs and scavenging leftovers from cafe trays.

When it came to his own family, however, Tommy's anecdotes were softened by sentimentality. Now, he described games of Racing Demon so heated the neighbours complained about the shrieking. A new family tradition of an outing to a theme park on Boxing Day, where Tommy was made to hold hands with a giant plastic potato. He and Karen had even viewed a house near to their daughter's, although of course they weren't in a position to move back until their bloody villa sold.

From the back seat, Anna looked at him as he spoke: the profile of his broad, freckled face; his coarse, sandy hair with its unfashionable wings. Creases were beginning to bank at his ears; the skin under his eyes was crinkled from half a century of amiability. His large, pink, freckled wrist at the steering wheel. The wedding ring embedded on his finger. It didn't take much for Tommy to seem like a stranger to her, and for her to feel ashamed that she had returned his affection, just because he wanted her so much.

'That phrase "family bathroom",' Anna said, suddenly irritable. 'It makes me think of you all crammed in there together, soaping each other's backs. Unable to bear being apart even for a moment.'

Tommy laughed obligingly.

'So, have you had any nibbles on the villa?' she continued, although she knew that, if he had, it would have been the first thing he'd told her.

He shook his head. 'A lady seemed quite keen. Came round twice before Christmas, we agreed to take another twenty thousand euros off, she said she'd be in touch. But nothing.'

'God. How annoying. It's been, what, a year now?'

'Nineteen months,' he replied, and then fell silent, concentrating on the road. Anna had successfully punctured his buoyancy but now she felt sorry for it; he was doing her a favour driving her, after all.

'Hey, shall I get in the front?' she said, leaning

forward between the seats. 'Live dangerously? I think we're far enough away from town.'

Tommy hesitated, before pulling in on the verge, beside a huge tangle of plastic wrap discarded from a lorry, the industrial tumbleweed that littered the coast road. Anna moved to the front passenger seat and touched his thigh in apology as she buckled up. She'd never been in the front of the Rover before. The seat was pushed back and as she leaned down to pull it forward, she realized that, of course, it was set to Karen's height. This was her seat.

Tommy kept a neat car, as necessary for a part-time cabbie, but Karen's side pocket, out of view of paying customers, was surprisingly cluttered. Amidst a mess of tissues and receipts and handcream, Anna spotted a packet of the menthol cigarettes that Karen occasionally smoked, and a couple of baby's dummies. She knew the grandchildren had never been to Spain – perhaps Karen had brought the dummies back with her to remember them by? She opened her mouth to make a silly comment, but, glancing at Tommy, saw that his hands were gripping the wheel too tightly. He was clearly disconcerted by her new position. He managed his guilt over his infidelity by glossing over the fact that he and Anna were doing anything untoward at all; the one time Anna had pushed him on the subject of Karen, genuinely interested in their relationship, he had first gone puce and then hidden his face in his hands, like a humiliated child.

She changed the subject and told him about her Christmas, what little she could wring out of it. When she mentioned her Skype call with Marie-Anne and her dad, Tommy laughed.

'I do find it funny that you and your sister have such similar names.'

'Half-sister,' said Anna. 'Yeah, well, Dad forgot that he had me.'

It wasn't too far from the truth. When Marie-Anne was born, less than a year after Anna, her mother was unaware that Derek had recently fathered another daughter with another woman. Derek didn't have the balls to tell her, or even the gumption to steer her away from a name that was so close to the one Janet had chosen.

'And then I went down to the beach and had a swim in the . . .'

'Jesus!' said Tommy, slamming on his brakes. They jolted forward so sharply that Anna braced herself for the airbag. In front of the stopped car stood a small pack of stray dogs. Anna and Tommy stared at them and they stared back, unperturbed, before casually continuing across the road.

'Suicidal dogs,' said Anna.

'I didn't see them at all,' said Tommy. A produce lorry beeped and overtook them, disappearing into a pink-tinted haze ahead.

'A *calima*?' said Tommy. 'At this time of year? Has it been very warm?'

'Quite,' said Anna.

The *calimas* – Saharan dust clouds – were much more common in summer, swirling over the Med and leaving a film of red dust in their wake.

'Bugger,' said Tommy. 'We've got people arriving to view a villa this afternoon. Mattie just cleaned it.'

'Oh no,' said Anna, clicking her tongue in sympathy.

'Now she'll have to do the patio and windows again.'

For a moment, sitting there in the front, Anna felt that she *was* Karen; this was the kind of conversation men had with their wives, not their mistresses. They drove on, Tommy now silent in concentration, passing through the row of huge greenhouses that were sandwiched between the coast and the mountains. Such was the dust, Anna could identify them only by the hiss of their sprinkler systems.

She switched on the radio. It was tuned to the local English-language station, and the closing seconds of 'Hotel California' faded to an ident: 'Warning, this product might contain nuts!' The host then continued what appeared to be a long-running phone-in game, titled 'What shapes are not what they seem?'

A woman called in. 'Trafalgar Square?'

'Very good, very good!' said the host, a one-time Radio One DJ from the eighties. 'We've had that one already, but it's a great one!'

'I've got another,' said the woman. 'The Bermuda Triangle.'

'Ooh, yeah!' said the DJ. 'What went on there, eh? Spooky stuff.'

Anna glanced over at Tommy. He had on his dolphin-like smile, but there was no sign that he found the question 'what shapes are not what they seem?'

absurd in any way. Maybe it wasn't and everyone got it except her.

As they approached the last garage before the mountain road, she asked him to pull in. The sight of the forecourt jarred her. She had come here almost every day during her time at the finca; not only was it the nearest place for food and fuel, it was where their mail was delivered. The same silent, wraith-like man was behind the counter and, although he didn't say hello, he recognized her, and brought out a bundle of post from the back of the shop, handing it to her without a word. She paid for two gas bottles and lugged them out towards the car. Tommy was texting – presumably Karen or Mattie about the cleaning – and didn't notice her for a few seconds, but when he did he jumped out to give her a hand putting them in the boot.

'Do you want to know why we're going up to the finca?' she asked, when they were back on the move. 'Someone's renting it.'

Tommy looked at her, finally torn away from thoughts of *calima* dust.

'A Spanish guy wants to stay, for at least three months.'

'Wow,' he said, frowning. 'Really?'

'Great, isn't it?'

'On his own?'

'I don't know. With his family, maybe.'

'Did he come through us?' He looked over at her, alert. 'Marea Moves?'

'No, no,' said Anna. 'There's a For Sale sign outside the house, on the gate, with my phone number on it.'

'So he would have gone past the house and seen it?'

'Suppose so.'

'That's a bit weird, isn't it?' said Tommy. They were climbing the mountain road now, and he winced at the sound of his exhaust pipe scraping the unpaved surface.

'I don't see why,' said Anna. 'Maybe he and his wife were on a walk in the hills and loving the scenery and thinking to themselves, wouldn't it be nice to live up here for a bit, so the kids can build dens in the woods and Conchita can write that novel she's been talking about, and then they passed a lovely looking house and saw a sign and thought, that's fate . . .'

'Yes, I guess,' said Tommy. 'Does he know you don't have a pool?'

'Yessss,' said Anna, drawing the word out like a teenager. Then she heard herself adding, 'Actually, he said he might buy it, afterwards.'

'Oh wow!' said Tommy. 'Really? Amazing! Well done, darling!'

He leaned over to give her a sporting kiss on the cheek.

As they climbed the mountain, deeper into the pine forest, the light dimmed and radio reception cut out. The gradient suddenly became steeper, the road narrower, the bends sharper and more frequent. Anna looked out of the window at the tunnel of trees and thought back to her first time on this road with Michael, their first visit to the finca together after she had found the place. It was infinitely more magical than the photos suggested, and she was sure he'd love it as much as she did. And now, she was going to see his reaction to their new home.

They'd stood side by side, gazing at that epic, soul-stirring view down the valley, and, more briefly, at the modest, derelict stone finca that had sat in this Elysian spot for centuries. The estate agent told them that the valley was known as the Magic Corridor, because it was on the migratory route for birds coming to and from Africa, and they were struck by the unexpected poetry. That's exactly what it was. On the way back down the mountain, however, Michael had sunk into silence, and she'd started to worry that he was having doubts, that the place was too remote, the commitment too big, the renovation too huge a project. But then, he'd stopped the car at one of the passing places along the road, turned off the engine and wordlessly pulled her on top of him. As they fucked, a cat had appeared from nowhere and mewed outside the door, and Michael had whispered into her neck, '*tu es mi vida*'. It was the most Spanish she ever heard him speak.

Then, there were all those journeys after they had moved in and were doing up the finca, when her ever-increasing familiarity with the twists and bumps of the road neatly coincided with the ever-increasing need to devote her thoughts to their relationship. Anna was barely conscious of the gear changes and hairpin bends as she turned over ambiguous things Michael had said, tried to second-guess his mood, mined her day for interesting anecdotes, planned how she could please him in bed that night. Later, towards the end, this road was where she got angry. Driving alone, she would howl and swear: the car was the only place in which she could safely vent her hurt and fury.

There had been more fraught journeys than joyous ones, but Anna's memory leapfrogged over those, back to those first heady months. She looked over at Tommy; his sunburnt neck; the way he winced as branches brushed the side of the car. It was a mistake to come up here now with him. She should have taken a real cab, found eighty euros from somewhere – she could have sold some things at the car boot sale, like the others did. Her feelings for Tommy were fine down in Marea, but up here in the mountains, fondness was not enough. The contrast between her situation then and now made her feel quietly devastated, realizing that the intensity with which she had once loved and was loved by a dazzling man would never happen to her again.

They approached the turning for the house. Wordlessly, Anna signalled to Tommy. The gate to the grounds was still secured by the inch-thick chains she had put on before leaving. A For Sale sign with her number, painted in leftover *Vert de Terre*, was propped against it.

As they got out, she saw Tommy boggling at the front garden, so wild and overgrown that the yellow front door was only just visible. The view to the left, down to the valley, was impeded by the rampant growth of the rosemary bush. Beyond, the almond grove had been thickened by rustling weeds, almost as tall as the denuded trees.

'Golly. I hope your new tenant has a machete!' he said.

Anna didn't reply. She was looking past the tangle of vegetation to the house, its blonde stones like rows of crammed, uneven teeth. Beyond it, the barren surface of a horseshoe mountain that led into a range, the tallest of them topped with helmets of stone. Above it, a pale blue sky, with scribbles of cloud. The finca's facade looked just as it had when she first saw it; as it had looked for centuries. Like the skin of an avocado, it gave no clue to its condition within.

'Chilly up here, isn't it,' said Tommy.

They each picked up a gas bottle. She unlocked the gate and led Tommy up the path to the house, the path that she and Michael had mapped themselves when drunk one evening, meaning it wasn't a direct route but a meandering river of gravel that twisted inconsequentially before reaching the front door. The air was, unusually, dead silent: no buzz of insects, no growl of distant farm machinery, not even a strangulated dog bark. The crunch of their feet on the stones felt horribly loud. She imagined the sound passing down the valley, the people in the next village pricking up their ears.

The wisteria she had planted beside the front door when they arrived had inched obediently up the stones, but it was still far from covering the house.

How foolishly optimistic she had been. She wanted to tell it not to bother growing any more.

'Don't you have any window grilles up, Anna?' said Tommy.

'It's shuttered from the inside,' she said, looking through the bunch for the right key.

He exhaled theatrically.

'You're lucky no one's broken in.'

'Listen,' she said suddenly, turning to him, 'do you mind if I go in by myself?'

'Oh! No. Of course not. I'll clean the car,' said Tommy, and gripped her shoulder before turning back. She couldn't tell whether he was upset or not, whether he understood. She had told him very little about what had happened up here, just that it hadn't worked out.

She stared at the glossy buttercup paint of the front door as she listened to Tommy crunch back across the gravel, and the creak of the gate. Then, she turned the key in the lock and slowly pushed the door open. It was a heavy piece of wood; as the cold, trapped air from inside reached her, she felt she was heaving off the lid of a tomb.

She stood on the threshold as light from outside washed the dim, shuttered sitting room. There had been no break-in. The place was as she had left it. Or rather, the furniture was still in position, pictures still hanging, jugs and books in place – but something essential had gone. The space felt embalmed; at once familiar and foreign.

She was reluctant to step off the threshold. To the

right, some bits of paper lay scattered on the floor. Michael's sketches, fallen from their string. She walked tentatively into the middle of the room. Dust shrouded every surface, as if the *calima* had found its way indoors. Beside the Knole sofa she noticed a forgotten empty bottle, and there was the smell of cold ash from the last fire. That would have been from just before Michael left: that weekend when his friends, Farah and Kurt, came to stay. It had been far too hot then to have a fire; Anna had lit it for something to do, for a few minutes of distraction from what was playing out around her. She remembered kneeling in front of it, unnoticed, as Michael and his friends talked, putting her face so close to the flames that her cheeks scalded.

Her memory leaped over that awful weekend to a happier time. Michael stretched along the sofa, shirtless, reading. As she came in from the garden, he put his book down on his chest to smile at her.

She shook her head, to dislodge the memory, and went back to the front door to pick up the two gas bottles. Struggling under their weight, she lugged them to the outdoor kitchen and set about replacing the empty one in the cupboard beside the oven. Crouched, she stared inside it, at the unsightly pipework. She had bought those valves herself; she could remember the particular plumber's yard. Pinned up by the cash register had been a calendar – not pictures of girls, as you'd expect, but of horses. Anna had made a joke about it to the plumbers, proud of her rapidly improving Spanish.

Everything in the finca – from the sink valve to the

roof tiles to the sofas and butter dish – had been chosen and paid for by her. Some items were directly associated with the pain of Michael leaving: the oak refectory table where she had found the note informing her the car was in the airport's long-stay car park and that he was not coming back; the toothbrush in the enamel pot in the barn, where he retreated to escape her, where globules of paint had hardened on the soil. But the entire place was infected. When she was telling him about her finding those nineteenth-century wine glasses at the market in Analonda, was he thinking about how dull she was? Was he despising her when she came in with a straining plastic bag of sand she had collected from the beach to mix in with the wall paint, in order to make the finish look authentically uneven? At what point exactly, whilst she was working to create the perfect house for them – organic, artless, stylish, timeless – did he stop giving her the benefit of the doubt? Why did she not see it? Why did she not stop it?

She heard a noise behind her and started. Tommy was standing a few feet away, looking sheepish.

'Sorry to disturb,' he said, wincing. 'It's just – could I have a pee?'

She stood up, feeling his embarrassment at being thrust into this new domestic setting. They had never been in the realm of banal bodily functions. She showed him to the bathroom. He went in and, a moment later, reappeared.

'Darling, I'm so sorry, but I think your bathroom has been vandalized.'

His face was creased with concern. She followed him in, and Tommy pointed at the shards of broken tiles over the bath.

'Why would someone do that?' he said.

At any other time Anna might have laughed. Now, she just shook her head.

'They're meant to look like that,' she said, and retreated, softly closing the door. She went into the main bedroom. Their bedroom. In the corner of the room, she noticed a semi-fossilized sock. Unthinkingly she picked it up and sat down on the clammy eider-down. Her body had done odd things in here, on those nights after Michael left. Lying on her back she felt her limbs and cheeks inflate, until her flesh seemed to touch all four walls. She had started to hear the traffic on the motorway, even though it was twenty kilometres away. The birds scratching on the roof felt like they were landing on her head.

The cistern groaned. She heard Tommy's steps across the flagstones stop, then start up again, and watched as the bedroom door was gently pushed open. Tommy stood in the doorway, with an uncertain smile on his face. He was almost as discombobulated here as she was, she realized.

'Come here,' she said, motioning to him with her head.

He approached hesitantly.

'Are you alright, darling?'

'I want to fuck your brains out.'

She had never talked to him like this before. She

watched as Tommy's excitement overcame his confusion, and he did what he was told.

Twenty minutes later, they were inching back down the narrow, rutted road when a truck approached. It was Alfonso, the finca's nearest neighbour. Of course they wouldn't get out of here without being noticed. Alfonso was claustrophobically concerned with everything that happened on the mountain. Somehow, he had even got wind of the fact that Michael had left, and, the day after, his wife had turned up on Anna's doorstep with a bag of oranges and a naked desire to get the gossip.

Alfonso pulled up beside Anna and leaned out of the window, his dog's face appearing beside him. Anna braced herself for one of his long chats about the problems with his septic tank, or the erratic timetable of the truck that delivered their fresh water. But instead he told her that he had seen men lurking around the house the previous week.

'Hero saw them off,' he said, proudly. 'You know Mariana, down in the valley? She had her trailer taken.'

Beside her, Tommy smiled blankly.

Anna thanked Alfonso profusely, as was expected, and added that, for the next few months at least, there would be no problem with burglars, as the finca would have tenants.

Alfonso raised his eyebrows. She said *adiós* before he could start interrogating her.

'Did he ask whether you had a machete for that

garden?' said Tommy, with a wink, as he pulled away. He had recovered his spirits and there was no need for them to talk about the awkwardness up at the finca, Anna thought. She rested her cheek against the car window – she was in the back seat, now – whilst he manoeuvred around the hairpin bends. As they neared the main road, the radio clicked in. The 'shapes that are not what they seem' phone-in was still on air.

'Ovaltine,' said a listener.

'Ha, that's a good one!' said the DJ. 'Everyone secretly likes Ovaltine, don't they?'

They passed by the greenhouses. The opacity and near-silence of the structures reminded Anna of the abattoirs near where she grew up. The *calima* haze had lifted now, and the opaque plastic was spotted with red stains from the dust mixing with the water from the irrigation systems. Blood rain, they called it, this after-effect.

'You'd think they could spare one of those sprinklers for the course,' said Tommy. Non-essential irrigation had been banned for months, because of the drought, and the golf course his villa overlooked was beige and desiccated: a source of much concern.

They fell silent until, ten minutes later, Tommy drew up at the bar.

'Well, thanks so much,' she said, reaching for the door. 'See you tomorrow night. Put on your party shirt.'

'Ah, Anna,' said Tommy, looking away, flushing. 'I'm so sorry to ask, but . . . Karen is doing the books now and she might wonder . . . of course it doesn't have to be the full amount, I'll sub it, but just a little contribution . . .'

When she cottoned on Anna dug for her wallet, flustered, and gave him twelve euros, all she had on her. The money was earmarked to pay for grapes for the New Year's Eve party tomorrow night; now she'd have to get them on tick. As Tommy drove off, she remained standing where she was and the thought slid from her mind. She was back sitting on the bed at the finca, alone, her finger stroking the eiderdown as she stared at the wall; its authentically uneven finish the result of sand mixed in with the paint, sand that she brought all the way up from the beach.

3

The following evening, New Year's Eve, Anna opened her doors at seven. By eight the bar was a quarter full. Her regulars – Tommy, Mattie, Graeme, Eddie – had been joined by various better halves and friends from the urbanization. The balcony drinkers, little seen in bars. The group had defected from Sweeney's for the occasion; he had been here for thirteen years and usually had the claim on big, potentially lucrative events. Anna knew she had Tommy to thank for that. She imagined him initiating the subject during one of the endless round of dinners he and Karen attended. 'Be nice to have a bit of change. And the poor girl's all alone, isn't she?' Even Caz the dog saviour was here, sitting at the bar by herself with a red wine and lemonade.

News of Anna's finca rental had got out. Their congratulations were qualified by barely concealed jealousy at her 600 euros a month. Not the jackpot of a sale, but a nice little prize nonetheless.

'And this bloke said he was interested in buying it too?' said Graeme, leaning heavily against the bar.

'Er, yes,' said Anna. And maybe Simón would. A

little mountain retreat for him and his family; an escape from Madrid, or wherever he was from.

'He knows you don't have a pool?'

'Yes!' said Anna, giddily. 'And he doesn't care!'

'You should dig one out, if you want to sell,' interjected Caz, ignoring what Anna had just said. 'People expect it. Even in character properties.'

It was the most Anna had ever heard her speak.

'I can't,' said Anna. 'It'd cost forty thousand euros. The place is so cheap, they can make one themselves.'

Caz shrugged. Beneath her heavy fringe, Anna spotted a smudge of mascara on her lids.

'All I'm saying is, it might be an issue.'

The way Caz pronounced the word – *iss*-ue, with a long first syllable – nudged a memory in Anna; not forceful enough for actual recall. She looked at Caz, but Caz had lowered her head to suck noisily on her straw, and the moment passed.

The conversation around them moved onto the generalities of house-selling; a subject the expats needed no excuse to pile onto. Someone said they were thinking about installing glass bricks in the bathroom, to give their place an edge. Another man, who had a 'strong expression of interest' on his place, started dispensing wisdom like a lifer who'd been granted parole, offering tips lifted from property shows.

'Declutter, declutter, declutter,' he told them, solemnly. 'You must have neutral décor, so buyers can project onto it.'

Anna had checked out the others' villas and apartments online and knew that this advice was hardly needed: their properties were united by an absence of personality. Three bedrooms, one en-suite. A terracotta tiled floor, orange pine dining table and veneered wardrobes. In the kitchen, obscure brand white goods and exactly six sets of supermarket white plates and cutlery and those too-small wine glasses. For decoration, a sprig of fake flowers in a glass vase and a single print. Outside, a seating area with a plastic table set and a defeated mini palm tree.

The expats' identikit interiors had bemused Anna – did they not care at all, or were they all expressing themselves but just happened to have the same bland taste? – until she learned that many of them, Tommy and Karen included, hadn't even chosen their furnishings themselves. Rather, when buying their new builds from the developers, they had taken up the option of purchasing a furniture package for 10,000 euros, which included everything from bed linen to coffee cups to artwork.

Tommy and Karen were here now, mingling with friends. Tommy had swapped his polo shirt for one with a snazzy pattern; Karen was in a glittery top and embroidered jeans, and Anna saw she had had her hair done with a handful of judicious highlights. As he talked with his friends, Tommy kept his back to Anna; he had to do this when in company, he'd told her, so that he didn't stare at her.

Conversation around the bar moved on, to the value of the euro that day – the expats watched the exchange rate like Wall Street hawks – and a juicy trial in the news, of an American girl charged with the murder of her friend in an Italian town. Mattie came up to charge her glass. She was relatively dressed down, for her: the last time Anna had seen her, on the lottery day, Mattie had worn a tennis dress on which she had pinned dozens of photocopies of their ticket, overlapping like scales. This evening, she had merely wrapped plaits of her waist-length, blue-black hair around her head, German-style, and was wearing a short, flippy skirt and a leotard top. Her interest was piqued by Anna's description of Simón.

'I like short men,' she said. 'We're on the same level.'

'I think he's married, Mattie,' Anna said, with unearned sanctimony.

Mattie shrugged, and then winked at Anna. Did she suspect Anna and Tommy? Impossible to tell. She presented herself as a cartoon, and kept her actual level of acuity close to her chest. She was similarly evasive on the facts of her life: her age, her background, why she had come to Spain; what was wrong with the never-seen mother she lived with and cared for.

'Your tits look fantastic in that top!' Anna said. It occurred to her that she may have started on the booze too early, but Mattie coyly accepted the compliment.

'Well, that's the advantage we have, isn't it,' she said. 'You and me. No udders.'

She nodded towards a huddle of wives from the urbanization, and Anna realized that she was referring to their lack of children. She would not be plunged into despair by this comment, the idea of her and

Mattie as two of a kind. She had, quite often, had uncharitable thoughts about her customers, but this evening, she was determined to be bountiful and see the best in them. In everything. To stay in the moment.

Her high spirits weren't entirely forced. The prospect of Simón renting the finca, that tear in the ordinary fabric of her days, had buoyed her: it seemed a symbol of hope, that someone might want what she had to offer. Earlier, when she was getting ready upstairs, she found herself unearthing a bag of clothes she hadn't touched since coming to Spain and putting on a dress from her past. Dark green wool, knee length and high-necked, its apparent primness was undermined by the tight cut and leather panels at the shoulders. Subtle and sexy; quite un-Marea. As she'd put on some lipstick and clipped up her hair, it occurred to her that she saw her remaining stock of attractiveness like an expensive candle, only to be lit for a few hours on special occasions.

She'd beautified the bar too, with a string of fairy lights around the optics, some balloons on the dartboard and ceiling fan, and a foil *Happy New Year!* banner on the wall.

The keys were sitting on a shelf behind the bar, waiting for Simón, and she found herself hovering close to them. Each time the door opened she expected him, striding in to give her 600 euros, but it was another Brit. It was getting on for a full house, actually, the best she'd ever done. Woozy and forgiving, she looked out at her customers. They may not be thrilling, or stylish, or clever, but they were decent folk making the best of things. They were all in the same boat: nursing dashed dreams, muddling through a situation beyond their control. Like a low-key Blitz, where the bombs came in the form of letters from the bank and reports of the daily euro exchange rate.

Graeme came over and draped his arms heavily around her and Mattie's shoulders.

'How are my two favourite females?'

Anna practised her benevolence by smiling at him, before twisting free in order to turn up the music – she had made sure to tune into the local radio station without presenters – and set about geeing up the room, offering around free cava. She had a surplus from the lottery day; although she couldn't bring herself to collude in the delusion of joining the syndicate, she'd ordered two extra crates, just in case they won. Why this gesture of hope had been superior to going in on a ticket, she didn't have the will or energy to explore.

Graeme, stationed at the bar, joined in conversation with a Scottish couple. The wife was twittering away about her Christmas in the UK.

'I never thought I'd actually be happy to see rain,' the woman said.

Graeme looked at her, eyes narrowed. This was dangerously close to treasonable talk. A former Merseyside policeman, Graeme was a self-appointed custodian of the expats' collective pride: a whip to keep them on message. Even as their dream was falling to pieces beneath them, and they were desperate to sell up, they mustn't admit out loud that coming here had been a mistake, or that they missed anything about home.

'Next thing you'll be saying you want to go back to live in the UK,' he said, quietly.

'Oh no, no,' said the wife, flustered. 'Of course not.'

Anna was about to defend the woman when the song ended and, on cue, like an ice-cream seller at a play interval, the door opened and in walked – not Simón, but a young African man shouldering a large bag. The hawkers generally kept to the steps leading down to the beach, but in lean months sometimes migrated up to the town centre.

Graeme took charge.

'No no no no no no,' he said, waving his arms with the authority of an air traffic controller. But the man was quick off the mark and had already produced his wares: a doll of a Rasta man, complete with dreadlocks and spliff dangling from his grotesquely oversized lips. On the flick of a switch, the doll started gyrating and singing 'Don't Worry, Be Happy'. The man pressed the doll towards Caz with a broad, beautiful smile, as if he felt honoured to be given the opportunity to offer her a racist toy giving inane advice.

'I said *no thank you*,' said Graeme. Putting his hands on the African's shoulders, he steered him back towards the door. The man left with no protest, still smiling. Graeme rubbed his palms on his trouser legs.

A moment later the door opened again. Anna perked up, but it was only Richard, the urbanization's

Mr Fixit. He was wearing a worn suit and his customary gelled quiff; he was proud of his full head of hair.

'Here comes trouble!' shouted someone.

When Anna had bought the bar the year before, Richard had been first through the door, offering her a cut-price Sky Sports subscription and then asking her out for dinner at Pinocchio's. She'd half-considered the latter, until Mattie had sidled over to inform her that she and Richard had had an on-off thing for years.

Now, with a fanfare, Richard upended the bag he was carrying onto the bar. Out spilled numerous pairs of red socks.

'Got a deal down the market,' he said, although for him to be giving them away, Anna thought, he must have got them for free. Another Spanish New Year's tradition, along with the grapes, was to wear a red undergarment, given as a gift. Richard ceremoniously handed the socks around and everyone put them on; even Caz, who laboriously unbuckled her walking sandals.

By 9pm the room was full with flushed Brits. The radio was playing back-to-back naff hits. Anna was overheating, her wool dress welded to her skin. She circuited the room with the cava – she must stop giving away free booze soon – and topped up Karen's glass. As she poured, Anna avoided Karen's gaze, staring at the cowl-neck of her top. Despite her height, Karen's shoulders were as narrow and sloping as those of a wife in a Renaissance portrait. A few fallen blonde hairs had caught on the sequins; Anna resisted the urge to pick them off.

'Ooops!' said Karen, and Anna snapped to attention just before the wine cascaded over the top of the glass. She apologized and retreated to safety behind the bar. She watched Karen lean in to say something to Tommy. Was she archly remarking on Anna's lack of pouring finesse? Or simply reminding him that their home insurance policy was due, or that he must check the oil in the Rover?

Anna didn't know this woman at all. She was guilty of reducing her to someone bloodless, without irony or sex appeal, to justify her dalliance with Tommy, but her few interactions with Karen had done little to counter the impression. Karen was not a drinker, preferring weak coffee. 'I like to see the bottom of the cup,' she'd told Anna once when asking for one and Anna, to her shame, had said, 'Oh, you want *instant*?' and had made a show of looking under the counter for the Nescafé, although Karen was hardly the only customer who had asked for it. Karen's conversation seemed to be limited to her grandchildren, and her mission to sell their villa so she could get back to them. The only time she had really talked to Anna was to ask if Anna could Photoshop the golf course in the images of their villa on the website, turning the course's grass back into the verdant green it once was.

'I know you used to be a graphic designer,' she'd said.

'I *am* one,' Anna had replied, but agreed to help out.

Now, Anna continued watching Karen, as she and Tommy talked, Karen holding her glass in the palm of her hand, its stem between her fingers. Did Karen sense that Tommy's affections had been diverted elsewhere? Anna imagined her discussing her fears, delicately phrased, with a trusted friend. Of course Tommy still adored her. They were a great team! Periods of drifting apart were inevitable in a long marriage. Maybe she should become involved in his hobbies, learn to play golf?

As if Anna's thoughts had summoned her, she saw Karen was making her way over to the bar, Tommy close behind.

'Karen has something to ask you,' said Tommy, too brightly. Karen produced a folder from her bag, and placed it tentatively on the bar.

'I was wondering whether, if you have a moment, you might be so kind as to take a look at my little book,' she said. 'I want a nice cover design, you see, and you were so clever with our website.'

Anna looked down at the folder. Printed in Curlz typeface was a sticker bearing the title: *Sun, Smiles and Sangria: Our Spanish Adventure!*

Anna glanced over at Tommy, who had his perma-smile on.

'I didn't know you were a writer,' she said to Karen.

'Oh no, no,' said Karen, horrified. 'It's just a silly thing. Only for family and friends. A little memento of our time here, before we go.'

'I'd love to,' said Anna, with as much sincerity as she could muster, and then felt awful, as if her uncharitable thoughts about Karen had been exposed for all to see. The next moment, she found herself clinking a glass to get some attention, before clambering onto a chair.

'*Señores y señoras,*' she said, looking down at their open, pink faces. 'I know it's not quite time yet but I think we should raise our glasses and toast the end of the year. And here's hoping that 2010 treats us a little better and we all sell our bloody houses!'

The crowd cheered. Anna raised her glass towards Karen, as the toast was really for her.

'Well, easy for you to say, Miss Six Hundred Euros!' heckled Richard, and Anna gave a coy shrug.

As she clambered down from the bar, 'The Power of Love' by Huey Lewis came on. Mattie and Richard started dancing, Richard with his knees chivalrously bent to ease the height difference.

Tommy was still standing at the bar.

'Happy New Year!' he said, glassy-eyed and soppy. He put his hand on her arm, then quickly turned to slap Graeme on the shoulder – 'Happy New Year, old cock!' – to cover his tracks.

'Two Hearts' by Phil Collins. Others joined in the dancing, self-conscious shuffling, the fairy lights casting a kindly glow over their efforts. People had started to buy rounds; in these straitened times, such largesse had become rare. They invariably bought a drink for Anna, too, and each glass she clinked and knocked back unleashed more fondness for these nice, ordinary people, who had accepted their lives weren't going to be magnificent, and were making of them what they could.

Just before 11pm, the door opened and Anna

looked over – surely, this must be Simón – but it was another African, young and rangy, a large bag slung over his shoulder.

'No thank you very much,' bellowed Graeme from the bar.

The man waved his hands.

'No, no,' he said in a muffled, unconfident voice, holding out a piece of paper.

Graeme took it, and frowned. He looked over at Anna.

'He has your name written down.'

Anna leaned below the bar to turn down the music and the chatter in the room died with it. She stared at her name, in large, unequivocal capitals.

'I have money,' said the African man, pulling a thick, folded envelope from his back pocket and offering it to her.

'Anna, what's going on?' said Mattie. 'Are you a drug dealer?' She gave a shrill little laugh.

'House,' said the African. 'House. Here for house.'

'Wait, I can't hear properly,' said Anna, although she'd heard just fine. She ducked down below the bar to turn the radio off and gather her wits. She stood up too quickly, getting a head rush. The man waited, holding the envelope. The room was silent.

'You're here for the keys to my house?' she said.

'Yes!' The man nodded, pleased to be understood.

Graeme was peering out of the front door.

'There's more of them out here,' he reported.

'You were sent by Simón?' Anna asked the man.

'Simón, yes, yes,' he said, smiling.

'Anna, do you want me to deal with this?' said Graeme, in police mode.

'No,' said Anna. She couldn't look at the Brits; she felt as if she had been pushed up on stage. She had not quite sobered up enough to deal with it.

'Where is Simón?' she said to the African. 'I ought to speak to Simón.' She spoke slowly and loudly, as if he was deaf, in the tone she hated to hear from others.

'Please,' said the man, and he pushed the envelope towards her. He looked at her, head slightly cocked, as if they were the only two in the room. He was standing directly under a clump of fairy lights, and the colours danced across his skin. He looked barely out of his teens, with a pointed chin and deep-set eyes fixed on hers, and in his look, Anna saw fear. She thought of her encounter with Simón: his coiled impatience, how she felt obliged to comply. And that was with her, a white woman from whom he wanted something. What would he be like with this man if he interrupted Simón's New Year's Eve to tell him he had failed to get the keys?

Beyond him, what was once a room full of affable individuals now felt like a silent, hostile chorus.

Had Simón even said the house was for himself?

'Please,' said the man again, quietly.

'Wait a minute,' she said, and turned, face burning, to find the card that Simón had given her. With her back to the room, she called the number. He answered after one ring – *sí?* – so quickly she was caught off guard.

'Oh, *hola*. It's Anna,' she said and, when he didn't respond, added, 'the finca woman?'

'Yes, I know,' he said. 'Everything alright?'

'I didn't realize you wouldn't be picking up the keys yourself,' she said, stumbling over the double negative in Spanish.

A pause.

'Yes. You met Almamy. He is an old employee of mine, a trusted friend. I am giving him and his fellows a holiday. A reward for their hard work.'

'Oh. Right. So you won't be staying there.'

'That's OK with you?' he continued. 'To be honest, I didn't think to mention it. With someone else, maybe – but you did not seem a narrow-minded person.'

'No, no,' she said. 'I'm not. It's not a problem. I was just . . .'

'You received the money OK?'

'Yes. Thank you.'

Anna glanced back at the room. Everyone was turning their attention on her, except for Mattie, who was offering the African man her glass. Anna watched him politely take a sip, whilst keeping his eyes fixed on Anna.

'If that is all,' said Simón, 'I will go back to my dinner.'

'Yes. Sorry,' she said.

'Well, *adiós*.'

He hung up.

Anna turned back to the room, glancing down at the thick envelope on the counter, its corner touching a slick of spilled cava that had soaked the paper. Then, looking only at the African, she smiled, reached over to the keys and handed them to him. The anxiety fell from his face. He thanked her profusely and hurried out of the bar, bag at his shoulder. The door banged shut, and the room remained silent. Anna ducked down behind the bar to turn the radio back on, loud.

4

The following week, Tommy drove Anna to the Plaza del Sol. On the way, he told her that his neighbour Sue Wallace was worried about some graffiti that had appeared on the side of her villa.

'She says she's heard that's what these gangs do – like, secret signals, telling each other how many people live in the house, whether they have a dog or what-not.' He checked over his shoulder as he steered the Rover into the entrance of the site, marked by a felled concrete girder. 'She thinks it's saying that she's on her own, because they know that Martin has gone to Cheshire for his knee op.'

'Oh, come on,' said Anna, from the back seat. 'It's just tagging, some kid bored over Christmas. Look.' She indicated the walls they passed as they crawled through the moribund estate. 'Graffiti everywhere.'

'She said it was different,' said Tommy. 'Like it was a sign.'

Anna said nothing.

They pulled up in their usual spot, the driveway of a house in a secluded plot on the north side of the development. There was no need for such discretion.

Although there were signs that others also used the place for illicit purposes – the graffiti, fly-tipped sofas, empty bottles and syringes – in all their visits, Anna had never seen another human. Even the cobwebs stretched across the redundant street signs and never-used benches looked long-deserted.

The Plaza del Sol was modest compared to other aborted housing projects in this part of Spain, the monolithic ghost towns whose only visitors now were dying cats and the news crews and student photographers drawn to the irresistible visual metaphor. Typically for Marea, this one was an also-ran. It consisted of a boulevard, a parade of bricked-up shops, a playground and around fifty housing units abandoned at various stages of their construction. Some had their ribs in place, the girders wearing a skirt of concrete. Some had only just been conceived, marked out squares on the bare ground. A handful were shells that at first glance appeared habitable, with windows and tiles in place, but these details only served to emphasize their deadness. The fierce wind that swirled down the thoroughfares and propelled the roundabout in the playground was the only vital force around.

'You'd think that they would have started using this place for cycling proficiency lessons,' said Anna.

She had made this observation before to Tommy. Once, she'd felt grateful she could repeat herself with him and he wouldn't pick her up on it.

'Anna . . .' started Tommy.

'I'm not going up there to check on them!'

She found herself on the verge of tears. This was a

new emotional tenor for them, and, in the rear-view mirror, she saw Tommy flinch. For a moment, sitting in the back seat, Anna felt like a teenager. First she was Tommy's wife; now his daughter.

'Thing is,' Tommy said, carefully, after a pause, 'people are worried that they might be plotting something. Getting their mates together, coming down to steal our stuff.'

'That's what black people do, is it?'

'Don't be like this, poppet,' pleaded Tommy. 'It isn't about that.'

'Right,' said Anna. 'So if Diane and Terry from Lowestoft had rented my place, you'd be suggesting I go up there and check on them, too.'

'Really, Anna,' said Tommy, turning to face her. This was forceful behaviour: the new side of her had brought out a new side to him. 'It's not about race. It's about being . . . realistic. Seeing the situation for what it is. You know as well as I do young African men do not rent crumbling old fincas for a holiday.'

'It's not crumbling,' she said. 'Besides, you're forgetting about Simón. The Spanish guy. He was the one who rented it. I googled him, he seems legit.'

She had actually done this, although *Simón Ruiz* had brought up hundreds of entries – the name appeared to be the Spanish equivalent of David Brown – and she hadn't waded through them all. She had, however, found one picture of Simón at a charity event, arm around the waist of his pretty, dark-haired wife.

'Karen was thinking that maybe they're growing drugs up there.'

Anna snorted. 'That's ridiculous.'

Was it? All Anna knew for certain was that she wasn't going to concede to Tommy. Just as she had refused to acknowledge the uneasy atmosphere in the bar on New Year's Eve after the African left, turning up the music and pretending not to care that several of her customers called it a night before the clock struck twelve, leaving their grapes unswallowed. In the days since, she'd reimagined the moment as similar to a test in a fairy tale; as she handed over those keys a fog had cleared, exposing a gulf between her and the rest of the Brits.

In fairness, she knew that Tommy's concern was less to do with race than her casual relinquishing of her house.

'Don't you care about what's going on up there, Anna?' he said. Although they were stationary, his hands were still on the steering wheel. 'You don't know these people at all. Have you even a deposit from them? References? It's your *property*. Your asset.'

Anna stared through the window at a set of tyre prints that contemptuously scuffed the prematurely painted street markings. Must be from joyriders: maybe the same boys who spent their days smoking dope by the beach.

'I hate the word "property",' she said, as if musing to herself. 'It's not an investment. It's a house. A *home*.'

She heard her maddening, flattening tone, and wondered if Tommy realized that it was masking her own uncertainty.

Tommy exhaled, bewildered. They sat in silence for a minute, as the wind bullied the immature, neatly spaced trees lining the road and whipped in and out of the empty windows above their heads. Then, Tommy opened his door and came round to join her in the back.

'I'm not very good at arguing,' he said, reaching over to her.

His hand slid up her thigh, and his freshly shaven chin nuzzled her neck. Anna usually enjoyed sex with Tommy – six months into their meetings, he still acted as if he couldn't believe his luck to be touching her – and at first she responded to him, pressing herself down onto his hand. Then, she stopped.

'We can't do this.'

'No,' he said, mouth at her jaw, 'let's not fight. I hate it.'

'No. This,' she said. 'Us. I'm sorry.'

He pulled away to look at her, and she watched his face sag as her words registered. His hand went still, a dead weight on her leg. Sweet, guileless Tommy. She was almost as taken by surprise as him; she hadn't planned this, or at least not consciously.

'I've been thinking about it for a while,' she said. How long? Since that awkward trip to the finca, where she was overpowered by the memories of Michael? Since New Year's Eve, when he formed part of that suspicious chorus? Since twenty minutes ago?

'But I thought we were happy,' said Tommy, quietly. And with that, a phrase more suited to the break-down of a marriage than the halt to a fortnightly knee-tremble, Anna realized that she should have done this ages ago.

'I can't stop thinking about poor Karen,' she added. It wasn't quite the truth, but it *should* have been the truth. It was the righteous explanation, and the simplest. Tommy winced, and then, in a sudden movement, opened the door and got out. He sank back into the driver's seat, fired up the engine, and drove her back to the bar in silence, abruptly changing gears, eyes glued to the road.

That evening, Sue Wallace's house was broken into. It wasn't a standard, opportunistic break-in, either – a door left foolishly ajar whilst Sue was picking mint on her roof terrace. This was a professional job, efficiently executed whilst she was out at the supermarket. Bolt cutters, security grille prised off. And they had cleaned her out. Her jewellery, the electronics, clothes – all gone. Even her collection of audiobooks.

Graeme came to tell Anna the news the following afternoon.

'Bit of a coincidence, eh?' he said, leaning against the bar. Anna pretended to be cleaning the Stella Artois pump clip in order to avoid his gaze. You had to be careful with Graeme: his geniality ran as deep as a single coat of paint. He was wearing a yellow polo shirt, and his gravy-brown forearms lay heavily on the counter, ostentatiously bare. He liked to tell people that on the day he arrived in Spain he took off his watch, never to put it back on again.

'I'm happy to go up there for you, my love,' he said. 'Just to check all's in order.'

'Thanks, Graeme,' said Anna, eyes still on the pump. 'But you're alright.'

'No bother,' he went on. 'I can nip up there now. Got the car outside. Up the A50 and then left, isn't it?'

Anna forced herself to look at him. His eyes were hardly bigger than buttonholes in his flushed face: a wonder he could see out of them.

'Well, there's no evidence my tenants were involved, is there?' she said. 'I don't want to harass them.'

'Thing is, Anna, it's not really just about you, is it,' he said. 'I wouldn't *harass* them' – he spoke the word with contempt – 'just ask them if they knew anything about it. Rule them out. You know.'

Anna had always doubted Graeme's claims to have been top rank CID – surely, even in Liverpool in the eighties, there were some standards – but now she could see him back in his heyday, the corrupt copper in a straining nylon shirt, ordering some casual violence with a lift of his chin. He was always nipping off down to Marbella and Estepona; he claimed to be birdwatching, but maybe he kept dodgy company there, and could enlist some bored muscle to accompany him up to the finca.

'You've been here, for what, a year?' he went on. 'Well I've been here a lot longer than that, my dear, and I can tell you that ninety-nine per cent of the trouble we get is from Africans. That's not racist, that's a fact.'

Anna didn't reply.

'I'll tell you now,' he continued, the fleshy triangles of his fingers pressing down on the bar. 'If anything else happens, anything at all – if a flowerpot goes missing – I'm going up there. OK?'

'OK, Graeme,' said Anna, forcing herself to smile at him, as if this was just an innocuous conversation.

He left, letting the door bang shut behind him. Jangled, Anna moved to pour herself a *copita* before deciding instead on a *carajillo*: an espresso with a shot of brandy, the breakfast of Spanish working men. As the coffee machine warmed up, she imagined her new tenants sitting around the oak table at the finca, sharing their intel as they marked a map of the area with one of Michael's sketching pencils. *Fat woman, arthritis, easy to overcome. Dog, but it's old. Golf buggy here.* Or maybe Karen was right, and they were establishing a hydroponic skunk farm up there. Windows sealed with gaffer tape, furniture thrown into the garden, light cables slung over the beams.

She drank the coffee and the brandy, one straight after the other, blinking as the alcohol blazed in her stomach like a match dropped on petrol.

She could call Simón. But to say what? During that New Year's Eve phone call, she'd given her agreement for his 'friends' to stay there. And what he'd said: 'With the others, I'd have mentioned it, but not you . . .'

And maybe the African men *were* his friends. His trusted ex-colleagues, whom he wanted to treat to a holiday. A three-month holiday. As he said. Just because something was unlikely, it didn't mean it wasn't true.

To suspect the worst – well, wasn't that just halfway to becoming Graeme, so blinkered he could barely see?

But, but. She thought of Tommy's uncharacteristic firmness at the Plaza del Sol: 'Anna, it's your *asset.*' Sure, the finca wasn't worth anything at the moment, but the recession wouldn't last forever. And the time, the effort, *the money* . . . She thought, again, of the sixty-mile trek to that plumber's merchant, the one with the horse calendar, to buy the sink valves. Of picking up those endless eBay purchases from the garage. Stamping on those bathroom tiles by the side of the road. What that money could represent – if she could somehow liquidate the place, and pour it back into London. Maybe not a flat in Islington any more. But something. A fresh start.

And Simón had lied to her, hadn't he, that first meeting on her doorstep? Or, certainly, he hadn't told the full truth.

She had another *carajillo,* found Simón's card, and called the number. He answered after less than a ring.

'*Sí?*'

'It's Anna,' she said. Silence. 'I own the finca?'

'*Sí,* Anna. How can I help you?'

'I was just wondering if . . . everything is OK up there. At the house?'

'Yes, it's perfect,' he said. 'I spoke to Almamy and they are very happy there.'

He was outside somewhere; she heard a car horn. His impatience vibrated down the line.

'Oh, good . . .'

'As we are talking,' he said, 'I should say – here in

Spain, the law is that the tenant has a right to peaceful enjoyment of their property. A landlord must get their permission before entering. It is the same in the UK, I think?'

'Yes, of course,' said Anna, although she didn't know.

'Is there anything else I can help you with?' he said, and then, when Anna didn't answer, 'OK, *adiós*.' He hung up.

A moment later, a loud burst of music from outside made her jump. A car radio? Too loud. The music abruptly cut off for a second, and then flared up again, long enough this time for her to identify the song – Whitney Houston, 'I Wanna Dance with Somebody'. Oh yes – Sweeney was hosting a karaoke night that evening, with one-euro shots. He'd written it on his window in wonky fluorescent pen. His attempt to re-establish his bar as the venue for special occasions; payback for her grabbing the custom for the lottery and New Year's Eve.

Another five-second blast of music from Sweeney's. Anna stayed where she was at the bar. She had a jittery, hollowed-out feeling, not helped by the brandy, but it was too late to regret that now. Her phone rang, still in her hand, and she jumped; for a stupid moment she thought it was Simón, calling back to give her the proper explanation she deserved. But of course not. The screen flashed *Derek*.

She let it ring out. She knew what her father wanted – to sound off about how lonely he was and be reassured that someone, somewhere, still cared about him. Derek didn't leave a message; he never did. If someone couldn't fulfil his needs at that very moment, he dropped it and looked elsewhere. He'd be on to Marie-Anne now.

Another abrupt, five-second blast of music from Sweeney's. Maybe he was torturing someone in there.

The afternoon lay ahead of her, a thick, torpid river to wade through. She sat on her stool, shoulders rounded, hands in her lap. The overhead light highlighted the wounds on the mahogany-coloured counter she had inherited: dents and scratches from God-knows-how-many seasons of contact with beer bottles, hire car keys, lighters, signet rings, false fingernails. The spirits on the optics had a sticky film, their metal casings corroded from the sea air. The fronds of the spider plant, which sat on top of the defunct fruit machine in the corner, were weighed down with dust. God, this place. But it was more than just dirt. Even if Mattie cleaned for six hours, it would still feel grimy, with its oily faux beams and yellowed walls, testament to the fact the bar's previous owner had opted out of the smoking ban.

She hauled herself up and went to the door, opening it to let the air in and glancing out at the square. Another mild, clear, unexceptional day. The woman in the You Chic gift shop leaned against the frame of her doorway, underneath her canopy of Peppa Pig towels. She glanced in Anna's direction, and gave what might have been a nod. Apart from her, Anna saw a solitary man with a shopping bag and, on the far side, Caz with the dogs, doing her circuit. The tiny birds sat patiently at the fountain. The square was clean, at least: the outlying streets, where the Spanish lived, were clogged with rubbish and reeked of urine, but the council still made an effort here. The trees had been adorned with fake plastic oranges; Anna hadn't even realized they weren't real until she saw someone replacing them the previous month.

Anna ducked back inside. Paperwork – that was her task for today. She printed off the till receipts. Under the bar, beside a box of years-old mayonnaise sachets, was a wodge of unopened mail. She fetched it, her laptop and a *copita* – no more brandy for now – and sat at a table, letting the envelopes fall in an unlovely pile.

In the early months of the bar, she'd been diligent and efficient, stock-taking and balancing books, enjoying learning the mechanics of her new project. But that seemed a long time ago, now; when this had all been a bit of an adventure. She pulled up an Excel spreadsheet and started opening the mail, scanning the bank statements and bills. The period just gone, between Christmas and New Year, was supposed to be one of the busiest of the year, when bars raked in enough to cover the lean months ahead. But even with New Year's Eve and the lottery night, it appeared she had taken in less than 2,000 euros in total over the month. And the fixed expenditure kept on coming. Rent, IVA, social security, fire insurance . . .

Terrace tax? She stared glassily at the letter, a final reminder for 670 euros. A yearly charge she'd forgotten about. That was the money from Simón, the first month's rent for the finca, gone: a thin cushion whipped out from under her.

She entered the debt on her spreadsheet. Next in the pile of mail was a thick, expensive A5 envelope, addressed to her personally and bearing the logo of a London fertility clinic. It took Anna a moment to recall its origin, and when she did, she put it aside, unopened. IVF information. In a moment of late-night weakness, spurred on by an email from Marie-Anne, who was as practical about Anna's childlessness as she was about everything else, Anna had filled in an online enquiry form. But even as she did it, she knew it would never go any further. Creating a child alone wasn't the answer. She wasn't put off by the burden of single parenthood – she liked a challenge and didn't mind hard work – but it felt like cheating to dive straight in there. Any fool could be loved by their children.

On the rare occasions she went out to restaurants in Marea, eating alone, Anna would smile at bored toddlers on neighbouring tables, whose parents were ignoring them, and they would look back at her, suspicious and implacable, before continuing trying to get their parents' attention. To earn that kind of indiscriminate devotion, she felt, you first had to do something infinitely harder: find someone you adored who adored you back, enough to want to be tied to you forever. Someone who would bring you into their family, and then create a new branch of it with you.

From outside came the sound of a truck reversing on the square and a shout, followed by the thud of beer barrels. A last-minute delivery to Sweeney's.

Clubbed by tiredness, Anna pushed the bills aside so she could lay her head down on the table. The varnished surface adhered to her skin, and her nostrils filled with the smell of wood permeated with sour beer. She felt herself sinking into a doze, before jerking awake at the sound of the door opening.

It was Cynthia, one of the Brits from the urbanization. In her seventies with thin, teased orange hair and a conurbation of lines on her chest, Cynthia frequented the bars and cafes in a rota, taking care to share herself out fairly amongst the owners. After tutting at the litter of envelopes on the floor, she planted herself at the counter, and ordered a Coke.

'Ice with that?' said Anna, moving behind the bar.

'Oh. Well. I don't usually,' said Cynthia, sounding aggrieved that Anna had to ask. 'But maybe one cube.'

I don't care whether or not you usually take ice! Anna shrieked internally, as she served Cynthia her drink. Cynthia proceeded to talk at Anna, aggressively oblivious to Anna's mood and her pile of paperwork, not caring that Anna might not give a toss that Cynthia had been hoping to get to the Morrison's on Gibraltar that day.

In the early days, Anna had felt enraged by Cynthia and her ilk; set in transmit mode, operating under the presumption that by buying a drink, they were owed Anna's time and interest. The long-term effects of the dynamic worried her, too: after all, how many times could you have dull conversations, or passively concur with opinions you didn't hold, before this became the level on which you permanently operated? But gradually she had become accustomed to it, accepting that the primary function of conversation in Marea was to pass the time. In the lead-up to Christmas, Anna had been asked dozens of times what she was doing for the day itself, and had given the same weak, evasive joke in response – 'staying here in case Santa needs a pint on his rounds' – often several times to the same person. They didn't seem to notice, or care, about the repetition. It almost seemed a comfort, like a child wanting the same story read to them night after night.

Cynthia was now expressing her views on Gordon Brown letting in too many immigrants and giving millions in foreign aid whilst her pension was cut. This was another thing Anna had got used to: expats complaining about immigrants being allowed to abuse and disrespect the system in UK, seemingly unaware that they themselves were doing exactly the same thing in Spain. Not learning the language or integrating; working illegally; dodging taxes. Today, she wasn't in the mood to let it go.

'But what are you?' said Anna, cutting through her. 'What are we?'

'Eh?' said Cynthia.

'We're all immigrants, aren't we? You and me. All of us. Do you think the Spanish shouldn't have let us in?'

'We're not immigrants!' said Cynthia, furiously. 'We're expats!'

Anna didn't have the energy to continue the argument she had started, and turned back to her laptop screen. Cynthia angrily unzipped her purse and threw a euro onto the counter, before banging out of the door.

The light was fading now, the window grilles casting weak shadows on the floor. Another day gone. The music had started up again at Sweeney's; a full song this time. 'Sweet Caroline'. Anna pictured him sitting in an empty room under a glitter ball, lyrics scrolling unsung across a projector screen. Then, finally, she allowed herself to think about the finca, and what might be going on up there in the mountains. But her mind was too leaden; she had passed the point of imagination some time ago. Leaving the litter of envelopes and bills, she took another bottle and headed upstairs, the '*ba-dum-dum-dum*'s of the song's chorus following her up the stairs.

It was gone 2pm by the time Anna heaved open the shutters the next day. Before the metal had banged against the top of the frame, Sweeney was on her terrace. He must have been waiting for her.

'Did you see the offer at Carrefour for grout cleaner?' he said. 'Three bottles for ten euros. Thought you might be interested.'

He was wearing his customary matted fleece; she had never seen him without it, even in forty-degree heat. The broken veins on his cheeks were livid in the sun.

'What can I do for you, Sweeney?' she said.

'So, your fellas were at mine last night.'

'What's that?'

'Black fellas who are renting your place. They came to the karaoke. All of them.'

'OK,' Anna said, at last. 'Are you sure it was the same people?'

Sweeney smirked. 'Oh yes.'

'But you weren't here at New Year's. You didn't see them. How can you be sure?'

Sweeney's smile widened over his chipped teeth.

'Mattie said they were,' he said. 'And she certainly saw your man, if you know what I mean.'

'What *do* you mean?'

'They were looking very friendly,' said Sweeney. 'And then they went off together. And I don't think it was to play Scrabble, if you get me.'

Anna tried to digest this, but something else was in her mind.

'What do you mean, *all* of them?'

Sweeney smiled, pleased to have got to her.

'Whole bunch of them. Six, seven. Said they were staying up at yours. Having a right laugh, it sounds like.'

He looked at her, arms crossed high on his chest, waiting for a response. She would not give it to him. He was winding her up. There weren't seven of them, surely. A couple, she had thought. And she couldn't imagine that diffident man who collected the keys at New Year's Eve confiding laddishly to Sweeney about the party he was having at her house. He barely spoke English, for a start.

'They're free to do what they want up there,' she said, primly. 'I'm glad they're having a good time.'

Sweeney smiled at her again before walking off back to his bar, stick legs invisible inside his jeans. She watched him pause to rub off the fluorescent lettering on his window with the sleeve of his fleece, before ducking back inside.

Anna remained on the terrace, looking out towards the promenade, at the tired palm trees and strip of placid ocean. Then she went back inside and made a call.

Twenty minutes later, she was in the back of a cab, on the coast road, watching the sea emerge and disappear in the spaces between the developments. The driver, a heavy-set Spaniard in his sixties, hadn't attempted to make conversation, for which she was grateful. The journey was costing Anna eighty euros, taken from Simón's envelope; so reckless a use of money it felt like stealing. But she couldn't ask Tommy for a lift, now. Nor could she involve any of the other expats; she didn't want anyone to know she was going up.

She just wanted to check everything was OK, for her own peace of mind. So she could look at the others straight when they tried to rile her or cast aspersions. She had her excuse ready for the men at the finca: she was just passing by, and needed to collect a document. Nothing odd about that.

Passing the greenhouses, they got stuck behind a lorry emblazoned with tomatoes, trundling below the speed limit. As they finally turned onto the mountain road and began to climb through the pine forest,

Anna opened the window and stuck her head out, inhaling the medicinal freshness that cleaning product companies spent millions attempting to mimic, trying to dilute her sense of trepidation.

'Not this one,' she said to the driver, as they neared the turning to the finca, 'Or the next one, but the one after that.'

She directed the driver to pull in at the verge and they sat in silence for a moment, as the car engine cooled. The gate was ajar, the house out of sight. From here, everything was innocent. The only change Anna could see was that her *Se Vende* sign had fallen – or been placed – face-down onto the ground.

'I won't be long,' she said to the driver. He shrugged; he didn't care how long she took, as long as the meter was still running. Maybe she should have asked one of the others; someone who would come to her aid.

She got out, closing the car door as quietly as she could. Remembering the creaky gate, she wove through the gap rather than pushing it fully open. Parked just beyond it was the first surprise: a new, expensive-looking pick-up truck, its back empty, tarpaulin lying loose. Another present from the men's grateful and generous employer? Skirting around the truck, avoiding the noisy gravel, Anna moved towards the house. It was a modest building but today it loomed, the pale stones of its facade like crocodile armour. Behind it, the sky was a delicate watercolour blue, laced with wispy clouds being pushed around by the wind. Some distance away, an eagle circled on the air currents. There was the faint sound of building work; Alfonso was probably making another chicken shed.

In the front garden, giant thistles rattled in the breeze. The dry leaves cracked underfoot, loud as twigs, and the rosemary bush jabbed her as she squeezed past it. Had the place been this wild when she was here with Tommy, just a week ago?

She saw that the outside light had been left on, and felt an involuntary flicker of irritation then unease. Somehow, this sign of occupation unnerved her more than the pick-up truck. The window shutters were closed.

Before she could wimp out, Anna lifted the tarnished knocker and let it fall, before clasping her hands behind her back and arranging a smile.

No reply. She knocked again, louder, twice. She knew exactly how long it took to get to the front door from any point in the house. After a moment, she reached for the handle and slowly turned. The door opened with a smooth, silent action – she had spent a lot of money on that hardware. She peered around the frame.

'*Hola?*'

The shuttered sitting room was dark but she could feel, instinctively, that there was no one there. She pushed the door a little wider, and as more light entered the room and shapes became distinct, she saw that the furniture had been rearranged. The two Knole sofas had been pushed together to form a bed, although the seats were different heights. A pillow and blanket from the bedroom cupboard lay folded at one end. The armchair had been pulled right up against the fireplace. On the floor was a pair of mattresses, barely thicker than towels. The air felt as if it had been stirred.

Anna stepped inside, leaving the door ajar, and her sense of unease merged into a forensic curiosity as she scanned the room. The flagstone tiles were gritty with dirt from outside. Lined up against the wall were three large, full, heavy-duty plastic bags – the tartan zip-up affairs sold in street markets – and several small rucksacks. A row of cheap sandals – she counted five pairs. Some toiletries and a plastic bag. She could smell that a fire had been lit recently; beside the grate were two of her saucepans and nestled in amongst the ashes were some tinfoil-covered objects. Potatoes?

On the bookshelf, two phones sat charging. Beside them, a book – *The Hours* – was pulled two inches out of its neat row, as if someone had quickly thought better of reading it. And hanging from the mantelpiece, looped around one of Michael's attempts at sculpture – a small abstract nude in clay – was what looked like a primitive necklace, with three little leather pouches tied onto a string.

This sign of a possible feminine presence reminded Anna of Mattie. Was it possible she'd been up here too? She crept across the kilims to check the other rooms. The guest-room bed was neatly made up, a pile of clothes folded on the chair, a smear of toothpaste on the Moroccan basin. In her room, the bedspread was half pulled onto the floor. The sight of it, fresh from someone else, gave her a lurch; a similar sense of queasy wrongness as when someone wears your shoes.

In the bathroom, a desiccated bunch of wild flowers sat forgotten on the windowsill; they must have been there a year. A bottle of shower gel sat balanced on the bath ledge, in front of the broken tiles. What must the men think of them? They now seemed a ridiculous affectation. There was a tidemark of dirt around the bath; unusually dark. What had they been doing? She noticed that the light switch was also smudged with dirt, and a blackened towel lay on the floor.

She left the house quickly, pulling the door closed and walking briskly down the path, this time not bothering to avoid the gravel. As she was passing the rosemary bush, she heard something and froze. Voices. They seemed to be coming from beyond the almond grove.

Before she had time to consider whether it was a good idea, she stepped off the path, pushing past the bushes and onto the terrace. The almond trees were bare of leaves and their white trunks were slender, offering little cover, but still she darted from one to the other as she moved quietly through the grove, weeds brushing her as she passed. Beyond the grove was the hill that marked the edge of the finca's land; linking the two areas was a small plain, where she and Michael had kept their short-lived chickens.

Before Anna saw anything, she smelled damp, mineral soil and heard the sound of metal striking earth. Slowing down, she crept forward, until she could glimpse the plain. The chicken wire of the abandoned coop – an ambitious two-floored structure she had built herself – came into view, and then, near to it, the top half of a man. His T-shirt was covered in smears of dark brown, and he was talking and gesticulating to unseen friends in a foreign language. She leaned forward further, clutching onto two tree trunks for support, and saw that the man was standing in a hole, about a metre wide.

Anna looked at the hole, and the man, and the marks on his T-shirt. Then she swung around and retraced her steps, picking up speed until she was springing through the grove as nimbly as a deer, barely panting. In no time she cleared the almond grove, and the gate came into view. The cab driver was waiting, staring into space. Anna dived into the back seat and pulled the door shut.

'Let's go,' she said.

She sat quiet and still until they reached the safety of the pine forest, and then she leaned forward to speak to the driver.

'Actually, can we go back to a different address?'

5

Marea Village Residential Caravan Park, where Mattie lived, was situated on the ring road, near the big supermarkets. Anna knew of the place but had never been there: she'd had no reason to. Although always quick to accept an invitation, Mattie had, to Anna's knowledge, never hosted anyone herself. Nor had Anna, come to that. They had tacitly excluded themselves from the expats' endless social reciprocity: Anna with the excuse of running the bar; Mattie, her ill mother and eccentricity.

The cab dropped Anna off beside the entrance sign. Small letters under the name stated that the park was a retirement community, for over-fifties only. Aha, Anna thought: a clue to Mattie's age. (But Jesus – in a decade, she too would be eligible to live here.)

Beyond the gates were three wide thoroughfares each lined with large static caravans, scores of them stretching into the distance, as uniform and tightly spaced as modern cemetery plots. Anna found a prefab reception block, which doubled as a shop and cafe. A man with eye bags like blisters took a lunch order from a table of four – 'Mash, roast, chips or jacket?' he asked each diner in turn – before telling her where to find Mattie.

Following his directions, Anna felt conspicuous on foot; judging from the other traffic on the site, mobility scooters were de rigueur, even for those at the younger end of the Marea Village demographic. Everyone here seemed to know each other, hailing those they passed or slowing to a halt to yak. They seemed different from the urbanization expats, Anna thought; breezier, less strained. She supposed it was because they didn't own property; they had the levity of people with little to lose.

Each caravan was around forty feet long, clad in dun-coloured uPVC, with a kitchen under an adjoining awning and a small patch of outside space. Almost all were hooked up with satellite dishes, and the sound of individual TVs merged as Anna went by. Passing one caravan, she heard a startling, guttural cackle from inside; from another came the smell of frying fish. Although a few of the caravans looked unoccupied, their white plastic outdoor chairs tilted against their table and still dusted red from the *calima*, the park appeared pretty full. Anna supposed that many of them were used as holiday homes, and now was when UK-based retirees came over to warm their bones, heading back home again during the unbearably hot summer months. Swallows, they were called.

A few inhabitants had personalized their plots with strings of lights and garden ornaments, but no one had gone as far as Mattie. Unit 443 was conspicuous from a distance: the outside space laid with AstroTurf, bordered with pinwheels and plastic flamingos. She had even squeezed in a freestanding pond, although it was empty, its blue plastic lining pathetically revealed. A few feet away, her neighbours, an ancient couple, sat in recliners under an awning, watching a TV fixed-up outside. The woman was wearing a strapless dress, her breasts like cushions on her lap. She smiled as Anna knocked on Mattie's door.

Within seconds there was Mattie, in a peach kimono.

'Anna!' she gasped, in overblown, delighted surprise.

Twinkling at her, Mattie leaned against the door frame, clutching its edge with one green-nailed hand. Her black sheet of hair hung to her waist, and the neckline of her kimono dropped almost as far; it was the kind of thing Anna had only seen before in 1940s films, or East London burlesque nights. There was a grease stain near its hem. From inside the caravan, Anna heard snoring. Mattie's disabled mother?

'What *are* you doing here?' asked Mattie.

It was a good question, and Anna hadn't prepared a reasonable excuse, as she would have done with someone else. She'd assumed that Mattie would take the visit in her stride: after all, she rarely questioned anything, seemed oblivious to social conventions.

'I . . . Sweeney mentioned that you talked to one of the guys who's staying up at my place. Last night. At the karaoke?'

Mattie sighed dramatically.

'Darling Almamy.'

'Yes.'

'Well, I suppose we did do a *bit* of talking, yes,' said Mattie.

Without make-up Mattie's face was even more oddly ageless; egg-like in its lack of pores and lines and shadow. Her eyes were faintly Asiatic and had very clear whites; you'd think she was a non-drinker.

'Did he mention what they were doing up at the finca?' said Anna. 'What was going on up there?'

Mattie cocked her head to one side.

'Did they mention digging a hole?' said Anna, feeling stupid. 'Like for a vegetable patch, or something?'

Mattie laughed. 'A *vegetable patch*?'

'Mattie, this is important.'

'No,' said Mattie, looking at her. 'We didn't talk about vegetable patches.'

There was a cough from inside the caravan. Anna had vaguely assumed that Mattie had brought the man, Almamy, back here, but could this be true? Marea Village offered as little privacy as a festival campsite.

'Where did you go with him?' asked Anna. 'Did you go up to the finca?'

Mattie paused, before leaning towards her.

'I went to Senegal,' she said, in a stagey whisper. 'And I tell you, Anna, there's no going back.'

Anna shuddered, visibly, at the vulgarity, and Mattie clocked it. Her eyes narrowed, and in her look Anna realized that whilst Mattie might have appeared impervious to how others saw her, at this moment at least, she was not. She knew exactly what Anna was thinking of her.

Then Mattie smiled, and said, in an artificial, sing-song voice, 'So, do you like my place?'

'Yes, it's lovely,' said Anna, just wanting to get away.

'I know!' said Mattie, as if the thought had just occurred to her. 'You should come and live here! Malcolm says there are a few plots going. People keep dying. One in, one out. I think you'll fit right in.'

Anna couldn't help herself, even though she knew she was lobbing Mattie an easy ball.

'I'm not old enough, actually,' she said.

'*Oh*,' replied Mattie pointedly.

Anna admitted defeat. She turned to leave, pushing open the pointless little gate in the miniature picket fence around the caravan and striding out into the park, speeding up until she was outpacing the mobility scooters. What a waste of time. Why did she expect any more from Mattie?

Furious, she marched home, barely registering her surroundings as she passed through the dark, narrow back roads of the town and emerged into the clean, open space of the square. Back at the bar, she sat at the counter and tried to calm down. She should call Simón again. But then she thought of their last conversation, his sharp, unsolicited warning against entering the property without permission. She should arm herself first.

So, instead, she called her *abogado*; the property lawyer she had dealt with when buying the bar. No reply. She pulled out her laptop and tried to get online to find another one, but the Internet was down. She scrabbled through the pile of papers behind the bar to find an old copy of the local English-language newspaper. Under the banner, *Everything Under the Sun!*, the back pages were dense with classified ads, tersely worded to come in as cheap as possible. *GARDENING, E5/hour. VILLA CLEANING, cheapest around. ODD JOBS – will do anything.* Tiling, airport transfers, pool maintenance, TV repairs, pet sitting, tennis tuition, cookery lessons, Zumba classes, AA meetings, British Legion events, house clearance, spare rooms, eBay listings. Then, For Sale: villas, bungalows, apartments, bakeries, bars, cars, jet skis, golf clubs, freestanding BBQs, plasma TVs, phones, dogs, puppies, dog baskets, fridge freezers, toasters, Soda Streams, hair straighteners, baby clothes bundles, crystal vases.

Standing out, pricily boxed in black, were the recession-proof services. Funeral directors (*specialists in repatriation*). Dentists. Pawnbrokers. *Get instant access to the latest bank repossessions.* And lawyers.

She called one at random and, when a woman answered, started to explain the situation.

'I will stop you there,' said the woman, her tone weary. The fee for a phone consultation, she explained, was thirty euros for fifteen minutes, 'in English.'

'Can we do it in Spanish for twenty?' said Anna, digging out her card. The woman was intractably silent until Anna had read out her details and the payment had gone through.

Then, she said, 'Is it in your tenancy agreement to prohibit digging on the land?'

'Well, that's the thing,' said Anna, triumphantly. 'We never signed anything. It was just a conversation.'

'What did you say in your conversation?'

'Just how long he would stay, and the rent.'

'Well, you know, a verbal tenancy agreement is as binding as a written one.'

Anna swivelled on her stool, astonished.

'Even with no witnesses?'

'Yes,' said the woman. 'That is our law.'

'That's fucked up!'

'Has the tenant been paying rent?' the lawyer continued, blandly.

'Well, the first month, yes.'

'It's very difficult to evict a tenant here,' the woman said. 'The law is on their side.' She explained that rent had to be unpaid for six months before proceedings could even begin, and that if Anna went onto the premises without permission, or shut off any utilities, she could be prosecuted for harassment. So, Simón hadn't been bluffing.

'If you believe you have grounds for damage to your property, we can begin proceedings,' the lawyer said. 'But I advise you, it will take a long time.'

'How long?'

'A year, at least, to get to the first court,' the woman said, and, unprompted, added that her fees from here on in would be eighty euros an hour. Anna couldn't tell whether the lawyer's abject lack of encouragement to press the case was born from kindness or, like a boutique assistant easing an expensive bag from the hands of a window shopper, because she had divined that Anna couldn't possibly afford it. In any case, the woman was efficient: with seven minutes remaining on the clock there seemed little else to say.

Anna finished the call and yelped with frustration. Whatever this faceless woman said, it was simply impossible that there was no recourse against a stranger desecrating her property. The law seemed insignificant beside the profound injustice of the situation.

All that time and effort and money, she thought. She had poured everything she had into that place. Not just money – all that love and care. She had polished the bathroom window's tiny brass latch with cotton buds, massaged the terracotta plant pots with yoghurt to give them an aged look. That place was *hers,* in the same way that her body was hers. How could she have been so careless, letting strangers in there?

With nowhere to go, her rage started to ebb. Suddenly, desperately, she needed comfort and found herself calling her mother. Janet answered cautiously. The TV was on in the background.

'Hello, darling,' said Janet, almost warmly, when she heard Anna's voice. 'I was wondering when you'd call. Let me turn this down.'

'Well, you could have called me.'

'Oh, you're always so busy. I never know when's best to catch you.'

Anna felt the familiar bolshy hurt beginning to brew and, when she spoke again, her tone was clipped.

'Can I ask you something,' she said. 'A friend of mine is having an issue with their tenants. They've damaged the property and are refusing to leave. Didn't you have a problem with some couple once?'

'The ones in Cheltenham?' said Janet. 'Who stole the bath panel?'

'I can't remember,' said Anna. 'Yeah, I think them. What happened in the end?'

'Well, they were a nightmare, weren't they?' Anna heard a faint grunt and realized Janet was directing her comment to Bill, beside her on the sofa, as ever. 'We had to go through the courts, it took months. They wanted to be forcibly evicted so they could get a council house. Don't you remember? I lost half a stone. Terrible. And people think it's easy money.'

'My friend doesn't want to take the legal route,' Anna said.

'Has she tried talking to them?' said Janet. 'We've found that issues can usually be diffused by a calm discussion.'

'Of course she has!' said Anna.

Janet gave a meaningless *mmmm* in reply, and Anna imagined her mother's gaze fixed on the muted TV, next to an impatient Bill. Suddenly, again she felt herself welling up.

'Surely I can get him out,' she burst out. 'It's *my house.* Do you remember, that bit just behind the almond trees? I just want them to go, Mum. They're doing something weird. There has to be some way I can make them go.'

Silence from Janet's end. Then she said, falteringly, 'Darling, I don't understand. Your house . . . ?'

'No, no,' said Anna, defused. She rubbed her face. 'Not mine. That's what she said to me. My friend.'

'Ah yes,' said Janet with relief, as if her daughter

suddenly recounting another person's distress in direct speech was nothing to question.

'Look, I can hear you're busy,' said Anna. 'Let's speak another time.'

'OK, darling,' said her mother. 'And how is everything with you?'

'Oh, fantastic,' said Anna. 'Wonderful. Great.'

They hung up, and she drank a *copita* in one, and then another straight after, trying to cauterize her frustration. Anna knew she had a part to play in her and her mother's feeble relationship, but her reluctance to confide in Janet was the result of decades of inadequate responses. She thought back to when she told Janet about Michael leaving. 'Well, he was very attractive . . .' her mother had said, sorrowfully.

She'd talked to Michael a lot about Janet, back in the early days. If Marie-Anne was a hammer drill when it came to what she thought Anna should be doing with her life, Janet was the opposite; so diffident that even if she did have opinions, she would think it presumptuous to offer them. As if she didn't feel she had the right to expect anything, or make a mark on the world. Anna had never heard Janet express any anger or disappointment over Derek's abandonment of her when Anna was tiny; she seemed to feel it was her due, that she'd never have been able to keep a charismatic man like him. When the dull, pedantic Bill came along, Janet allowed him to sweep her up, without resistance, not questioning whether he was right for her or not.

Michael had once declared that 'self-absorbed people make the best parents, because they see their children as extensions of themselves.' At the time it had seemed wise and incontrovertible, like everything Michael said, but actually, thinking about it now, it didn't make sense at all. Both Janet and Derek were self-absorbed, in their different ways, and where had that got her?

Anna had another *copita.* Another mental wound reopened. During the early days in Spain, she and Michael had explored their new country, spending the night in little towns, getting drunk in neighbourhood bars with strip lighting and toothpick wrappers on the floor and greasy legs of *jamón* above the counter that knocked them on the head when they stood up. In one of these places, the song 'Just the Way You Are' came on the radio.

'This is our song,' Michael had murmured to Anna, as she pressed against him. The comment surprised her – it seemed too sentimental a thing for him to say – but she was delighted and kissed the side of his neck.

He corrected himself. 'I mean, it's *your* song.'

At the time, tipsy and love-drunk, Anna hadn't thought that much of it – he had realized the phrase 'our song' was a cliché and changed his wording. But in light of his desertion, the hints he had given about their intellectual incompatibility, the comment took on a different hue. The song's lyrics proclaimed a lack of need of clever conversation; it was a patronizing tribute to the non-challenging partner from her out-of-her-league love.

Anna necked another glass, furious at the memory. On top of the condescension, the sentiment was a lie:

clever conversation was apparently just what he did need, and she was not enough for him, as he gravely explained when he finally deigned to answer her calls, four days after bailing out.

Anna noticed she'd finished the bottle. White wine didn't really count; it was just one step up from water.

The next morning Anna woke with a jolt, so early it was still dark. The vivid dream did not immediately dissipate and it took the steady red light of the security alarm on the wall to reminded her where she was, and that she was alone. On the arm of the chair sat her phone; on the floor beside it, an empty glass which had held the final, beyond unnecessary nightcap. Checking the time on her phone – 5.20am – she saw an unfinished, unsent text to her father. *Hi Dad, I was just thinking about something. You know I went to Bali, too? In my year off? I only chose it because you had lived there and I believed you when you said you would meet me out there and show me around and I . . .*

If she had even considered airing a twenty-year-old grievance with her father, what else had she done at the thin end of the evening? Warily, she checked her sent texts. Yes, there was one to Tommy at 1am: a lengthy justification for dumping him, laden with clichés. *You're such a lovely man. It's not you, you must know that.* Even, *I want us to be friends.* Far too overwrought for what was just a casual affair. Anna knew that her motive in texting him was not noble; she was after reassurance, for him to tell her how much he adored her. She thought of him waking in a couple of hours, rolling over in bed to check his phone; propping himself up on his elbow to shield the screen from Karen as he read it.

She shifted, and her laptop dug into her side. It was under the duvet with her. Once, drunk online shopping meant underwear or vintage lettering sets from eBay. In the recent past, it was usually a flight back to the UK. At a certain time of night, it seemed so irresistibly easy. For as little as €24.99, she could be out of here; at 2am, after a couple of bottles, all the counter-arguments faded into the background. She could just bail. Cut her losses and get out, like so many others had done. Pack a carry-on bag and spend the last of her money on a flight home, leaving the keys in the lock. Be on the Gatwick Express by tomorrow lunchtime. Start again from scratch. The next day, her sense restored, the flight time would pass by, the ticket wasted. Over the past year, four empty seats had headed back to Gatwick, carrying her ghost.

She prised open the laptop, the screen lit up in the darkness. Yes, she saw, she had tried to get onto the airline website, but her escape attempt had been thwarted: the €64.99 payment had been blocked by her bank. God, she really was in the red.

There was no point in bailing out, anyway. The bills from the finca and the bar would follow her. Tommy had told her about one woman who had done a flit and found herself being door-stepped by debt collectors in her flat in Southampton. Anna pictured herself in a single room in a house-share in an outer-London suburb, opening an *electricidad* demand. Standing in the queue at the discount supermarket, ignoring a +34 call on her phone.

The laptop screen went to sleep. Looking at the red eye of the security light in the corner of the room, she was struck by an intense loneliness. Stronger, even, than those awful few weeks up at the finca after Michael had left. It was like an out-of-body experience; a different and more frightening feeling than the panic she often felt in the dead of night, as if her rib-cage was full of moths who lay dormant during the day.

The impotent fury she had felt towards Simón, the feeling she had gone to bed on, was now turned on herself. What a fool she had been. Maybe this was just what she deserved for putting everything in one basket. Two baskets – Michael and the finca. Maybe it was some sort of poetic justice if the finca was destroyed. The place had been made to measure for a life she was no longer going to have – why not let it be torn apart and put to different use, like an unworn wedding dress cut up for tea towels?

But it was the nearest thing she had to a home. This apartment wasn't one, and neither was London any more. That, as much as the practical reasons, was what stopped her taking all those one-way flights she'd booked. She wanted, desperately, to get back to London – but the London she'd lived in before Michael. Before her friends started buying leather sofas and using phrases like 'forever home' and spending all weekend with their families. When arrangements didn't have to be made three weeks in advance. When things were there for the taking. Before Anna had realized that, just from one ill-timed decision to trust a man when he told her that she was his future, she'd missed her chance to be one of those women cycling around with an empty baby-seat on the back of their bikes, advertising both the fact they had procreated and that they had someone at home looking after the child.

And now, all her friends were onto their second. At least with the first, there still seemed time to catch up, and the personality changes motherhood wrought on her friends – preciousness, fussiness, insularity – could be blamed on lack of confidence. Come the second, it felt like they were gone for good. During her last visit home, the previous Christmas, Anna had understood that it wasn't that Jess and her other parent friends pitied her; rather, that they didn't have the headspace to think about her at all. When Anna talked about Spain they said, 'Oh, how wonderful! We must visit!' No one said, 'What the hell are you doing? What's really going on? This isn't you.' How lonely it was, to be taken at face value.

And on that last visit back, she had felt left behind by the city itself, too. Just a few years away had turned her into a tourist, walking too slowly, getting flustered at ticket machines, disapproving of the amount of packaging in supermarkets. Her clothes didn't look right. The good places she knew to get a drink were no longer good. She would meet friends on newly fashionable market streets and be overly conscious of the twenty-somethings flitting around. Lithe, insouciant, potent, they still had the power to dazzle and disorder.

Watching them, her situation appeared stark. She saw herself through London's eyes: an almost middle-aged woman. She could wander around the city for weeks by herself, dolled up, lingering in galleries and cafes, making eye contact, and not be picked up by anyone she wanted to be picked up by. Things would no longer happen to her.

And out there somewhere, maybe in the next street, ready to be bumped into, was Michael. Men like him had no shelf-life. He would be adored until death. Women didn't care that he was a tosser. *She* hadn't.

After that visit, she found herself longing to get back to Marea, where standards were low, where she was still considered hot stuff and the days were not mined with painful memories. Getting through customs at Gatwick felt like shrugging off a hefty backpack and, for a half an hour, sitting in the seafood bar at Terminal 3, she felt at peace. Anyone looking at her would see a lone woman, still relatively attractive, who could be going anywhere, to meet anyone. They didn't know the truth.

Anna realized her heart was pounding fast; she pressed a cushion against her chest to try and smother the hammering. Outside on the window ledge, pigeons cooed.

At 6am the heating clicked on, and as the radiators warmed up they woke the peculiar scent of the apartment: traces of past inhabitants that had settled into the pores of the place. Instant soups, Lynx, duty-free perfume, aftersun, dirty nappies.

No. She couldn't bail. She had her pride. She was

someone who did things properly, saw them through. She must salvage something from her time here, otherwise the waste would forever weigh on her. She'd give it six months. Stay focused and concentrate on squeezing everything she could out of the bar. Open every day for the full twelve hours, make an effort, be charming to the customers. Copy Sweeney and put on theme nights, do some two-for-one offers. Make a renewed effort to sell the finca. No booze; or at least, in the evenings only. Go back on Facebook, reconnect with old colleagues, start putting out feelers for possible work in London. Then she would be returning with something; or, at least, the knowledge that she had done all she could.

Anna had made such resolutions before: there had been any number of early-morning epiphanies, witnessed by the red eye of the security alarm. Was it a case of them stacking up to a tipping point, she wondered. Or was it more mysterious, like conception; after many shots, one would randomly take hold. Hopefully, the key was just meaning it enough.

Beyond the thin curtains, the light was rising, bringing out the shapes of the furniture. She would begin her new start now, she decided. She would go for a swim.

Anna had never seen Marea this early. The street cleaners must have just been, as the promenade tiles were slick and gleaming, but she felt as if she was the only person in town. A couple of stars were still visible and there was a bite to the air. The palm trees stood motionless. The sea would be freezing, but she needn't stay in there long: this was more of a symbolic dousing than a proper swim.

As she walked down the steps to the beach, the rising sun was reddening the sand and casting a golden film over the textured sea. On the other side of the bay, the outline of the mountains was vivid against the brightening sky, but the apartments and hotels clustered at their base were still indistinct; for a moment, the scene was as nature intended. A flock of tiny birds zipped around overhead, in too much of a hurry for this time of day, as if they were rehearsing for the evening ahead. In the absence of any man-made noise, the waves seemed as loud as an aeroplane taking off.

Anna stood still, using the beauty of the moment as an excuse to delay getting in the water. The sky above the sea was now slashed with violet and pink, as lurid as an inspirational poster: an unnecessarily epic show for low-maintenance Marea. Don't waste it on us here! she thought.

That weekend at the finca when Farah and Kurt came to stay, Michael had been telling his friends about his decision to paint the greenhouses rather than the natural landscape, because beauty was banal, and there was only one response to it. Kurt had quoted Oscar Wilde in response: 'No one of any real culture talks about the beauty of a sunset.' Trailing behind them, Anna had thought of the notebook she had kept from her trip to Bali when she was nineteen, filled with lengthy, unoriginal, deeply felt attempts to pin down the wonder she was experiencing, trying to squeeze every drop out of a trip she had spent two years saving up for.

Within minutes, the dawn spectacle was over, leaving in its wake a plain old blue morning, like any other. The air was briny and fresh and the sea had a serene, pearly quality that belied its frigidity.

She had to go in. Leaving a puddle of clothes in the middle of the beach seemed too much of a statement, somehow, so she took off her shoes to feel the chilly sand between her toes and headed for the cluster of dark rocks at the far end of the beach.

As she approached, she glimpsed something move beside them. A cat? But as she drew nearer, a boulder-size shape straightened to the height of a man and looked in her direction.

Paco. Anna stopped, feeling wrong-footed and intrusive, as if the off-peak beach was his domain. She raised a hand in greeting but before she could decide whether to carry on, he started towards her.

'Hey hey,' he shouted, in Spanish. 'Miss, come here, quick!'

When Anna didn't move, he shouted for her again, more agitated, beckoning with both arms. He was wearing dark clothes, a long-sleeved top and trousers, and there was little contrast between them and his tanned skin. She glanced over her shoulder – the town waking up now, a few lights on in the nearest hotel – and then started walking quickly towards him.

'Are you OK?' she asked, as she came close. 'What's happened?'

As she spoke she glanced beyond him. She saw something green – some discarded clothing? – and then, in a lurch of recognition, saw that the cloth was a T-shirt and that the T-shirt was clinging to the body of a man on the sand. An African man who, from his stillness and the way his legs were splayed at an agonizing angle, was almost certainly dead.

Anna stared at the body, her chest heaving. She looked back at Paco. His eyes were wide and he started talking fast, stumbling over his words and gesticulating.

'Wait, slow down,' she said, shakily. She put her hand on his arm. 'I can't understand.'

He expelled a breath before starting again, at the same speed. As he talked, they edged closer to the body. One arm was raised over the man's head, shielding most of his face. He was young, in his teens. He was wearing jeans and his sprawled limbs were uncommonly long and thin. Beside him, where the rocks met the water, bobbed a collection of plastic bottles, like a cluster of spawn.

'Who is he? Do you know him?' asked Anna.

'*No!*' barked Paco, perturbed, and started explaining again, this time just slow enough for her to understand. He had been sleeping under the tarpaulin in his boat, as usual, and had woken to the sounds of voices nearby. When he looked out he had seen two men carrying something across the beach, towards the rocks. He had called out, and the men had dumped their load, run back to a car on the road and driven off. He had then gone over and discovered the body. That's when Anna had arrived.

As he babbled, Anna's gaze was locked on the body. It was impossible that someone so young, so viable, could be dead. His dark, delicately muscled arms were as hairless as a child's. The T-shirt had a logo on the chest pocket – a grinning hippo brandishing a paint-brush. She felt compelled to take in every detail of him.

'They carried him,' Paco was saying again. 'I saw. They came from there.' He pointed inland.

Anna nodded absently, still transfixed on the corpse. She shifted slightly, so she could see the eye that was shielded behind the man's raised arm, and recoiled. The whole iris was bright red, so that the pupil floated in a pool of blood. Nausea rose in her throat and she clasped Paco's shoulder – even under his top she could feel the wiry hairs. She wanted to cover the man's eyes, pull down the lids like she had seen in films, but she didn't know how to do it, how much pressure to use. Besides, it seemed an intrusion.

It also occurred to her that, if this was a suspicious death, she shouldn't touch the body.

She looked away from the man's face. An extra waistband poked over his jeans; he seemed to be wearing two pairs. The jeans were thin, and there didn't appear to be anything in the pockets. Then she saw something else, at the top of his exposed slice of stomach, half-covered by the T-shirt. It looked like a string around his waist, tied tight, cutting into his flesh. She moved closer, to touching distance. There was something attached to the string that wasn't immediately visible against his dark skin: a leather pouch, about the size of a matchbox. Under the T-shirt were the outlines of several more similar shapes.

The mantelpiece at the finca. That necklace.

Paco pulled at her arm. He was babbling again, more distraught than ever.

'Have you called the police?' she said.

'*Señora*,' he said, holding up his hands. 'I have no phone.'

'Of course,' she said, surprised at how together she sounded. 'Mine's at home. I'll go back and call them. Will you be alright?'

Without waiting for his answer, she turned away and started running up the beach.

6

La policía didn't seem too interested in the body. When, back at the bar, Anna got through on the phone, the woman took down the details and said they would send someone to talk to Paco, but her tone was more suited to the news of a squashed cat on the ring road. It happened quite regularly, the policewoman told her, migrant bodies washing up on beaches. Didn't Anna know? They sailed over from Africa at night in flimsy, over-stuffed boats.

Anna hadn't thought about it before, had never considered how the men arrived here, and found herself getting defensive. Yes, she replied, of course she knew that – but it wasn't the case here. The body had been driven over from inland and dumped. Surely that deserved some attention?

She was also conscious of the hypocrisy of being frustrated by the police's lack of concern whilst withholding a crucial, damning piece of information: that the string of leather pouches, tied too tightly around the man's stomach, had until recently been hanging from her own fireplace. But, she thought, she must be careful. She needed to ensure the missile would hit the right target before setting it off.

Sitting on a stool in the shuttered bar, she nursed the knowledge, her thoughts circling the only narrative that made any sense. The dead man had been part of the group up at the finca; the owner of one of those five pairs of sandals she had seen lined up by the door. When he died – or was killed – the others had decided – or been ordered – to dump him down on the beach, to make it look as if he had drowned en route from Africa.

Her thoughts turned to the hole the men had been digging. Had they tried to bury the man before realizing it was too risky, and taken him down to the beach instead?

The bald scenario seemed plausible, but she could barely guess at the rest of the story. What had this man done to be killed? And what part had Simón played in it?

Two days after the discovery, the weekly expat newspaper was published. Anna bought a copy and, perching on the edge of the fountain, leafed through it. The paper devoted half-pages to stolen mopeds and disappointing pizzas, but failed to give the death more than a sentence in its *In Brief* column. It told Anna less than she already knew: a body had been found on Marea's beach, believed to be an African migrant. No mention of his name, or that any further action was being taken.

Maybe things were going on behind the scenes, she thought. In some police mortuary, rubber-gloved hands were carefully unpeeling the thin leather on those pouches. Did they contain tightly folded identity papers? Perhaps the man had already been named, his family informed. Anna imagined a wailing woman in a dusty, remote village.

She stood up, threw the paper in the bin and walked across the square. It was another mild, ordinary day, the sky an insipid blue, the palm trees barely stirring. Sweeney out sweeping his terrace. The gift shop woman, leaning glumly in her doorway. The coin-operated child's train, jiggling and flashing its lights as it solicited for custom. Caz doing her circuits, the dogs crowded around her like bodyguards. On a bench on the promenade sat Anna's neighbours, Rose and David, who raised their hands in unison to greet her.

Anna leaned against the railings, looking down to the rocks at the far end of the beach. The body was long gone but the sand was still scored by tyre tracks. Would they have taken him away in an ambulance, at least, or was he just flung in the back of a truck? Further along the beach sat Paco's blue boat and beside it Anna could see him crouched, tinkering with something. Should she go down and talk to him, check on how he was? No. There was no time. She felt fired by responsibility, her mind operating in a new high gear as she considered her next step.

Simón *must* have been involved. His rental of the finca had unsettled her from the start; and then there was the caginess and impatience during their phone calls; his warning to her about going up there. But if she sent police up to Yalo now, without any proof, wouldn't the Africans invariably get the blame? She imagined an officer coming across that hole, just as she had; fingerprinting the mud-smudged light switches; sliding a spade in an evidence bag.

Anna looked out to sea, watching a gull drop silently down onto its flat, gilded surface. She needed to go back up to the finca and talk to the men, to find out what had happened. They'd talk to her, she was sure. She'd proved herself on New Year's Eve, when she handed over the keys; she was kind, one of the good ones.

So, transport. Not Tommy. He was so amenable that if she asked him for a lift, explaining it was an emergency, he would probably stifle his confusion and hurt and take her. But the journey would be painful for both of them. She imagined ninety minutes of stilted small talk and his brave, dolphin smile; the inevitable questions that the 'emergency' would throw up.

She could call a proper cab, like before, except that she appeared to have reached the limit of her overdraft, and all she had to spend was the cash from Simón. There was just over 400 euros left, to last God knows how long. She couldn't spend a quarter of that on one journey.

She looked down onto the beach steps. Unusually, there were no handbag sellers stationed there today; just a trio of young Spanish men, smoking and talking quietly. Smoke from their spliff drifted over in her direction. An idea came to her and she walked down the steps to where they stood.

'Hey, can I ask you guys something?' she said, in Spanish.

The men stopped talking and looked at her. Were they teenagers? In their twenties? They made no attempt to hide their joint.

'Do any of you have a car?' she said. 'I need a ride.'

'Oh yeah,' said one of them, with close-cut wiry hair and very light-blue eyes. He laughed, looking at his friends. Ignoring him, Anna continued to appeal to the other two.

'I can pay thirty euros,' she said, and explained where the finca was.

'I'll do it,' said one of them. He was tall and narrow and wore his hair shoulder-length and tucked behind the ears, like a nineties tennis player. He didn't seem surprised by the request; maybe these sorts of deals were common in the post-crash Marea economy.

'Petrol's expensive,' said the pale-eyed one.

'Thirty-five, then,' said Anna. 'But that's really all I've got.' They could see she was telling the truth: the guy, her driver, gave an assenting shrug.

'You want to go now?' he said, and when she nodded he carefully handed an inch of spliff to his friend before leading Anna over to a Renault Clio, parked on the next street.

Anna started to climb in the back seat, before changing course and getting in the front. She didn't want to appear aloof. The car interior was extremely neat; there were even little pinnies on the headrests to protect the fabric. As they buckled their seat belts, Anna said, 'Sorry, I don't know your name.'

'Jaime,' he said. He didn't ask hers. He drove expertly through the town's narrow streets, one arm laid along the open window. His long nose was flattened at the top, as if someone had pressed too hard on it when he was a baby, and his eyebrows looked as if they had been plucked in the middle. Is that what young men did these days?

As they reached the coast road, he asked if she minded some music, and slipped in a CD of something fast and urgent: a dance sub-genre Anna couldn't name and wouldn't choose to listen to. Now, though, the music suited her mission; it was a soundtrack to action.

As the roadside scenery slid by, Anna tried to prepare for what she might discover up at the finca, but was too fired-up for speculation. She couldn't begin to bridge the gap between that body down on the rocks and a man who had been living in her house; because she hadn't known him in life, she couldn't picture him laughing with his friends on the sofa, or looking out over the valley as he stirred his dinner on the hob, or stooping to plug in his phone charger at that irritatingly low socket next to the bookshelves. Her zeal to investigate his death felt oddly impersonal, but no less imperative for it

She'd have to think on her feet in order to get the men to tell her what had happened, but she felt confident about that. After all, if Simón was abusing them

– if he had *killed their friend* – they would want the world to know.

Simón. What if he was there, at the finca?

For the first time that day, she felt a surge of anxiety. They were on the single-track road now, in the pine forest, stuck behind a lumbering water delivery truck. Anna glanced over at Jaime. He was nodding – in response to the music, she thought, rather than impatient at the delay. His lips were pursed and he looked closed off, on autopilot. For thirty-five euros, could she expect him to come to her aid?

Too soon, they were at the house. Anna asked Jaime to turn off the CD, and directed him to park on the verge, outside the gate.

'Listen, I shouldn't be long,' she said. 'But if I'm more than ten minutes, will you come and look for me? And if I shout, will you come?'

Jaime raised his eyebrows. His eyelids were large and convex, with a mauve tinge.

'What's going on in there?'

'Nothing,' said Anna. 'But – will you?'

Jaime looked at her for a moment, and shrugged, in what Anna took to be assent. She smiled at him, bravely, before getting out and closing the car door as quietly as she could.

A flood of relief: Simón's BMW was not there. The pick-up truck had also gone. Beyond the wild garden, the finca glowed pinkish in the late-afternoon sun.

There was a nip in the air, and the crisp, clear day was softening into something more nuanced and mysterious. Around that time, the light in the valley changed continuously, the complexion of the mountains shifting between blue to peach to grey to rose. Above the house, an eagle circled. Anna could hear a faint strain of music. Had Jaime put on a CD? Maybe it was from another car, elsewhere.

Anna inched up the side of the path, avoiding the gravel, pressing herself against the rosemary bush. Her foot hit something unexpected and she yelped: looking down, she saw an empty rusted sardine can, discarded by one of the builders. Anna had found dozens of them when they had finally finished. Ahead, amongst the foliage, she glimpsed some white cloth, and froze, but then saw it was only a washing line, string up between two birch trees. A neatly pegged row of T-shirts, pants and trousers hung limp in the still air.

On the facade of the house, a nuthatch was pecking at the mortar between the stones, looking for caterpillars. The sitting-room shutters had been left open, and Anna approached the window from the side, cautiously peering in. The room appeared empty. She stepped lightly across to the doorstep and slowly turned the door handle. As the door swung open, she held onto its edge to stop it banging against the wall.

Standing on the threshold, Anna scanned the room. The dirt that had strewn the flagstones on her previous visit had been swept up, but the room was not as neat as it was before. The sheepskin rug that used to lie on the top of the Italian merchant's chest had slipped off; one of the sofas was askew. A speckled jug, which she had once used to hold wild flowers, sat on the floor, beside a couple of glasses. A beard clipper – Michael's – was plugged into a socket. There were still five pairs of sandals lined up against the wall. On the side table by the door was a little pile of papers. Michael's sketches. The string and the pegs had gone from the wall. She stared at the empty space, before recalling the washing line outside. The pegs that had once held up Michael's drawings of her high heels were now gripping strangers' underwear.

She glanced over to the fireplace and . . .

'Oh!' she said, out loud.

There, hooked over Michael's feeble sculpture, was the string of three little leather pouches.

Derailed, she stared at it. Then, she stepped over to the fireplace and reached out to touch one of the pouches. Her fingertips stroked the stiff, rough leather.

As she did so she heard the familiar sound of the toilet cistern flushing. Her heart jolted. She turned to see a man emerge from the bathroom.

Anna heard herself making a noise – not a gasp, but a strange, low groan, like a release of pressure.

They eyed each other. The man's T-shirt was streaked with something dark. The old Anna would have started apologizing for her presence, but in that split second she knew she had to put on the cloak of someone different. After a long few seconds, she said, brightly, 'Hello, I'm Anna. This is my house. I just wanted to check everything is OK?'

'Don't touch it,' he said.

She withdrew her hand from the leather pouch and stepped back into the centre of the room.

'I'm sorry,' she said.

The man's eyebrows knitted together. His body was wiry but his face round, with a neat beard. Was it he who used Michael's clippers?

'I call Mr Ruiz,' he said.

'No, no, no need to call Mr Ruiz. I just wanted to check you were settling in OK. I'll go.' She stepped backwards towards the door and the man moved forward, maintaining the same distance between them, ushering her out. Now all she could focus on was those dark marks on his T-shirt. What was in the bathroom?

She turned and walked a few paces down the path and then glanced back. The man stood in the doorway, watching her, his arm resting proprietorially on her door frame. She continued towards the gate, the crunch of gravel horribly loud. Then, she heard the music again, faint but distinct, and voices on top, carried on the breeze. She stopped to listen. It wasn't coming from Jaime's car, but from the other direction, beyond the almond grove.

She looked back at her house, at the man still standing in her doorway, and suddenly changed course, veering off to the right. She squeezed through a gap in the bushes, dropped down onto the terrace and ran to the almond grove. She wound between the trunks like a slalom skier, not looking back to see if the man was following, and burst out onto the dip, where she had seen the men digging.

Panting, she sunk to her knees, the scent of damp,

mineral soil filling her lungs. Before her, three men in stained tops stood, startled, beside a mound of earth. Nearby lay some machinery, and a large coiled mound of plastic piping. She could see the hole properly now. It wasn't a grave: unless the bodies were to be buried vertically. It was around four feet in diameter, with ropes and a pulley system feeding into it. As she stared, a pair of hands emerged and gripped its edges, and a man hauled himself up, as if he were being born from the earth. It was the one who had come in for the keys on New Year's Eve, Almamy, his face flecked with mud. He scrambled to his feet and joined the others, staring at her. Inappropriately jaunty music played from one of their phones, which lay on a pile of clothes and water bottles.

'*Hola*,' she said, eventually, stupidly.

She appealed to Almamy. 'What are you doing?'

One of the other men said, quickly, '*No comprende*.'

'You speak Spanish?' she said.

They all shook their heads. The music continued to drift. One of them reached down to turn it off, and, she noticed, kept hold of the phone.

'What is this?' she said, pointing at the hole.

The one holding the phone said, 'You talk to Mr Ruiz.'

He started to scroll through the numbers.

'No,' Anna said, putting out a hand. 'Please. We don't need to call him.'

She heard a sound behind her and looked to see the hostile man from the house approaching. He stopped a little way from her, as if to guard her exit through the grove. She looked back towards the hole and the still, tense men around it, and then away from them, towards the chicken coop, as she tried to collect her thoughts. The coop's wire was dented, a small hole under one side the legacy of the fox that dug in to kill their hens. Their droppings were still there on the ground, dried – it reminded her of the globules of paint on the earth in Michael's studio. Amazing that they were still preserved, out here in the open, after two years. Had there really been no rain since then?

Then she looked back at the hole; the pulley system; inhaled again that unfamiliar scent of damp, sweet earth.

'It's a well, right?' she said. 'For water?'

The men glanced at each other.

'Why here?' she said.

'*No comprende.*'

One of them, at the back, very young, glanced nervily behind him, towards the hill, as if expecting someone. Almamy pulled up his T-shirt to wipe his face, and the sight of his stomach reminded Anna of the body on the beach and the leather string; the original reason she had come up here. But there was no time to think about that now.

She changed tack.

'Listen,' she said, addressing Almamy. 'I know Simón is not a good man . . .'

'Mr Ruiz is a good man,' he said.

'You don't have to say that to me,' said Anna, suddenly desperate. 'I'm not trying to get you into trouble.

It's not your fault. It's just – this is my home. It's my *home.* You understand?'

'It is not your home,' said the man with the neat beard from the house, who had stepped forward so he was beside her.

'Yes,' she said, carefully. 'This is my home.'

'You do not come from here. From Spain.'

'Oh no,' she said, understanding. 'No. I come from England. But this is my home here in Spain.'

Another silence. The very young one again glanced behind him, towards the hill.

'Where are you all from?' she said, finally.

'Africa,' said the man with the neat beard.

'Which country in Africa?'

'Africa,' he repeated slowly, spelling out each syllable.

'You must miss home,' she said, ignoring the mockery in his tone.

There was no response. They had closed down entirely, now. The very young one at the back was still compulsively glancing over towards the hill. The one with the neat beard started talking to the others in their own language – no doubt, ordering one of them to alert Simón. She should go back to the car. But, she thought, if Simón was coming anyway, and she was screwed, then she might as well see what was behind that hill.

Anna started walking forward, past the men and the well and the coop, and began climbing the hill. Her hill. She forced herself not look back to see if the men were following or making that phone call, focusing instead on the movement of her legs and the view ahead of her; the yellow, dry grass; the curve of the top of the land; the crisp outline of the mountains beyond it. Perhaps Simón would be standing there, arms folded, waiting for her.

She reached the top, and stopped short. Before her was a sea of grimy plastic. The greenhouses that had so upset Michael two years earlier had vastly expanded – they now covered every inch of land between the bottom of the hill and the edge of the forest. The nearest structure was close enough to see the blurred shapes of workers moving around inside. Giant tins of fertilizer lay discarded around the perimeter, and she heard the hum of some irrigation system, like artificial cicadas.

She heard a sound behind her and turned to see Almamy draw up beside her.

'You work here?' she said. 'Simón owns this?'

He nodded.

'How long has this been here?'

He shrugged. 'A long time, I think.'

The late-afternoon air nipped at her; from somewhere in the valley came the sound of goat bells. She glanced over her shoulder towards the finca, its stone roof visible beyond the almond grove. What was once her home now seemed like a folly, innocent of the monstrosity that had crept up beside it, rendering it next to worthless. No pool was one thing; a well feeding three acres of dirty plastic another. Not to mention a legion of exploited workers as neighbours.

She turned and started slowly back down the hill. Almamy followed her.

Back at the well, the other men were sitting on the ground, waiting. The phone was back on the pile of clothes.

'I'm leaving,' she said, not looking at them. Her voice sounded reedy and defeated. 'Please don't tell Simón I came.'

It was a vain hope, she knew. Not looking at them, she walked back into the almond grove and started towards the car. She noticed that Almamy was still following her.

'You don't have to see me out!' she said, stung at being escorted off her own land. But he had another motive.

'What is your password, please?' he said, in a low voice, as they wound through the trees.

'What?'

'The password. For Wi-Fi.'

'Oh,' said Anna, nonplussed. She told him, and he nodded his thanks. Then she remembered she had closed the account a year ago, when she'd left. 'Sorry, forget that. It doesn't work any more.'

He shrugged good-naturedly, and continued to walk with her. Then, in the same conspiratorial tone, said, 'And how is your friend Martha?'

'Martha?'

Almamy nodded eagerly.

'You mean Mattie?'

'Yes, yes,' he said, smiling. 'How is she?'

'I don't know,' said Anna. Then, seeing his face fall, added, 'I mean, she's fine.'

'Tell her Almamy says hello, please.'

They continued walking through the grove, more companionably now. The finca came into view, and this time the sight reminded Anna of why she had come. She seized the opportunity.

'That necklace. In the house. Over the fire,' she said, casually. 'Do you know what I'm talking about?'

Almamy frowned.

'Gree gree?'

'The necklace thing,' she said. 'Leather. I saw one like that the other day. On a man. It was around here.' She touched her stomach and paused. 'He was on the beach.'

Almamy's face, so alive when asking about Mattie, clouded over.

'*No comprende*,' he said.

And with that he turned and slipped back through the grove.

Jaime had got out of his car and was leaning against the gate, hands stuffed into the pockets of his Adidas top. He took one look at Anna's expression and her stiff, fast walk, and turned back to the car to start the engine. Without a word, she climbed in the back door, and he reversed down the path.

Moments later, just after they had turned onto the mountain road, another car approached. Jaime pulled in to let it pass. A black BMW. Anna caught a glimpse of the driver, that seal-like black hair with no parting, and flattened herself down in the back seat.

Jaime glanced back at her, bemused.

'You know him?'

'Who?' she said, hearing the BMW's expensive roar subsiding into the distance.

'Mr Ruiz.'

'You know Simón?' she said, still not lifting her head from the seat.

'Sure,' said Jaime. 'Everyone knows him. I used to work for him. He was in construction, before that was fucked. Is he going to tear down your house?'

He seemed faintly amused by it all. Anna remained flat on the back seat and didn't reply. After a while, Jaime put on the CD. The fast music fed her agitation and as she stared at the roof of the car, her body jolting as the wheels bounced over the unpaved road, she thought: if Simón was going to tear down the finca, she could hardly feel more outraged than she did now.

7

As they reached the outskirts of town, Anna asked Jaime to drop her off at the police station. It was only as he drove off that she realized she'd been too distracted to pay him his thirty-five euros.

The *comisaría* was one of Marea's grander buildings, with a neo-classical facade in custard yellow fronted by high gates and a row of limp flags. But attempts to impress ended at the automatic doors. Rows of screwed-down seating, vending machines and an ever-present cleaner mopping the floor gave the reception area the ambience of the departure gate for a delayed night flight.

Anna had been here before, for the registration procedures required of all foreign residents, and for the drink-driving matter, although the finer details of that night were hazy. Her enduring memory was of Michael taking a seat two away from her, and his expression as he looked at her across the gulf of moulded plastic.

'It could have been you,' she'd said, flushed with shame.

Spain's alcohol limit was strict – a single glass of beer would push you over.

'Well it wasn't, was it,' he'd replied, as if having the bad luck to be caught was yet another failing of hers.

Today, there were half a dozen people waiting in the reception, including a couple who looked as if they had bedded down for the day, with foil-wrapped food on their laps. The spicy smell mingled unhappily with the lavender-scented chemicals from the cleaner's bucket. Anna joined those hovering around the window. After the elderly woman ahead had given a long account of a theft by her lodger, Anna stepped up to the glass. The policeman was writing something, head bowed, but from his careful side parting Anna recognized him as the man who had dealt with her on the night of the drink-driving incident. Of course she would get him. She didn't have time to move before he looked up.

'*Sí?*'

There was no flicker of recognition. It had been almost two years, she thought; he must see dozens of people a day.

'I wanted to ask about the man whose body was found on the beach,' she said. 'The African.'

'That case is closed,' he said. Although somewhere in his forties the man had a disconcertingly cherubic look, with full cheeks and dark-pink lips.

'What happened to him?'

'I can't tell you that,' he said. 'But the case is closed.'

She frowned. 'But what if I have new information?'

'What exactly is the information?' he said. He didn't bother to inflect the end of the sentence, such was his lack of interest in her reply. He'd had the same tone during their interview, when Anna had stammered away about how sorry she was, how she really wasn't the kind of person who did that sort of thing.

'You should look into Simón Ruiz, he's a tenant up at my house. I think he might have something to do with it. I don't know what, but I think there's something going on up there. And he's digging this well . . .'

The policeman's chin lifted.

'Simón Ruiz is your tenant?'

Anna nodded, although there was something in his tone that made her falter.

'As I say, Miss Moore, the investigation is closed,' he said.

His eyes were on hers. She hadn't given her name this time. So, he did remember her. The look he was giving her now had the same level of disgust as when, during their previous encounter, he'd given a slow, deliberate account of the time he'd had to scrape a six-year-old drink-drive victim off the road.

Behind her, Anna heard a sigh, and the policeman looked over her shoulder towards the next person. Anna turned and left, waiting impatiently for the automatic doors to release her and then, on the street, picking up speed until she was at a sprint. The soles of her five-euro supermarket pumps were so thin she might as well have been hitting the pavement barefoot. Pedestrians stared and cats fled as she flew past: people didn't tend to move fast in Marea. She ran through the pinched streets, under washing lines, past a Spanish boy kicking a washing-up sponge; a weightless football. She didn't know exactly why she was running, whether out of shame at her past or frustration with the present.

As she turned onto the road leading to the square, she slowed down, panting, as a thought came to her. That glimpse of Simón in his car, as he headed to the finca. There was no doubt that the men would tell him she'd been there. If not Almamy, then certainly the hostile one from the house. She imagined Simón striding over to check on progress at the well, and receiving the news in furious silence.

She checked her phone, but he hadn't called.

Anna walked gingerly to the end of the road and looked across the square. The bar was shuttered, as she'd left it. No BMW purring outside. Out in the square, pensioners pottered around the barren fountain; the mild weather was holding up. The ice-cream parlour had opened for the first time that year; a serving girl stared blankly out over the pastel mounds. Sweeney brought out pints for a couple on his terrace. The church clock chimed 3pm.

Anna fought the urge to retreat, to duck into one of the anonymous little old-man bars she'd passed and stay there forever. Instead, she made herself move forward, stepping out from the safety of the dark side street and padding across the square to her bar. She was crouching down to open the padlock on the shutters when she heard the slam of a car door and there he was, striding towards her. He stepped smartly up onto the terrace and stopped a few feet away. Too close. Anna stood up and backed into the shutters, the metal jabbing her shoulders.

'My men say you were harassing them,' he said, pulsing with anger. He was wearing a polo shirt, his delicate forearms crossed at his chest. 'Do not go up there again. I'll have you arrested.'

'I'll have *you* arrested,' said Anna, although she had just attempted and failed to do exactly that. 'You can't just dig a hole in my land.'

'A "hole",' he said, with contempt.

'OK, a well. Whatever.' She flushed. 'You can't do that.'

Simón smiled mirthlessly.

'It's a borehole, actually. And if you knew anything about "your land",' he said, 'you would know that it is sitting on a reservoir which belongs to the valley. Anyone growing agriculture nearby is entitled to draw from it.'

'That's not true!' she said, but she heard a quiver in her voice. Was he right? Was this in the small print of their contract when they bought the place; one of the clauses she had skimmed over, half-understood?

'It's been true for eight hundred years,' he said. 'Maybe you should have done your research. You want to look out at lovely views in your little paradise, but we need to eat, I'm afraid. And we were here first.'

He had relaxed now; arms uncrossed, a condescending smile. Anna looked away from him, over his shoulder. The T-shirt woman was at the door of her shop, watching them; meeting Anna's gaze, she ducked inside.

'How long have the greenhouses been there, that size?' Anna said. 'When we arrived, they weren't that big. They weren't anywhere near the bottom of the hill.'

'You are wrong,' he continued. 'They have always been there. Long before you came. I think you are confused.'

He took a step towards her and sniffed, pointedly.

'Perhaps you are drunk.'

'No, I'm not!' cried Anna, before she could stop herself. She knew she had lost now. Her forearm twinged; she realized she was squeezing the padlock key hard in her fist.

'You are disgusting,' he said. 'You Brits. Coming here, because you've failed at home. Becoming drunkards. Driving drunk. You could have killed my daughter.'

Anna stared at this loathsome, precise man. How did he know about her conviction? She recalled the policeman's face that morning when she mentioned Simón's name; his refusal to even hear her out.

Simón started walking back to his car with the air of someone who held all the cards. But he was wrong.

'I know what you did with that man,' Anna called after him.

It was a long shot. But Simón stopped, his back to her.

Triumphant, Anna pressed on.

'I saw the body myself, on the beach,' she said. 'You should expect a call from the police.'

Even from behind, she saw Simón relax. He continued walking to his car.

'I have no idea what you're talking about,' he said, over his shoulder. 'I think that you are still drunk.'

His BMW was blocking the side street and a queue had formed behind him; drivers began leaning on their horns. Anna stayed standing until the car had pulled off, and then crouched back down at the padlock, calves trembling. She opened her tightened fist; the key had left a reddened imprint on her palm.

Once inside, Anna locked the door of the bar and sat at the counter with a *copita.* As the shock of the encounter with Simón wore off, she felt stranded, like a child at the high end of a seesaw outweighed by an intransigent bully at the bottom. The only point she had scored against him was ephemeral – that pause when she had first mentioned the dead man, before he had relaxed again and delivered his parting shot. But what could she do with that, without any proof of his involvement or anyone willing to investigate?

As for getting back the finca, the options open to her looked unappealing and pointless. She imagined herself in some municipal library, leafing through pages of dense, technical Spanish, trying to find the relevant section on land laws. Selling her remaining possessions at the car boot sale in order to raise enough for a session with a lawyer; one tiny step on the lengthy, uncertain, expensive journey to evict Simón and the men.

The bar was horribly quiet. Anna got up and turned on the radio, heard a blast of manic chatter, and snapped it off again. Instead, she switched on the glass washer, for its low, comforting rumble, and refilled her *copita.* God, how she longed for someone to share the burden, and tell her what to do. Or, better still, to deal with it themselves. Impulsively, she called Tommy; his phone rang once before she came to her senses and hung up.

How would Michael have reacted, if he'd been here for this? She'd rarely seen him tested, had always tried to shield him from difficulties. Even when they'd been threatened by a junkie with a scaffolding pole in Granada, she had instinctively stepped in between the two men. Presumably, once upon a time, when he still loved her, he would have been at her side, battling to evict Simón, vowing to get justice for the dead man on the beach. But such speculation seemed perverse: after all, if he still loved her, she wouldn't be in this position.

In the square, the church clock chimed the half hour; Marea had excessive timekeeping for a place where most residents had little to do. Anna thought back to that moment when she and Michael first climbed the hill beyond the almond grove and glimpsed the greenhouses. Simón claimed the structures had always been bordering their land, as large as they were now, but Anna didn't remember it like that at all. Back then, they were just a flash of plastic, far off in the distance. She was sure of it.

The size of Simón's agriculture empire was unimportant in the scheme of things, but, in the absence of solutions to bigger issues, it moved into the foreground. It worried her, the prospect that she might have so badly misremembered. Had that plastic ocean really been there all this time, just out of sight behind the hill? A vast presence, teeming with silent men, pressed up against her land? She found she was swivelling back and forth, violently, on the stool. Maybe this was how it felt at the beginning of losing your mind, realizing that your memories could no longer be trusted.

Her phone was there on the counter. She could call Michael, and ask him to put her mind at rest and confirm that those greenhouses were just a speck in the distance when they first arrived. But even in her fevered state, she knew this wasn't wise. As far as she was aware, Michael had no idea of what she was up to now. For all he knew, she had blossomed in his wake and was now shacked up in the finca with a dashing Spanish intellectual, surrounded by babies and chickens and interesting friends and incomparably better off than when she was with him. Even the scantest information about her circumstances now would puncture any such visions, let alone the fact she was living in the derided Marea.

She stopped swivelling. His paintings. He'd captured that view behind the hill, many times. He had an agent, and a gallery; or at least, he did. The pictures might be online. Galvanized, she found her laptop and tried the Internet, in the hope that it might have started working. When it didn't, she put her laptop under her arm, unlocked the bar door, and ran over to

Sweeney's, perching on the edge of his terrace to catch his signal.

She'd done this several times before when her Internet was down, but now Sweeney's network appeared to be locked. As she tried again to connect, a shadow fell over her: Sweeney, the crotch of his baggy jeans level with her face.

'You've put a password on?' she said.

'Indeed,' he said.

Anna smiled up at him, expectantly.

'Ten euro minimum spend to use the Wi-Fi,' he said.

'Oh, come on, Sweeney, don't be like that,' she said. 'I've helped you out loads.'

He looked down at her, face drawn and implacable.

'I gave you all that vinegar, remember?' she said. 'Dozens of bottles. I didn't ask you for money.'

'Out of my hands, I'm afraid,' he said. Anna let out a growl of frustration and snapped the laptop closed.

'There's an Internet cafe in town,' Sweeney added, as he turned away.

Anna had walked past the Internet cafe before, registering it only to wonder how such places still survived when even her ancient neighbours, Rose and David, had broadband at home. Its narrow, out-of-the-way street seemed a fitting location for such an anachronism.

Arriving there now, Anna winced at her lack of imagination. Of course, it wasn't aimed at her, or the other Brits. The windows were plastered with posters offering mobile phone deals and money transfers to Africa, using photos of winsome young girls in plaits and old women in tears of gratitude. Around them, making use of every available inch of glass, were homemade notices on scraps of paper in a variety of languages. Similar to the small ads in the back of the English newspaper, she supposed, but most were even more general and terse: the single word *Work*, followed by a mobile number. Then, there were enigmatic notes targeted at one other person: *Julian, Oct 24, get in touch*, with a phone number. Anna thought of the notice boards in travellers' cafes during her Bali trip in the late nineties; those pre-email forums for rekindling lost connections.

The cafe was three quarters full, the customers all African men. A Spanish girl behind the counter took Anna's money and pointed her to a spare terminal. A melancholic pop song played, lyrics in Arabic, and there was a delicious smell in the air: on the counter was a large bunch of fresh mint that the girl was making into glasses of tea. Bottles of water and soft drinks were also on sale. On a table near the front desk, a dozen mobiles were attached to charging leads, like dogs tied to a railing.

A couple of the computers were housed in private cubicles, and their occupants sat in silence, heads bowed and shoulders hunched to further block the view of whatever they were looking at. Amongst those out in the open, however, the atmosphere was lively. The men chatted to each other as they typed whilst some, wearing headphones, talked loudly to people on Skype. Anna recognized their animated manner from her own similar calls back home. *All good! Best thing I ever did. Oh yes, work's going well.* Postcard conversations, sent over a wall of dishonesty. People back home didn't want to hear the full truth, nor did anyone want to admit it.

Anna logged on at the terminal, beside a man playing a furiously fast card game online, and stared at the empty search box. After Michael had left, she had, inevitably, spent the odd evening at her laptop, looking for clues to his life without her. He wasn't on social media, so she had combed his friends' profiles searching for photos of him. Even the most innocuous mention of his name, any sign that he was existing without her, threw her off course for hours. In the end she had given up googling him, and it was one of the few resolutions she had stuck to. It had been over a year, now.

Be strict, she told herself, as she typed in his name. Focus. She'd search only for Michael's paintings from his time at the finca, nothing else.

There was a yowl from the man beside her as he lost his game. Anna leaned closer to her screen. The first two results under Michael's name were a website and a Twitter feed. Neither had appeared when she last searched for him: it was like going back to a familiar neighbourhood and seeing new buildings had sprung up. She opened the website. It was of the stylish, minimalist variety, the home page just a single image of one of his paintings with his name laid across in lower case Courier. Anna was reminded of Simón's business card; the arrogance of that lack of information.

She clicked on *recent work*. And miraculously, there it was, third from the top – exactly what she was looking for. *Plasticulture: greed v nature.* Six paintings of the landscape of southern Spain, exhibited in a group show at an East London gallery the previous autumn.

'Yes!' she exclaimed out loud – after a morning of disappointments, something, finally, had gone her way. Infected by the animation of her card-playing neighbour, she even found herself giving a self-conscious air punch. Without stopping his game, the man looked over and nodded his approval.

As she enlarged the thumbnails, however, her sense of triumph evaporated. She had seen some of Michael's paintings in their early stages, up at the finca, and remembered them as mildly expressionistic yet still representative of reality. But either her memory had deceived her or Michael had reworked the pictures once back in London, as the images in front of her now were abstract to the point of incomprehensibility. The land and sky were painted almost identical shades of grimy off-white, whilst the greenhouses were a formless, bright green mass. And crucially, far from being a distant aberration, the structures now appeared vast, a blob devouring the countryside. As huge as the one there now, if not larger.

The scene was distorted for emotional effect, surely. Deflated, she looked around the cafe, this time taking in the chipped MDF partitions and grimy, clunky equipment; the thick snakes of exposed wires along the skirting and the tile which had come off the wall, revealing the hardened glue beneath it. The man next to her gave a jarring shriek, slapping his hand on the table and gleefully cursing his opponent.

Anna turned back to her screen and moved the cursor towards the log off button. Then, she paused. Clicking on Michael's website, she'd felt barely anything – a faint flutter, perhaps, but it was more like a reflex, a muscle memory, incomparable to the pain of her previous online excursions. Had time finally done its work, and inured her to him?

She clicked the *about* tab on Michael's website. Under some terse biographical details, there was a photo of him at his easel: black and white, a heavy contrast lending him deep hollows under his cheeks and brow. His forehead was furrowed and he wasn't looking at the camera, too engrossed to even give a minute to his own publicity.

Anna gazed at the photo and felt a pleasing sense of detachment. The sight of him left her unmoved, as if she were looking at a mere arrangement of different tones, rather than an image of the man who had demolished her. Maybe she had been over him for months, but hadn't realized, like a leg fully healed within its plaster cast.

Emboldened, she opened another tab and looked at the second search result under his name, his Twitter profile. So he had taken Farah's advice. She quickly scanned the first few dozen entries. They appeared to be confined to his life as an artist: re-tweets of praise for his work, quotes from magazine articles, droll opinions of shows he had seen, the odd aphorism. Here he was, building his brand. The most personal it got was the news that he was going on an artist's retreat in Bordeaux.

Anna kept scrolling. There was nothing here she wished he were saying to her, or that made her miss him in the slightest: in fact, the opposite. Wasn't it a relief not having to pretend she got his jokes? To knew what he meant by *liminality* and *negative capabilities*?

Then, she spotted a re-tweet that jarred amidst Michael's sober content. *Homemade crumpets? Damn right. Recipe here. #lotsofbutter #simplysatine.*

Anna clicked through to a photo of a winking young woman with a sharp jawline and short dark hair in a punky undercut. Her bio read *Satine Simpson: cook, blogger, campaigner, overachiever.* The name rang a bell. Frowning, she turned back to Michael's website and checked the credit on the photo of him at his easel. Yes, it was her.

Anna's inner smoke alarm went off. No good could come of further investigation into this woman, she knew, but it was too late. The noise in the cafe faded to nothing and she stared at the screen, scrolling through Satine's tweets.

> Hey, men in the British Library – I'm here to WORK, ok?

> Oh Copenhagen, we will only be together for 18 hours – let's make the most of it. #getreadyvesterbro

> Nice profile in ES mag today (ignore the 'high priestess of hipsterdom' crap)

Props to the Observer for the baddass review of #simplysatine

Apols to everyone who couldn't get into my launch last night. #bullshitfireregs

Happiness is: when you and your man both get onto the same artists' retreat. #mercibordeaux!

Anna's chest filled with concrete, but deep within was a pulse of satisfaction at having been proved right. *Merci Bordeaux!* She opened a new tab, searched Google Images and there they were, Michael and Satine, at a gallery party just a fortnight earlier. Beer bottles in hand, they posed for the camera, tucked into each other. Satine was wearing a fedora and denim dungarees, a slice of her pale, bare torso on show. Was she early twenties? Late twenties? Young and beautiful enough, in any case, to look good in dungarees.

Michael's trousers were rolled up to expose his bare ankles and brogues and he had grown a substantial beard. Anna recognized the look from her last trip home, when a pocket of East London appeared to have been colonized by the Amish. Annoyingly – inevitably – it suited him. And he was smiling. Beaming, actually. When Anna had been with him, he had seen photos as a chore.

So, Michael was now a happy hipster with a hot hipster girlfriend. His hand was on Satine's arse. Her left arm was curled around his waist. And on her hand, just visible, something glinted.

Anna leaned in for a closer look, her face only a few

inches from the screen. Maybe it was just a normal ring. But her investigative energies had been diverted: she needed to know. There were three minutes left on her time at the terminal. She turned to Satine's blog, *Simply, Satine.* That enraging comma! The subtitle was *Food, feminism and flights of fancy.* She scrolled through recipes and opinions, photos of dogs, canals, bikes, cocktails, gaunt body parts and young people in neon Ray-Bans, until she found it, dated the previous month.

An Announcement

Time: 2230. Place: E5. Occasion: dinner with the A team. We're putting the world to rights over lamb chops and strong liquor. We talk dogs, Bieber, the future of radfem. We act out scenes from The Wicker Man in memory of Ted Woodward. Have the obligatory dance-off to Run DMC. It's all good.

Then, I call for silence and get up on the table. I can put it off no longer. Suddenly, for the first time in years, I feel nervous.

I have to tell them that M has asked me to marry him, again. And this time, I've said yes.

Me. The girl who rants about the patriarchy at any opportunity. Who led the Ms Selfridge campaign. How am I going to tell them I have finally been persuaded to get hitched? And that the only reason I can give defies rational analysis.

Simply, love.

Without warning the screen went blank, as if the computer was taking Anna's wellbeing into its own hands. Anna continued to stare at it.

Simply, love.

The din around her was suddenly unbearable. She pushed back her chair and stood up. As she moved towards the exit, threading around the terminals, the cafe door opened, and Paco entered.

Anna stopped, shaken out of her absorption by the incongruity. She had vaguely assumed he never left the beach, let alone went online; it was like seeing a sea mammal walking on dry land. He looked different today, more muscular, as though his head were welded straight into his neck.

Anna looked away in the hope he wouldn't notice her; she wasn't in the mood to talk. But Paco seemed to be in a hurry, taking a bottle of water from the desk and sitting down at a terminal, with no offer of payment. The girl behind the counter just smiled at him.

Anna slipped out of the cafe and trailed home along the dull, dim streets. The streetlamps around these parts weren't lit at night, to save money. It wasn't quite warm enough for people to be outside at this time yet; the windows she passed glowed with TVs and the bursts of laughter tracks. The buildings looked as if they were all constructed in the same fortnight in 1982, and painted sickly yellows and pinks. When she and Michael had first visited Marea, she'd made a wry observation about how Farrow & Ball could bring out a range for the town: Own-Brand Mustard, Tinned

Salmon. Through a window, she saw a man hold a baby up above his head. An elderly man lay splayed in the doorway of a shop, snoring. A butcher's shop window was filled with spongy duvets of tripe. As she got closer to the centre, to the old town, the streets widened and turned from rough, uneven paving stones to cobbles, buffed from half a century of the soft-soled summer shoes of tourists. She passed the window of a sweet shop, fizzy cola bottles arranged beautifully on a silver platter, as if they were oysters. Here, the streetlamps were left on.

Anna was still in a daze. Not because of Michael – she barely recognized that bearded, beaming man. She missed how he had made her feel, for that first year, but she didn't miss him at all. No, it was Satine who had thrown her.

She'd had the same raw materials as Satine, once. She'd been young and good-looking and bright. But she'd lacked the crucial binding element: the self-belief that made you think the world needed to hear your take on feminism or your twist on a bacon sandwich, or know what your feet looked like wearing a toe ring. It was the glue that held a person together and made them someone to be reckoned with, and convinced men to stay with them forever. Without it, you could be demolished with a few blows and left for rubble.

Satine wouldn't have let Simón into her house. She wouldn't have embarked on an affair with Tommy because she was grateful someone wanted her.

Anna thought of one image of Satine she had seen

on her blog, sitting on her father's lap, arms around his neck. *My main man.* She reminded Anna of one particularly confident girl at school, who had told the others that her dad constantly said to her: 'Sissy, when you walk into a room, those people are lucky to have you there.' Others at Anna's school would bemoan their dad's over-protectiveness: how they would vet their boyfriends, threaten to kill them if they hurt their baby girls. They told Anna she was lucky not to have to deal with that.

Back at the bar, Anna shut the door behind her, and poured a *copita.* She noticed a strong smell of damp. Was it always like this, or was there a leak?

Outside in the square, the church bells started ringing the hour. Anna counted the chimes – nine – and thought of all the couples in the world sitting together on the sofa, watching TV. She rose off her stool and leaned forward over the bar to inspect the optics. Tequila! That was it. Fetching a glass, she pressed until it was half full. Far too much, but it would save her coming back again. She took a sip, and winced as the spirit pinballed up against her neurons.

Another few mouthfuls, and she was buzzing. After months of wine-sodden days and fuzzed discernment, leading inexorably to a melancholy bedtime, this state of sharp, exhilarating intoxication seemed a revelation, a bracing smack across the chops. And it had been just here, within her reach, all this time! She took another gulp and got to her feet. The bar was like a tomb: she needed to get out. And she needed company.

*

The beach steps were ill lit at night. In the dense darkness beyond them, the waves roared. As she approached, Anna could see three vague male shapes and the glowing tips of a couple of joints. By the time she was close enough to realize that her driver was not amongst them, they were looking at her and it was too late to retreat.

'Where's Jaime?' asked Anna, in Spanish.

'He's not here,' said one of them, in English.

'I can see that,' she said, in Spanish. 'Do you know where he is?'

'At home, I guess,' he said, in English.

Anna looked at the guy, and he looked back at her. Was that a smile or a smirk? He was the one with pale eyes; dark and stocky, with short, curly hair. Maybe she should ask him back? No. She sensed a lack of kindness in him. He was playing to the other two: they would mock her later.

So might Jaime, of course, but better the devil you know. Not that she really knew him at all.

One of them gave her directions to a street in the new part of town, a few minutes' walk away. Anna glided across the square, the cobbles slippery underfoot. The tequila was still working: she felt heady and boosted. Outside Sweeney's, a couple in their fifties sat in silence over their beers. You're not going to have sex tonight, thought Anna, but I am.

She found Jaime's street, even though there was nothing to distinguish it from the others in the new town: narrow, strewn with washing lines like bunting; lit windows behind grilles and net curtains.

At Jaime's house, Anna paused only for a moment, in case she lost her nerve, and rang the bell. In so far as she had imagined it at all, she thought he might share a flat with friends, and was prepared for more smirks and joshing. But the door was opened by a woman, her age or a bit older, with two-tone dyed hair, like a badger's nose. The woman looked at her quizzically, and Anna opened her mouth, about to give the excuse of a wrong address, when a young girl appeared, pressing herself into the woman's side and staring up at Anna. Of course: this was his mother.

Anna smiled and, trying to sound casual, asked if Jaime was home.

The woman's bad hair didn't obscure the fact that she was extremely beautiful: fine-boned and doe-eyed. Born in another place, she could have been a hedge funder's wife or a news anchor. The little girl at her side was holding a green bean, twisting it around her fingers. Behind her, in the room, Anna could see a cat eating from a bowl, pulling a piece of meat onto the floor to better concentrate on it.

'He's in his office,' Jaime's mother said, indicating across the road. 'Knock before entering.'

Anna looked across to a parked car. Jaime's car. The interior light was on and there he was on the passenger side, reading a book. The seat was pushed right back and his shoeless feet were wedged against the dashboard.

Anna thanked the woman and crossed over the road. She tapped on the car window, and Jaime jumped.

'I didn't pay you this morning,' she said, when he opened the door.

'No,' he said, unfussed. 'I was going to find you tomorrow.'

Anna realized she didn't even have the money to hand; that's how flimsy an excuse it was.

'I left my wallet at home,' she said. 'Do you want to come back with me?'

Jaime looked at her and she added, for the avoidance of doubt, 'We could have a drink?'

'Sure,' he nodded, and it was definitely with a smile, not a smirk. He put a bookmark in his book – *The Power of Now* – and placed it in the door's side pocket. She opened her mouth to tease him about it but then thought better of it. He locked up and they headed off towards the bar, walking close together. His top carried the scent of fabric conditioner.

As in the car, Jaime seemed content not to speak, and Anna resisted filling the silence, instead savouring the headiness of the moment. Of all the drugs concocted by man, none came close to this: knowing that someone you fancied was a sure thing. God, how she'd missed this! There had been an element of it with Tommy, but her attraction to him had been rooted in gratitude at his excitement over her. This felt more elemental and potent.

'Your mum's really beautiful,' she said, finally, as they crossed the deserted square, grazing hips.

'God, not you too,' he said, amiably.

'She must have had you young.'

'Yeah.'

'What I'm really asking, Jaime, is – how old are *you*?'

Jaime glanced at her and laughed.

'Old enough,' he said.

Anna grabbed his arm.

'Fuck, that means you're like, eighteen or something.'

Her voice sounded loud and theatrical in the empty square. She knew that this alien man at her side, with his tracksuit top and footballer's hair, was not a teenager – rather, somewhere in his twenties. What he had told her in the car that morning, about working for Simón during the construction boom, made that clear. Still, she felt the need to test him: to make sure the age gap between them wasn't a big deal. To try and ensure that later, when she was up close to him, he wouldn't gaze at her and say, after a beat, *um, I don't want to be rude but – how old* are *you?*

Jaime passed the test. Or rather, he just laughed and shook his head, and they continued walking.

Anna hadn't mentioned that she owned a bar, and thought Jaime might be impressed. But, as he helped her pull up the shutters, his only comment was, 'This place used to be a bakery, when I was a kid.'

Once inside, she swiftly attempted to create some ambience, which, in the absence of side lamps, involved switching off the main overhead light and leaving on the one in the kitchen. The room would not be mistaken for a bordello, but it would have to do. She put on a CD, *Harvest.* Everyone liked Neil Young, didn't they?

Jaime sat on a stool and produced a pouch of tobacco.

'This OK?' he said.

Anna nodded, and filled two glasses with tequila.

'Do you have a beer?' he said.

'Oh, come on,' she said, 'have a shot with me.'

'A shot?' he said, looking at the amount she had poured, but he accepted it, and, from their neighbouring stools, they clinked glasses and knocked them back.

'Whoa,' he said, flicking his wrist in the air, and the boyish gesture gave Anna a flash of him with his gang on the beach steps, telling them about this evening, about her, to a chorus of sniggers and high fives.

'So what's with the other place this morning?' he said, fingers working on a joint, back to his air of benign nonchalance. 'That was nice. How come you're down here?'

'I was living there with this guy, but then he decided he didn't love me any more and left,' she said. 'He didn't even tell me. Just drove off early one morning and left a note on the table. I didn't want to stay there after that.'

She was surprised at her frankness, but it was liberating, knowing her relationship with Jaime would go no further than this evening.

Jaime frowned as he licked the Rizla.

'On behalf of men, I apologize,' he said.

She laughed at his quaintness.

'I bet you're not a bastard,' she said, inanely.

Jaime lit the joint and then passed it over to her.

'There are girls who would disagree with that,' he said. 'But I am trying to be good.'

'Is that so?'

He raised an eyebrow in reply.

This suggestion of past bad behaviour was, Anna felt, as good a cue as any. She took a puff on the joint, although she didn't like dope, and attempted to exhale with style. Then, as she handed it back, she kept his gaze and leaned forward to put her hand on his thigh.

Unflustered, Jaime put the joint on the counter and got to his feet, and she slid off her stool to meet him. He pressed her up against the bar and kissed her. His mouth tasted of weed, oddly sweet; hers must too, she supposed. She slid her hand under his hair to feel the nape of his neck – almost indecently tender, after Tommy's – and with the other pulled up his top to feel his warm, lean back. His fingers stroked her breast, under her T-shirt, and she wrapped one leg around his, clamping onto him as tightly as she could.

This clearly wasn't going to take long, and Jaime broke off to glance around the room, presumably looking for a soft surface. Knowing there wasn't one, Anna tugged him down onto the floor. She lay back, feeling the cold, gritty tiles through her clothes – how long had it been since she had swept? – but Jaime took her forearms and pulled her up, deftly swapping places so she was on top. Whether this was a gentlemanly act or not, Anna didn't know, or care. Straddling him, she sat still for a moment, looking down at his young, unreadable, semi-handsome face. On cue, the CD started on the opening bars of 'Old Man', and she laughed at the timing.

Then she started to undo his belt buckle and he shifted to take a condom out of his back pocket. He must do this all the time, she thought, and for a moment felt stung, although she had no right to.

She was wearing a skirt, and so was spared an ungainly struggle out of jeans. As he put on the condom, she looked away – there were bag hooks under the lip of the bar counter, she'd never noticed them before – and then closed her eyes to focus on the physical sensation, and to feel less self-conscious as he looked up at her. Moving faster she reached out for support and grabbed the leg of the nearest stool, and then felt it topple and opened her eyes to save it just before it fell.

She came indecently quickly, just before him. 'Old Man' hadn't even finished.

'Sorry,' she said and they both laughed at her Englishness.

She climbed off him, adjusted her clothes and got to her feet. Jaime went to dispose of the condom. Anna felt flushed and unglued and suddenly quite sober.

'Well. Thank you,' she said, when he came back.

'Hey, you kicking me out?' he said, frowning.

'Oh, no. I just thought . . . no, of course. Stay. Let's have a drink.' She reached for the bottle.

'Actually, do you have a Coke or something?'

As she went behind the bar to fetch it, he said something she didn't catch.

'What was that?'

'Where are you from?'

'London. Well, not originally, but that's where I was living before.'

'You like it here in Marea?'

She had a brief flash of Simón, on her doorstep, asking the same question.

'Have you always lived here?' she asked, sidestepping, as they sat back on their stools, with their knees pressed against each other.

Jaime nodded. 'A lot of the guys, they want to go abroad to find work. They think you can't have a good life here. Carlos – he was down at the beach, too, you met him – he's going to Canada next month.'

'You don't want to go?'

'To Canada? No. I don't like ice hockey.'

'And too many bears.'

'Man, I hate bears,' he said, shaking his head.

'No bears in Marea,' she said. 'Or ice hockey, come to mention it.'

He smiled. 'It's not the greatest place, but it's my home, you know? I'd miss my family.'

'Must be cosy, all living together,' she said.

'Cosy?' he said, not understanding the word, and his repetition of it made her realize how patronizing it sounded.

'I mean, how is it, living with your parents?' she said.

He shrugged. 'It's OK. For now. I hope it's not going to be forever.'

'So, you used to work for Simón?' she said, moving on.

Jaime nodded, and told her he and many of his friends had dropped out of high school to work in *ladrillo,* the construction industry, during the boom years. Developers like Simón had hung around school gates, recruiting, with promises of fortunes to be made.

'And it was true,' said Jaime. 'I was on three thousand euros a month. We used to pay for beer with five-hundred-euro notes. They had to ban them in the town because we took all their change. We were the cool guys, you know? For, like, five years. There were so many cranes around, wherever you looked, we called them the national bird of Spain. I bought this beautiful old Fiat. Man, that was a nice car. Then we were working on the Plaza de Sol, out there.' He waved his hand vaguely north.

'I know it!' said Anna. It was the place she went with Tommy.

'And then the boss – Ruiz – he turned up one day and said work was stopping and that was the end of it,' he said. 'Two years ago. Nothing since. We hoped Madrid might win the Olympics, and then there would have been work, but . . .' He shrugged. 'When they announced Beijing had got it, Carlos kicked a wall so hard he was in a leg brace.'

'If there's no building work, can't you do something else?' said Anna. 'I mean, if Simón's now into greenhouses, can't you work there?'

'You're joking, right?' In his voice, for the first time, was a hint of derision. Anna thought back to those hunched dark shapes she had glimpsed labouring behind the filthy plastic.

'But you're all so young,' she said, taking a slug of her tequila.

'What use is being young if you don't have possibilities?' he said. The phrase sounded stiff coming from him, as if he'd heard it somewhere else. 'Being young isn't an advantage here. My dad had a kid and his own house when he was my age. It's fucked up.'

'So, you're a *nini,* right?' she said, pleased to have remembered the word. She had caught a news story about the plight of the unemployed generation, condemned to live at home into their thirties, spending their best days in their childhood bedrooms, fruitlessly applying for minimum wage jobs.

His face fell.

'I guess,' he said. 'I haven't given up, you know. I'm starting a business. Selling scrap.'

'I'm sorry,' she said quickly, chastened. 'I'm not judging. I mean, fucking hell, we're no better! Look at us. The Brits. Isn't there a word for us, stupid Brits over here . . . what is it?'

'You mean *guiri*?'

'That's it,' she said. 'You must hate us.'

'No. Why?' he said. And just when she was worried she had punctured the mood, he added, 'Although you do all wear awful shoes.'

They both looked down at her bare feet.

'Not you, of course,' he said.

'No, I have no shoes at all.'

'You have nice feet,' he said. 'You're pretty. I think you look like the girl in *Shutter Island*. You seen it?'

Anna shook her head. 'All of me looks like her, or just my feet?'

'Just your feet,' he said, and leaned over to lift her left foot onto his lap.

'Anyway, you never said what you think of Marea,' he continued.

'Well, the weather's good . . .'

He gave a jokey sigh, squeezing her instep.

'Yes, and?'

'And . . . you're all so nice to each other here!' Anna said, sentimentally. 'There's community spirit. Like, I was in the Internet cafe earlier and Paco came in and they just let him use it. You don't get that in London. We'd just step over him in the street.'

Jaime looked up at her. 'Paco?' He laughed. 'You know who he is, right?'

Anna nodded. She didn't need to hear the story about the town celebrity discovering the shipwreck again. For a moment, she considered telling Jaime about the body, but she was enjoying not thinking about all of that. She wanted to keep things light. She felt a surge of warmth towards this self-possessed young man, who asked questions and liked his parents. She took her foot off his lap and slid off her stool to stand in front of him, wedging herself between his knees, and they started to kiss again.

8

Anna snapped fully awake, as if she'd spent the whole night primed for this moment. She registered that she was in her chair in the apartment – there was the red eye of the security light. She tilted her head from side to side, and then stood up, but there was no trauma. In fact, she felt unnaturally fresh, as if she had gone to bed at 8pm after two pints of water. Maybe she was still drunk.

The doorbell rang, and she realized it was this sound that had woken her. She crossed to the window and looked down. Coarse sandy hair, receding at the temples. Tommy. Why was he here? She watched as he bent down to tie his shoelace and saw his top ride up, exposing a section of bare lower back, dotted with moles. It occurred to her that she'd never actually seen Tommy with his shirt off: she'd seen far more of Jaime in a couple of hours than she had of Tommy in six months.

Images of the night before rose up but she pushed them to one side. Not now.

'One minute!' she called down, and pulled on some clothes.

Tommy gave a dislocated smile when she opened the door.

'You called,' he said, averting his eyes and jiggling the car keys in his hand.

Had she? She leapfrogged over the night before to her panicked phone call to Tommy, aborted after one ring.

'Oh, I was . . . I shouldn't have. I'm sorry. I was in a state. I'd just found out about that guy, up at the finca, he's digging a whopping great hole in the land. A borehole. And I just got flustered. I'm sorry.'

Beyond him, she saw that the sun was high and the sky a solid, unequivocal blue. A couple was sitting on the edge of the fountain, working their way through ice creams. The drought-defying bougainvillea bush on the building opposite was a froth of lurid purple flowers.

'A borehole?' said Tommy.

'To beat the drought. Apparently there's a reservoir under the ground. He owns the greenhouses next door. I guess he's going to pipe the water to them.' She tried to summon her outrage of the day before but the battery was flat; she'd need to rev it up again. 'It just seemed horrific, you know, to dig on my land without permission. And it looks like I can't get him out without hideous legal proceedings.'

Tommy's face screwed up with concern; there was no hint of satisfaction at his misgivings being proved right.

'Anyway, how are you?' she said, feeling guilty at eliciting such sympathy.

'Oh good, good,' he said. 'Someone's interested in the villa. Seems genuine. He's flying over to have a look. Got family in the area and wants to retire out here.'

'Great!' said Anna, with the animation of a primary school teacher. 'Well done!'

After a pause, Tommy said, 'Do you want me to talk to him? This guy at your place? See if I can help?'

'Oh, no, you don't have to do that,' she said.

'It's no trouble,' he said. 'I'd be happy to.' He smiled sadly at her, and she remembered that this was how Tommy operated: to be bright and helpful, to rise above his feelings.

She nipped up the narrow staircase to the apartment to get her phone. When she returned, Tommy was staring hard into the space over his shoulder.

'Listen,' said Anna, benevolently. 'I'm sorry about before. But I do think it's for the best. Don't you?'

Inputting Simón's number, he gave a dry laugh.

'I'll never think that not seeing you is for the best,' he said and, still not meeting her eyes, turned back to the Rover.

Back upstairs, Anna had a shower and tried to wash away the awkwardness of Tommy's gallantry. Then, finally, she allowed herself to gingerly recall the night before. The second time they had sex, after taking off all his clothes, Jaime had undressed her, too. She'd felt exposed, standing naked in the dirty bar, conscious of the strip light in the kitchen, but had made herself bring her arms down from her chest. If she was the kind of brazen person who picked up a man like she had, she couldn't suddenly become coy. There was an immature V of chest hair on his torso. The muscles from his labouring days had softened in the months of inactivity since, but she could still feel some buried strength when his arms tensed around her.

Scrubbing her hair, Anna winced at the details, but realized her embarrassment was more for form's sake. In her experience, the price of casual sex was lingering mortification, and the absence of it now was as surprising as her lack of hangover. She could only put this down to Jaime's good manners. The night had been about sex and, as the loose condom in his pocket attested, he seemed practised in brief encounters. (As he left, she'd teased him that he clearly did this sort of thing a lot. 'A bit,' he'd corrected her.) Yet, in contrast to the one-night stands she'd had before, in which the pretence of interest in her life and opinions was abruptly dropped at the first grope, and after which she'd walk home through deserted East London market streets feeling as valuable as the stained cardboard boxes in the gutter, Jaime had affected an interest in her above and beyond the call of duty.

She walked outside into the square, to dry her hair in the sun. A cat was lying outside a shuttered shop, impossibly large as it stretched out, filling the length of the step. There was the gift shop woman standing in her doorway. The birds and pensioners resting at the fountain. It was Saturday, but here that was the same as any other day. Anna stopped at the promenade railings. The sea was blue-grey today, its surface coarsened by the breeze. A liner inched along the horizon. A pair of gulls perched on the railings along from her, having an irritable conversation.

Anna looked over to the steps. No sign of Jaime – he'd told her he was on a course today – but a pair of beach hawkers were stationed there. One had counterfeit DVDs neatly arranged in front of him, the other handbags. Both of them sat with bent legs apart, their heads dipped.

Anna's high from the night before was dissipating and now, looking at the hawkers, she thought again about the body on the rocks. Those painfully splayed limbs. His blood-filled eye. The string of leather pouches, biting into the flesh at his waist, just visible under his hippo T-shirt. The identical set, up at the finca. What had Almamy called it? A gree gree.

Her discovery of the borehole, and then the discovery of Satine, had sent her off on a diversion, but now, today, she must find out what a gree gree was and what it meant. She thought, for a moment, of asking the hawkers, but then remembered the reaction of the bearded man at the finca, when he caught her touching it; Almamy shutting down when she brought it up. Instead, she turned from the promenade railings and started back across the square.

The Internet cafe was not as full as yesterday, and the atmosphere more sedate. It was mid-morning, so she guessed more men must be out working. The same girl was behind the counter, but there was no bunch of fresh mint, nor any music playing, and what conversation there was amongst the men at the computers was muted. Only four phones were charging on the table.

As Anna paid her euro, a man hurried out of one of the private terminals, and she took his place. The computer was screened by five-foot-high barriers to the side and saloon-style doors at the front. As Anna sat, she realized that the men whose hunched backs she'd seen in these booths on her previous visit must have been tall: in the low, rickety office chair, she was barely visible to the room.

Boxed in by grubby MDF, she felt grimly aware that there were only a few reasons anyone would require this level of privacy. There was a heavy chlorine tang to the air around her that she tried not to inhale. Perhaps she was the first woman who had ever been in this booth. Perched on the edge of the chair, she lowered her hand onto the mouse, grasping it with just the edges of her fingers, like a spider sizing up its prey, and then, when she logged on, typed with pernickety speed, not leaving her fingertips on the keys for a millisecond longer than was necessary.

Google told her a *gree gree* was something to do with a monkey character in a computer game. A different spelling, *Grigri*, was the brand name for some rock-climbing device, and this gave her pause – but no, that definitely wasn't what she was looking for.

Then, she googled *gree gree* and *Africa* and – bingo. The word was most commonly spelt *gris-gris*, and referred to the little leather packets on the string. Voodoo amulets offering spiritual protection, given to the wearer by their holy man, and often worn when travelling. The packets could contain various things: herbs, earth, hair, bone, lines from the Koran . . .

'*El Tio!*'

Anna started, and looked over her shoulder, craning to see over the partition doors. Paco had entered the cafe, and was being greeted by an African man at a computer terminal. The man had stood up and was leaning towards Paco, hand outstretched, but, as she watched, Paco ignored him. No, more than ignored him – he aggressively brushed past the man's hand, like a celebrity furious at being approached on his day off. The man sank back into his chair.

Slouching lower in her seat so she wouldn't be spotted, Anna continued to watch as Paco walked up to the counter, gave a perfunctory nod to the smiling girl and leaned over to the till. Opening the cash drawer, he took out some notes before slamming it shut, saying something to the girl and then leaving the cafe. The whole thing had taken less than a minute.

Anna turned back to the screen, thrown. So, Paco was not just tolerated by the staff here. To take money from the till in such an offhand manner could only mean he owned the place. Or, at the very least, worked here, as some sort of sideline. But if that were the case, and the girl was his fellow worker, why would he be so curt with her?

Anna thought back to Christmas Day. Paco with his

sardines, her drunken dash back to the flat, where she scooped up the money on the counter – money she really needed, that could have paid for her broadband for a month – and ran back to give it to him. The way Paco clutched her hand to his chest and thanked her, tortoise eyes glistening with sincerity. He had accepted her money like a pauper, when really, all the time, he was connected to a thriving business in town.

And how Paco had acted just now, with the man who'd stood to greet him. *El Tio!* Simón had called Paco this, too, the first time she had met him. Distracted by Simón's request to rent the finca, Anna hadn't given it any thought. Now, in her booth, she typed the phrase into Google. Apparently there was no one fixed meaning; it could signify *friend, boss, uncle* – even *demon.*

Why would Simón call Paco *El Tio*? And why the African? She supposed he might know Paco from the beach; or maybe, if he came into the cafe a lot, knew him as its owner. But if that were the case, then why would Paco react as he did to the greeting?

One thing seemed clear: Paco was not just a simple man of the sea, scratching a living from selling paella on the beach to tourists.

The man who had been shunned by Paco was now staring at his screen, jaw tense, headphones on. Anna stood and wound her way through the terminals towards him. Behind the counter, the girl's chin was raised, gaze fixed pointedly on Anna. She stopped in her tracks. The room was so quiet, filled only with the light tapping of keys. Anna carried on to the door, as if she was just taking a circuitous route out of the cafe. As she squeezed past the shunned man, she glanced down at his screen and saw he was reading what looked like a news site in French, *Dakar Online*.

Dakar. That was in . . . she couldn't think. Come on, she thought, come on. General knowledge had never been her strong suit. It was only after she had left the shop and was walking slowly along the street, face screwed in concentration, that the answer came to her. Senegal. Dakar was in Senegal. Wasn't it?

The image came to her of Mattie, wide-eyed in her peach kimono, at the doorway of her bungalow. *Once you've been to Senegal, there's no going back.*

The plastic flamingos in Mattie's garden seemed to have bred since Anna was last here: there were at least half a dozen of them dotted around the Astro-Turf, necks bent back in perpetual surprise as Anna approached. She knocked on the door of the caravan. The couple next door were outside, watching TV. This time, absorbed in some news programme, they didn't greet her.

The door opened, just the width of a security chain. Only a slice of a woman was visible, but Anna could see enough – a large pink arm, some grey-blonde hair – to know it wasn't Mattie. Her mother?

Anna said hello, and asked if Mattie was in.

'I'm afraid not,' said the woman. Her voice came

as a surprise; careful and well spoken, not unlike Janet's.

'She's at the market,' the mother continued.

'The supermarket?'

'No, the market,' she repeated, in the same measured tone.

Anna realized she might mean the weekly car boot sale, where Brits went to flog their stuff. She had never been. Salvage yards and vintage shops were one thing; the bric-a-brac of desperate expats quite another.

'Do you happen to know when she'll be back, by any chance?' she asked, mirroring the woman's formality.

'I'm afraid not.'

There seemed to be only a few phrases the woman was comfortable saying: a script she had learned for when she was home alone and the doorbell rang.

'Well, thank you very much and I'm so sorry to bother you,' Anna said. 'Oh – and I didn't catch your name?'

The woman hesitated.

'Deirdre,' she said, finally.

'Well, thank you, Deirdre,' said Anna. 'I'll leave you in peace now, but before I go is there anything I can help you with?'

'No, thank you very much,' said Deirdre. But she didn't shut the door, and kept on looking at Anna through the gap.

'I love your garden,' said Anna, in case she wanted more conversation. 'Did you do it yourself?'

The woman nodded.

'Me and Martha. It's not finished yet.'

There was a pause, and as Anna was about to say goodbye, Deirdre spoke again, in a different tone of voice, more anxious, as if she'd let the carapace slip.

'Is the earthquake over?'

'Sorry?'

'All those poor people. What can we do?'

'There's no earthquake,' said Anna, gently. 'It's lovely outside, actually.'

'No, no,' said Deirdre, more agitated. 'Not here. On the TV. All those poor people. What can we do?'

Anna didn't have a clue what she was talking about. She smiled and reached her hand through the gap in the door, to touch the woman's arm.

'It's all OK.'

Anna felt Deirdre flinch at her touch, and then the woman withdrew, back into the dark of the caravan, softly pulling the door closed. As Anna left, pushing open the pointless gate, she glanced at the neighbours' TV, and glimpsed pictures of rubble and desperate faces; a news banner about a disaster in Haiti. Deirdre was right – something had happened. Anna paused, and then kept walking. She hadn't watched the news for months, but now wasn't the time to start. The wider world would have to wait.

The car boot sale was held further down the ring road, not far from the police station. As she walked, lorries growled along the coast road above her, exhaling black exhaust fumes and leaving slow-to-settle dust clouds in their wake. The shop units in this part of town were almost all empty; a charity shop and a bookmaker's were the exceptions. A Spanish mother and daughter passed her, lugging a gas canister. Would Jaime go shopping to help his mum? He gave that impression. But then, thought Anna, aren't we all different people with our parents? The self-possessed, surprising young man who'd taken off her clothes against the bar might well be a mulish disappointment at home: locked onto his PlayStation, ketchup-encrusted plates shoved under his bed.

As Anna was considering giving in and asking for directions to the market, she saw some parked cars and activity in an empty lot up ahead, beyond a beige slab of a warehouse. From a distance, the sale looked like the ones back in the UK – piles of junk and low-key milling about. But, as she drew close, she noticed that although the lot was relatively small, the contents of what seemed like several entire houses had been hauled onto the tarmac – wardrobes, washing machines, dining tables with matching chairs. The furniture was all of a type – white MDF or cheap pine, modern and flimsy. Maybe they had all been part of a furniture package when bought, Anna thought, like the one Tommy and Karen had.

Alongside these house clearances were trestle tables offering the more usual car boot stuff. Sentimental but useless objects, like medals and horse brasses; gadgets that now seemed foolish luxuries, coffee machines and foot spas. Hobby apparatus. Power tools. And a lot of everyday items that could only fetch cents – clammy piles of clothes and warped shoes, magazines; even an old broom and mop.

Whilst the expats were selling the contents of their houses, the Spanish were into a different game. Their stalls offered wholesale quantities of sunglasses, factory pottery and knock-off football tops.

As Anna passed through the market, she recognized a couple of half-known faces from the urbanization sitting on folding chairs beside their goods. Several of them had swooped down on her the moment she had opened the bar, offering unskilled services – cleaning, driving, odd jobs – and she hadn't seen them since. Then she spotted Richard, sitting behind a trestle table spread with rows of DVDs and CDs. There were so many of them, newly produced, that they were clearly not his personal collection. He didn't have the same beleaguered expression as the other Brits and, on spotting Anna, waved a greeting.

'*Hola!*' he said.

'Gosh, what a lot of films you have, Richard,' she said, slipping into her default bar banter. 'The long winter nights must have just flown by.'

'Oh yes,' he said. 'Nothing like a good movie. You should come over and watch one with me one night.'

He smiled, showing lots of teeth. Anna had rarely seen him out during daylight hours – he wasn't a daytime drinker, and was always somewhere 'on business'. The sun shone off his gelled hair and highlighted the desiccation of his large, handsome face.

'You're a particular fan of *Finding Nemo,* I see.' She indicated the four copies on the table.

'Oh yes,' he said, and then, after looking theatrically around to check they weren't being overhead, told her how he had an arrangement with his mate Ron, who'd bought a laminating machine during the boom years. Richard burnt copies of the films at home and printed out the covers on his colour laser printer, then ran them through the laminator for the professional touch.

'Can clear ninety euros here on a good day,' he said. 'What do you think about that? And then there are the ones down at the beach. Looking at sixty euros a day when the season starts.'

'What, you supply the guys selling them on the beach steps? The looky looky men?'

Richard winked. 'I'm saying nothing.'

Anna knew that Richard was up to dodgy stuff, but the fact he was supplying the African beach hawkers was a surprise; she'd assumed that was sewn up elsewhere. She asked if he'd seen Mattie, and Richard gestured down to the far end of the market.

'She likes it down that end, near the food. Can't stand the smell myself.'

Anna walked towards the other end of the car park, and saw what he was talking about. Discreetly situated under some trees, out of sight of the main road, were a handful of food vendors. All dark-skinned women, they sat beside stainless steel vats. So this was where the female migrants were.

Close to them, at the edge of the official market,

was Mattie. Unlike the other Brits she wasn't stationed at a table but on a rug, sitting back on her heels, face hidden under an unnecessarily large sun hat, her dress fanned around her. She was surrounded by amateurish beaded jewellery, the kind that thirteen-year-old girls make during school lunch break.

Anna called her name, and the sun hat tilted back.

'Hi!' said Mattie, looking up from under the brim. She didn't seem at all surprised to see her.

Anna crouched down beside Mattie, being careful not to mess up her display.

'Listen,' said Anna. 'I need to ask you something.'

'Do you now.'

'That man you saw. Almamy. Do you have a number for him?'

Mattie looked at her, expression unreadable.

'Are you hungry?' she said.

'Er, no,' said Anna. 'I'm fine.'

'*I'm* hungry.'

Anna caught up.

'Shall I get you some lunch?' she asked.

Mattie smiled and nodded graciously.

'The Ghanaian is best,' she said, pointing at the food vendors.

The Ghanaian woman was wearing too many layers of clothing for the mild weather. Her vat of food was also bundled up: in the absence of a fire to keep it warm, it was insulated by layers of plastic bags. The woman took Anna's order without making eye contact, and as she stirred the stew, releasing tantalizing vapours of oil and meat and unknown herbs, Anna changed the order to two. The woman dolloped the stew into two china bowls, instructing Anna to bring the crockery back, and added chunks of thick, spongy bread.

Her neighbour was selling sliced avocado and plantain. Both women seemed on edge, checking the crowd. The lack of relaxed conversation between them was a contrast to the men in the Internet cafe – this was clearly an unofficial operation.

'Are you here every week?' said Anna, as she returned to Mattie.

'Of course!' said Mattie. 'I don't want to let my customers down.'

They sat together, companionably eating their stew. It was very spicy and, Anna thought, delicious, but that could be down to its novelty. Her taste buds were more accustomed to *jamón* and *queso.* For all her mannered refinement, Mattie ate indelicately, dripping liquid onto the rug. Anna wondered whether their previous meeting's awkwardness need be mentioned.

'Listen, I need to ask you something,' said Anna, starting again. 'About that guy, Almamy. I saw him yesterday, up at my finca, and he said hello.'

'Oh, how nice,' twittered Mattie. 'Such a sweet boy.'

Bowl now empty, she had gone back to threading beads, her tiny hands suited to the task.

'Do you know how I can get in touch with him?' said Anna.

Mattie looked at her quizzically.

'But you just saw him,' she said.

'I mean, I saw him at the house, my finca, but I need

to talk to him again . . .' Anna slowed down, feeling herself getting tangled up. 'I wanted to ask him something about . . . the others were there and their boss hates me, you see, so I think he couldn't talk freely . . .'

'Their boss hates you? Then of course they won't speak to you,' said Mattie. 'He's given them work, put them up in a nice house – of course they're going to be loyal to him.'

'He said that?' said Anna.

'He mentioned that his boss had promised them a permanent contract if he was happy with their work, so of course they want to please him. That's what they want, you know. A contract.'

'How do you know all this?' said Anna.

Mattie shrugged. 'We talked. I'm a people person.'

'So you don't have a number for him, or anything?' said Anna.

Mattie shook her head and continued with the beads. Anna looked at this strange woman, with her newly revealed qualities.

'Do you know anyone else from Senegal?' she asked.

Mattie tilted up her hat, with a sly expression.

'So you *do* want one of your own.'

Anna didn't react. This was a test: a reminder that Mattie hadn't forgotten their previous encounter. After a pause, Mattie relented.

'Most of them live around the greenhouses,' she said.

Anna had noticed lean-tos clustered around the edges of the greenhouses, constructed from corrugated iron, old plastic wrap and even metal from tins of fertilizer. They were straight from the Third World. Was she really going to knock on the doors of one and ask its inhabitants if they knew of a Senegalese man who'd died?

But Mattie hadn't finished.

'And they all congregate in the morning, to get work,' she said.

'Where?'

'I don't know, but Richard will,' said Mattie. She stood up and shouted for him. Richard sauntered over, hands in his pockets, and stood over them, legs apart.

'Where do the Africans meet to get picked up?' asked Mattie.

Richard described an intersection about a mile out of town.

'They arrive early,' he added. 'Before seven.'

'It's Sunday tomorrow,' said Anna. 'Will they be there?'

Richard gave her a pitying look.

'Yes, my dear,' he said. 'They do work weekends.'

Walking away from Mattie and Richard, Anna mused on how the pair seemed to know far more about the plight of the African workers than she did, yet appeared so unconcerned. It hadn't once occurred to her to confide in them, to appeal for their help. Then, she wondered how she would get to the intersection. She couldn't ask Tommy, and felt loath to request another lift from Jaime; she didn't want him to think her presumptuous. Besides, she doubted he would get up that early.

She left the market and started back down the ring road. Ahead of her were the limp flags of the police station, the scene of her humiliation, and a thought came to her: perhaps she didn't have to rely on anyone else to drive her at all.

9

It had seemed such a brilliant, obvious plan. But as the airport bus pulled away, leaving Anna alone at the entrance to the long-stay car park, her spirits dropped. This was partly a natural response to the sight of a land ruled by concrete, metal and plastic bollards, where nature was represented only by a few pushy weeds breaking through the baked asphalt and, just visible in the bleached-out sky, the outline of distant mountains. She also realized it was not going to be at all easy to find her car.

Before her were acres of vehicles, similar as newborns. Most people coming here would, of course, have some vague idea of the location of theirs. Anna could remember the first three numbers of the plate, but the vehicles were packed too tightly together to be able to view them from a distance. She wandered through the ranks, the bag she was carrying bumping against her thigh as she pressed the key fob in the direction of any red car, hoping that one of the anonymous metal lumps would flash and become hers.

The car would be filthy after eighteen months, she thought, and narrowed her search to only the dirtiest vehicles. Still nothing. It occurred to her there was a chance the car wouldn't be here at all: maybe they were junked after a certain amount of time. But she was its registered owner. Surely they would have contacted her? She thought of the pile of unopened post on the shelf behind the bar.

She kept walking, smelling warm dust and leaking fuel. Some of the cars bore finger graffiti, of the usual *I wish my missus was this dirty* variety. Surely the Spanish youth, however bored and disenfranchised, didn't come all the way out to the airport to draw on cars?

God, this was depressing. There was a story behind all of these abandoned hulks, variations on hers and Michael's. Each one marked the grave of a dream. That silver Citroën, with an ejaculating penis etched on the back windscreen: she imagined it bought with high expectations; the seats impregnated with the owners' sweat and suntan lotion and melted ice lollies. The inside of the boot scratched from the ornamental water feature bought on giddy impulse for the garden of their new villa. Now, that villa belonged to the bank and its former owners were back in the UK, three kids crammed in a two-bed flat, strained and bickering, snapping the telly off at the opening credits of *A Place in the Sun.*

On she went, pressing the useless fob and wiping windows to peer inside until, suddenly, there it was.

The interior was no different to the others yet it felt instantly familiar, its identity confirmed by a jumper of hers in the footwell of the passenger seat. Anna laughed with delight. Unlocking the driver's door, the car's trapped air hit her: an unholy mix of milk, old socks, cement, paint. A stew of her past. As Anna sat in the driver's seat and adjusted it to her position, she realized that she was surrounded by Michael's stagnated breath: an hour and a half of his exhalations as he made his escape from her. She opened the windows to disperse the funk, and put the key into the ignition.

Nothing happened when she turned the key and it occurred to her that, after eighteen months, the battery might be dead. Cursing, she got out and checked that the jump leads were still in the boot – they were, along with a spare can of petrol – but there was no one around. She got back into the driver's seat and, after several more tries, stamping on the accelerator, the engine kicked into life. The car was suddenly full of music – Michael had been listening to a CD on his journey. It was one of hers: the music to the film *Magnolia.* A suitably plaintive soundtrack to his desertion. She snapped it off, and then noticed the fuel gauge had flown to the right, as far as it could go. So, Michael had stopped to fill up at the garage just before the airport, as if he was returning a hire car. A small, surprising act of consideration.

Anna put on the wipers, and took the parking ticket from the dashboard as they feebly scraped the windscreen of some of its sticky film. *28 August 2008. 08.14.* Not many people knew, to the minute, the time their lover bailed out on them. She picked up the jumper in the footwell: a delicate, grey-blue cashmere number that had cost her over a hundred pounds. An unthinkable amount now, and imprudent back then, but she'd justified spending money on clothes because she wanted to look right for him.

Also on the floor was an empty plastic film envelope, which she recognized as the packaging for *The Economist.* She wouldn't have left the wrapper like that; it must have been Michael. She imagined him parking up, spotting the unopened magazine on the floor and deciding to take it for the journey. Whilst she was waking up at the finca to find her world had caved in, he was settled on the plane, catching up on the Latvian referendum. It cancelled out any credit for the full fuel tank.

When the windscreen was clean enough to see out of, Anna put the car into gear and slowly drove over to the exit gates. High up in the booth sat a young woman, her hair scraped back and gelled, like an air hostess'. She wasn't looking at her phone or reading, as one would expect of an underemployed person in a long-stay car park booth, but staring into the middle distance. After a beat, she glanced down at Anna and held out her hand for the ticket. Her white shirt, cut too tight at the shoulders, strained at the movement.

Anna got out of the car and stood at the window, level with the woman.

'Look, I can't pay this,' she said, in Spanish, showing her the ticket. 'I'm sorry, but I don't have the money. Could you possibly let me out, anyway?'

The woman said nothing, just tilted her head to one side, as if she had been here before. As Anna started to explain why the car had been left for eighteen months – omitting the drink-drive element – the woman looked to the side, not making eye contact as she listened. Despite heavy make-up, the bumps of acne were visible on her forehead and chin, and Anna felt sorry for noticing them. She looked barely out of her teens, but was wearing an engagement ring. Would a young woman in love, working with only a thousand dusty cars for company, be sympathetic or repulsed by the plight of an almost-forty-year-old at the other end of the line?

As she finished the story, Anna held up the carrier bag containing the bottles she'd brought, left over from the lottery night.

'I can offer you some cava,' she said, wincing to acknowledge the feebleness of the bribe. The girl didn't say anything. She took the ticket from Anna's hand and scanned it under her machine.

'It's four thousand one hundred and forty euros,' she said, raising her eyebrows. 'Wow.'

'Is that the biggest you've had?' said Anna.

'Personally, yes. But you are not the only person who has not wanted to pay their ticket.'

Anna nodded, carefully, waiting. She wondered whether the girl was purposefully drawing this out, relishing her power.

'Last week, I was offered a pair of shoes, from someone's feet,' the girl continued. 'Old smelly shoes! And the lady was annoyed I didn't want them! "They cost two hundred euros new," she said. "You can sell them." Like, thanks!'

Anna laughed at the outrageous cheek of this other woman, as she was meant to.

The girl held out her hand for the bag.

'I will drink it with my fiancé later.'

Anna smiled hesitantly as she lifted the bag up to the window.

'So I can go?'

The girl nodded.

'If a guy did that to me, I would destroy him,' she said, matter-of-factly, as much to herself as to Anna. Then, waving away Anna's repeated thanks, she opened the barrier to let her drive away.

Turning onto out the coastal road, Anna felt wobbly behind the wheel, driving as hesitantly as a tourist fresh off a charter flight. She turned on the radio and then snapped it off – she wanted to concentrate. The plastic grain of the gear stick grew familiar again under her palm, and soon she was in third, then fourth, and it had all come back to her. Uncertainty turned to exhilaration as she hit the speed limit, settling back into her seat as if she and the car had never been apart.

The fugitive element added to the thrill. Although her driving ban was long up, Anna suspected that she would need to have her licence officially reinstated and what she was doing now was, strictly, illegal. But it was only a matter of paperwork, surely: in the unlikely event she was pulled over, what was the worst that could happen? Nonetheless, she found herself checking her rear-view mirror every few seconds.

A wind had started up, sending dust devils whirling

down the scrubby baked verge. Although never busy at this time of year, the road was unnaturally quiet: Anna felt that hers was the only car for miles. She drove past billboard adverts for fertilizers, past shallow pits where building excavation had barely begun. Past the entrance to the Plaza del Sol, marked by that fallen concrete obelisk. And, at the edge of town, the fanciest restaurant in the area, the entrance flanked by two concrete lions, where she and Michael had gone to celebrate buying the finca.

Anna found herself steering into the car park of the restaurant and turning off the engine. She felt hyped and discombobulated, not yet ready to go back to the bar. On the gravel beside her, a vast seagull stood for several moments – as motionless as she was – before letting out a loud caw and lifting off vertically.

She hadn't been to this restaurant since that time with Michael. They'd been so ecstatic that night. The maître d' had taken one look at them and given them the best table in the house, on the terrace overlooking the sea. He later told Anna, when she went to the loo, that he had presumed they had just got engaged, and indeed that was exactly how it felt. That evening, as they ate bisque in the evening breeze, the sky a water-colour blotch of pink and blue and the sea churning beneath them, they had started discussing their building plans, but the conversation soon turned to each other, asking questions and listening enraptured, as if it were their first date. Everything she said was fascinating and valuable and, as they talked, Michael had taken out his pencil and, without a word, started sketching her on the paper tablecloth, as if it were impossible to be opposite such a face and not try to capture it.

Now, the single-storey building looked woebegone and disrobed, its ferns dying and the lions chipped and stained, like a nightclub when the lights are turned up.

Still unwilling to move, Anna saw some bits of paper tucked in the driver's door pocket, and pulled them onto her lap. Relics from her old life; receipts from builders' yards, supermarkets and garages. An electricity bill that had somehow escaped her lever arch file. An appointment card from a cruddy beauty salon in Marea, now closed down, where she'd slipped off to get her legs inexpertly waxed. And, on the back of the card, in her own handwriting, Anna noticed a list of words: TOMATO-ZIZEK-GYPSY.

She had long forgotten what exactly these words signified, but knew what the list was. A crib sheet of conversation topics for an evening with Michael in the dying months of their relationship, when she was desperate to keep his interest.

Looking at the words, Anna felt pity for the person who wrote them, and a more abstract sadness for how life could turn out. Of course, neither that glorious, heady dinner in the restaurant nor those miserable final evenings were the nub of her and Michael's relationship. The truth lay at some point in between. She didn't know where that point was, and, unlike her car, she'd probably never find it. Maybe it didn't really matter now. She turned the key in the ignition, and continued her journey into town.

The next morning Anna set off at 6am, driving slowly through Marea's dark, empty streets. The only sign of life was a cat tearing into a bin bag, which fled at her approach. Without traffic it took only ten minutes to reach the spot Richard had described: a featureless intersection just off the coast road. Parking up on the verge a discreet distance away, she turned off the engine and wound down her window. The road was deserted. There were no sounds of nature down here; the scrubby grass on the verge was too denuded to support even a cicada. Even the wind had stilled. Suddenly chilly, Anna put on the cashmere jumper from the footwell of the car. Unworn for so long, it felt clammy and foreign against her skin.

The moon was still visible, holding out as the morning lightened around it. The plot of land beside her car bore a shallow excavation pit. A few discarded sacks of concrete powder sat on its perimeter. The developers behind that one were relatively lucky: they'd barely started before everything combusted. Nonetheless, the land remained fenced off, with security notices warning of guard dogs. As if anyone would want it now.

She thought back to her studio in London. From the outside, the flats didn't look like much: the original Victorian bricks of the building facade were chipped and the small windows were permanently dirty from the bus route outside. Some of them had spider plants pressing up against the glass, as if the flats had been overrun by vegetation. Anna's was tiny, but it was hers, and she had made it beautiful and loved it. Although she didn't have much contact with her neighbours beyond nods on the stairs, she'd felt an inherent sense of community. Most of the people living there looked to be single, or just starting out. The building's age had made her feel connected to history, carrying on the tradition of people coming to London to make their way.

She had given that life up for Michael, and now, here she was.

She felt a rush of profound loneliness. Never mind her mission to uncover the truth about the dead man: she had to leave this dead place. She turned the ignition key and then stopped, one notch before the engine turned on, as she spotted something ahead. There, in the distance, it was coming down the road from the east, where the sky was flushing. Something yellow. Two things. Three. They weren't cars, but much smaller and slower. She watched as the specks grew larger, and were revealed to be African men on bicycles, wearing high-vis jackets.

Anna clicked back into focus, and watched. When the three reached the intersection, they carefully laid their bikes on the ground and leaned against the safety rail. One had a smoke. Then they waited, in the pearly dawn light.

A minute or two passed. Anna jumped as another bike flew past her window. She turned to see more coming from the opposite direction, and more still arriving along the main road from inland. A dozen, twenty, thirty men: all on bikes, all in neon jackets, all converging on the intersection. Anna watched as they got off their bikes, some talking to each other, others sitting by themselves on the ground.

Another five minutes passed. Then, a large pick-up truck rattled past Anna's car, shaking the window, and slowed to a halt at the intersection. As the men clustered around it, Anna was reminded of scenes of refugees converging on food aid. A man got down from the driver's seat and talked to a group, and after very quick negotiations, seven men lifted their bikes onto the back of the truck and climbed in after them. The truck pulled away, heading west.

The sun had risen now, and its rays glinted on the spokes of the bikes belonging to the men still waiting. Five minutes later, another truck appeared and the same transaction took place, only this time the driver didn't even get out of his seat and did all the talking from his window. Eight got into that truck.

A silent voyeur, Anna watched as a third truck came and took five more men, leaving around a dozen. The sky was now fully light, and other cars were zipping past her at infrequent intervals. She waited with the men, growing restless along with them. Out of the window, she watched a dung beetle laboriously roll a brown ball along the tarmac.

By half past seven, there hadn't been a truck for a while and it all seemed to be over. Some of the men picked up their bikes and resignedly rode away. This was Anna's cue: she didn't want to leave it so long that they had all cycled off and she had to chase them in her car. She started the engine and drove the short distance to the intersection, turning into the spot vacated by the trucks. The remaining men stopped and stared at her with reserved interest as she pulled up.

Anna undid her seat belt and put on a smile. At least these men didn't have a boss. And this time, she had given some thought as to what she was going to say.

She got out of the car, said *hola* and asked if any of them spoke Spanish.

A handful nodded. They all looked at her, waiting, wary. What could this woman want from them? Like the men at the finca, they were young – all under thirty, she guessed, and some much younger. She saw that several of them had protective goggles and flimsy paper masks looped over the handlebars of their bikes.

'I wanted to ask you some questions,' she said. 'Will any of you talk to me?'

'Who are you?' said one.

'No one,' she said, raising her hands. 'I'm not the police.'

There was no response. A few glanced at each other. One picked up his bike and threw his leg over, preparing to cycle off, and this seemed to be a signal, as the rest of them turned away from her and headed over to their bikes.

'Wait,' said Anna, aiming at the man who had first picked up his bike, the ringleader. 'Listen. Don't give me your names. You won't get in trouble, I promise. And I have money, I can pay you.'

The man – short, with a snub nose – stopped and looked around.

'How much?'

Anna took out the folded notes she had ready in her pocket – the last of the envelope Simón had given her.

'Thirty euros if you talk to me, just for a few minutes.'

The man hesitated for a moment, and then swung his leg off his bike and laid it back down on the ground.

'No names?' he said.

'No names,' said Anna.

He nodded and moved towards her, and then the others did too, grouping in front of her so she felt in the position of the men in the trucks, soliciting.

'What do you want?' said one.

'Are any of you from Senegal?' she said.

'I am,' said one, and two others put up their hands.

'I'm trying to find out what happened to a man. I think he was from Senegal.'

'What is his name?' said one.

'I don't know,' she said. 'But, he's dead. He died around a week ago. Have you heard anything?'

'He died at sea?'

'No,' she said – and then she thought of Paco's tearful account of the body being dumped from inland, and his unsettling behaviour in the cafe. 'Well, I don't know. Maybe. But he was found on the land, on the beach. He had a *gris gris* around his stomach.' She put her hands to her waist.

'Many people have those,' the snub-nosed one said, dismissively.

'Did he die in the boat?' said another.

Three of the men started talking in their own language, and then one said, 'Ibrahim, he died. On the boat. He was at the bottom.'

'I was in the boat,' added another.

'You were in the boat when the man died?' asked Anna.

The man nodded. He had huge eyes: you could see the white all the way round the iris. In his over-large fluorescent jacket, he looked like a schoolboy.

'Can you tell me what happened?' said Anna. Her suspicion of Simón's involvement in the man's death had now fallen away.

The man started speaking, first slowly then speeding up, keen to get the words out. At first others chipped in, and once or twice Anna interjected, when she couldn't understand his slow, imperfect Spanish. The huddle of men listened, although, Anna presumed, they must had heard it before, or had similar stories themselves.

After a few minutes, she stopped him.

'Wait, can I call you something? Anything. Not your real name.'

One of the others said something indistinguishable and they all laughed; a private joke.

'Call me Mickey,' the man said, to Anna.

Mickey came from a village in the east of Senegal. He was nineteen, the oldest of five brothers and sisters and had considered becoming a fisherman, like his father and grandfather. Life was OK – they had a house and food and a television – but he wanted more than that: he wanted a nice life. After seeing pictures of Barcelona on the TV, of clean roads and gleaming buildings and shopping centres, he'd decided to join many of the other young men in the village and make the journey. Barcelona was the goal – everyone wanted to get there – but any part of Spain would do.

His mother had been sad to let him go but having a son migrate to Spain was a badge of honour. Those boys who got to Europe wired money back, and bought their families fridges, cars, new houses. With his first pay he was going to tell his mum to buy herself a mobile phone. The cost of a passage to Europe was $1,200; his uncle loaned him the money. His cousin was coming too.

He packed a small rucksack with some clothes and 200 euros and first they travelled to Dakar and then boarded a small boat. There were twenty of them. The first bit of the journey, to the Canary Islands, took a week, and wasn't so bad: the captain let them sit upright, and they laughed and joked around, spirits still high. When the boat landed at the Canary Islands, the group was split in half and transferred onto two boats. His cousin was on the other one. The nice captain disappeared; now it was another man, who wasn't kind, who didn't allow them to come out above the tarpaulin even at night. They lay next to each other, packed together like fish, and tried to keep their good humour, talking about what they were going to do when they arrived in Spain, the money, the women.

Then as the hours went on, they stopped talking, and just lay there, silent, willing the time away. If they were sick, they had to lie in it. In their piss, too. They ate only biscuits they had brought with them – they had been told to eat a special kind because they stopped up your bowels. They tested each other on their Spanish numbers, using a pack of cards. *Eight and six equals what?* They stored their phones in balloons wrapped in tape, so they wouldn't get wet.

He thought this was the last boat, the boat that would take them onto Spanish sand, but he was wrong because after forty-eight hours at sea, in the middle of the night, they were told to get up and, in complete darkness, pushed into an even smaller boat.

'They packed us tight in rows, like we were already dead,' Mickey said. He was now sitting down on the dusty ground; Anna had crouched beside him. 'There were two layers and I was on the top layer: I knew I was lucky. Then there were many more hours.'

During the day they all used their phones for GPS, to see where they were going, and to text and play games, but at night, the captain wouldn't allow it, in case the police saw the light from the screens.

'But one man kept looking at his phone when it was dark, and the captain got so angry he threw him overboard and left him to drown,' said Mickey, quite matter-of-fact.

Squatting on her haunches, Anna felt her legs quiver, and sat down next to him.

Mickey kept thinking about the mobile he would buy his mum when he started work in Spain: the expression on her face when she saw a Spanish number, his number, come up on it. He tried to relive his favourite films, scene by scene. The man next to him was sick in his ear, in his hair. The biscuits didn't work for everyone, and there was a terrible stench of shit. One man kept on saying, 'We are dead, we are dead,' but everyone ignored him.

And then, finally, there was an awful jolt as the boat hit land. Mickey banged his head. The tarpaulin was ripped off and a man told them in Spanish to scarper immediately, to get out of his sight. Mickey tried to stand up but his feet were on the other men below him and his legs were wobbly so he fell over, and then some hands dragged him off the boat, painfully. There was wet sand in his mouth and he could immediately taste it was European sand, and, despite the terrible journey, he felt a sense of joy. Even in the half-light he could see the sea was blue, unlike the grey water around Africa.

'Then the Spanish man told us again to go, to get out of here, and started hitting us on the back, and so we all ran up the beach and then into the bushes,' Mickey said. He gesticulated as he spoke, waggling his fingers to mimic moving legs.

'What did he look like, this Spanish man?'

Mickey rubbed his head. 'No hair. Old.'

'What was his name?'

Mickey shrugged. 'We just called him *El Tio*.'

So, Paco had been their ferryman. Although she'd been expecting it, the news was a punch. She remembered the feel of Paco's stiff chest hair under her fingers, as he pressed her hand against his heart, and flinched.

The other men had joined Mickey and Anna sitting on the ground now; Anna noticed the snub-nosed one tracing patterns in the dust. Another man, with a wan expression, brought an inhaler out of his pocket and took a deep lug.

Mickey continued his story. A contact already there in Spain had told them where to go, so when it was daylight they followed his directions and found his shack. They shared a room with him for now, but after he'd earned enough, Mickey would rent a space in a different shack with eight other men, for €100 a month.

Everyone wanted to reach Barcelona. But to get a proper job you needed papers, and to get papers you needed a permanent contract. Down here, in the greenhouses, they didn't care whether you had papers. And so the men found work there, bent over in forty-degree heat for nine or ten hours a day, for pay of around thirty euros. Some bosses were OK, decent enough. Others were mean, spraying pesticides over the crops when the men were working; many of them got ill. If they complained or refused to work, their names were put on a blacklist.

'Have any of you worked for Mr Ruiz?' asked Anna. 'Simón Ruiz?'

The men conferred between themselves; a couple then nodded.

'He is OK,' said the man with the inhaler. 'Not a bad one. He didn't spray pesticide.'

'Oh,' said Anna. So Almamy hadn't been lying before, when he said that Simón was a good boss. She tried to adjust her perception of him; he was awful only to her, not his workers.

'The bad ones – can't you go to the police?' she said.

'No,' said the inhaler man. 'The police turned a blind eye, because the area needed people working in the greenhouses and Spaniards didn't want to do it. Sometimes, for show, they rounded people up: but everyone knew that if you were caught, the police couldn't deport you if you had no passport and didn't tell them your nationality. So, they either kept you locked up until you decided that your old life was better than being in prison and told them where you were from, or, more often, they let you go.'

He paused in his story to catch his breath. One of the others gave him a bottle of water.

'And you said you saw the dead man?' Anna asked Mickey.

'Yes,' he said. Mickey's friend had been at the bottom of the boat and told Mickey that the man next to him, Ibrahim, had died during the journey. The friend had been whispering to Ibrahim, and heard Ibrahim's breath in his ear, and then Ibrahim made a weird noise and the breath stopped. He had been suffocated by the men on top of him. As Mickey was on the top layer, he may have been one of the men who crushed Ibrahim. He didn't want to think about it.

Mickey's cousin was probably dead, too. Mickey saw him briefly in the Canary Islands but then he went on the other boat and it never arrived in Spain. For a week he went down to the beach early every morning, searching for his cousin, but then he gave up. No body was found, as far as he knew. There were few bodies recovered, because most of the migrants couldn't swim, or were scared, and so clung onto the boat as it sank. When rigor mortis set in, they stayed clinging to it as it rested on the seabed.

'Does his family know?' asked Anna.

Mickey nodded.

'What about the other man, Ibrahim?'

'I don't know. Maybe. Back home in my village, the families gave it a long time, but if a year goes by, and there are no messages, no money being sent to them, then they accept their son had died doing his duty.'

Anna thought of Paco, dipping into the till at the Internet cafe; the money transfer posters; the phones lined up charging beside the desk. How resourceful he was! First making money off the migrants by smuggling them over, and then profiting from them again when they sent money back home and Skyped their mothers to lie about their great new lives in Europe.

Anna noticed some of the other men had begun shifting whilst Mickey had been talking. They had been listening for twenty minutes: the sun was now hot.

'But I am not dead!' Mickey said, smiling, as if he was keen to end on a positive note.

They all stood up, and Anna handed him the money.

'Thank you for talking to me,' she said.

He nodded, folding the notes carefully away in his pocket. 'We will share it.' He shook her hand, and Anna stood watching as he and the others got back onto their bikes and cycled off into the dazzling sun, in their now unnecessary hi-vis jackets.

10

From the top of the beach steps, Anna looked out towards the rocks. There was Paco sitting beside his boat, legs apart, hands between his knees, and, even from this distance, it was obvious that he was looking at his mobile. She thought back to the discovery of the body on the rocks, how he'd sent her running up the beach to call the police. *Señora, I have no phone!* And she tried to imagine the terror of the man he threw overboard, in the middle of the ink-black ocean, when the man didn't stop using his. Two deaths on one journey: all in a night's work.

Behind her, the church struck 9am. Anna had come straight from the roadside, and although the dawn excursion had already taken on an unreal dimension, the hours it occupied had not: she felt she had lived a day already. The sky was the colour of stonewash denim and the sea gently agitated, the palm trees quivering on their concrete anchors. On the beach, nearer to her, a pair of detectorists were out, testing the sand. One of them was limping. Graeme.

Anna hadn't anticipated anyone being around when she confronted Paco – nor imagined she would ever be grateful to see Graeme – but she felt relieved she was not alone. She remembered Paco's expression when approached by the African in the Internet cafe, swatting away the man's outstretched hand.

Waving at Graeme to make him aware of her presence, but staying out of chatting distance, Anna headed down the steps and towards the back of the beach. Shielded by the ranks of thatched umbrellas and slumbering banana boats, she walked stealthily towards Paco, as quickly as the sand allowed. Because of the angle of her approach, she was only ten feet away when Paco lifted his head. Discreetly pocketing his phone, he got to his feet and held out his hands.

'*Señora!*' he said, warmly.

Anna didn't reply, and watched as he took in her expression, his dark eyes narrowing into slashes.

'*Cómo está?*' he said, evenly.

'I know what you're doing,' Anna said in Spanish, coming to a halt a few feet away. 'What really happened to that man.'

Paco gazed at her steadily, silent. The skin on his head looked polished; the trenches on his face so deep they looked drawn on with marker pen. She forced herself to not look away. Then, finally, he shrugged and shook his head, as if bemused – crazy English! – before turning away from her. The gesture also served to remind her of his strength: his bare neck and shoulders were a triangle of solid brown muscle.

'You have nothing to say?' she continued.

'But, *señora,* I do not understand what you are saying,' Paco said, slowly, turning back to her.

'How's business?'

'*Señora, no comprende.*'

There was something mocking about his repeated, overly formal *señora*s. Anna looked away from him, over to his boat. There was a tidemark of sand on its blue painted hull. Did that mean the surface was wet, that the boat had been out that morning? She stepped forward and crouched to wipe at the sand.

'You're cleaning my boat for me? Very kind.'

The sand felt powdery on her fingers. Maybe the morning sun had dried it out? Without making eye contact, in case she lost her nerve, she stood up and leaned over to peer inside the boat. At the bottom was a tarpaulin, neatly folded. Nothing else. The interior space was not much bigger than a single bed: it seemed impossible that there could have ever been ten men in here, however tightly packed. For the first time, she felt a pulse of doubt.

Maybe the inside of the boat was wet? Mickey had talked about waves crashing over them, making them feel they were going to capsize. She leaned inside to touch the base, knowing she was being ridiculous – even if it was damp, it wouldn't prove anything – and braced herself for Paco's hand clamping down on her shoulder, hauling her backwards onto the sand.

But there was no hand. For whatever reason, he had decided not to intervene. Her fingers stretched down into the dark hull and grazed against the wood. It was damp and she felt something on her fingertips – something gritty. Sand? No, it was the same colour, but softer. She pinched some and brought it up to her face. It smelled sweet and yeasty.

Biscuit crumbs.

'Why are there biscuits in your boat?' she said, turning back to Paco. He'd taken the phone out of his pocket and was scrolling through it, like a bored commuter.

'It's my lunch,' said Paco, not looking up. Now his tone was unquestionably mocking. 'I am just a poor man. No sardines today.'

'You're not going to get away with it.'

Paco's mask had been slipping. Now, he let it drop.

'*Perra estúpida*,' he said, slowly. Stupid bitch. The look he was giving her was the one she saw in the Internet cafe. His voice had changed: it was stronger, less gravelly. 'You know nothing. And if I were you, I would fuck off right now.'

Then, unexpectedly, he smiled, and took a single, deliberate step towards her. Anna felt a punch of real fear and whipped around to shout for Graeme, but the beach was deserted.

She started to retreat backwards across the sand, facing Paco, who watched her, arms out by his sides like a body builder, phone in his fist. Even from several metres away, she could see the veins on his forearms. When there was enough distance between them, she turned and started running back up the beach, as fast as she could. Her shins felt as brittle as sticks; the powdery sand clung to each foot as if colluding with Paco, making her stumble and lurch. When she finally reached the steps and took purchase on firm ground, she gasped with relief. Not looking back, she scrambled up the steps and burst onto the promenade, startling a flock of little birds and Rose, her elderly neighbour, who was sitting on a bench. As she ran to the safety of the square, she heard someone calling her name, but she didn't look back.

Anna sat on the edge of the fountain and closed her eyes until she felt able to speak. Then she took out her phone and dialled the police. When the call was answered, she started explaining, in Spanish, how she had reason to believe that Paco was involved in people smuggling, and had had a hand in the deaths of at least two men.

'What is your name?' the policeman asked, when she finally paused for breath.

'No names,' she said, like the Africans earlier.

'Do you have any evidence for these claims?'

'Testimony from one of the men on the boat,' she replied. 'But he won't give his name.'

'So there is no evidence?'

'Why not call this a tip-off, then,' Anna snapped. '*You* find the evidence. You're the police.'

'One moment,' the policeman said, and put her on hold.

Anna found herself pacing around the fountain, absently scanning the square. In Sweeney's window, a new sign had been put up, advertising a puce-faced, superannuated lounge singer. There was the ice-cream parlour. The You Chic gift shop. The little coin-operated train. Her bar . . .

She stopped. Something white – a piece of paper? – was stuck on the window. A passing woman paused to look at it, before shaking her head and moving on.

Still on hold, Anna walked towards the bar. When she got close enough to read the large sticker, she hung up, still staring at it.

Closed by Order of the Commissioner of Health and Mental Hygiene. Imminent Risk of Injury to Health.

A mistake. It must be. Anna tried to unpeel it from the glass with her fingernails, but it was designed to stay put, like a car-clamping notice. She couldn't even fray the edges. Over on her front door, she found another notice. It was a letter addressed to her, densely typed and written in officialese. But for all the text, it didn't give much more information than the sticker, merely stating that serious concerns had been raised about the standard of hygiene and presence of pests in the bar, and she was ordered to close for investigation until further notice.

Anna's first instinct was a flush of guilt: the same she felt when a security alarm went off on leaving a shop, despite having stolen nothing. Then, indignation. The bar wasn't spotless, true, but – *pests*? Surely, if any of her regulars had spied a mouse dropping, they'd have mentioned it to her, not called the authorities?

Unless it was untrue. A malicious complaint from someone with a grudge.

Sweeney. Of course. Anna thought of his triumphant looks of late. She marched over to his bar. He wasn't yet open, so she banged on the window until he came to the door, holding a packet of Yorkshire pudding mix.

'Is this really what you do for kicks?' she said, holding up the letter.

Confusion clouded his face and he craned forward to see what she was brandishing.

'You've gone too far,' said Anna, weakly, but turned away as she spoke. She walked back to her bar and wrenched down the shutters to conceal the sticker, making no attempt to cushion the bang of the metal against the tiled terrace, and went upstairs to the apartment.

Locking the door, she curled herself into the Frank chair and closed her eyes. Much as she'd like to believe that the hygiene notice was Sweeney's latest swipe, or the consequence of one of the urbanization lot mistaking a shrivelled grape in the corner for a mouse dropping, she knew that wasn't true. She thought of her last encounter with Simón. That sniff. He'd known about her drink-driving conviction: he must have links to authority. Could he have asked them to close her down? Did he have that sort of power?

Smothering her nerves was a profound, paralysing tiredness. It reminded her how she'd felt during a brief period when she was going out with a cokehead from the RCA. She'd disliked the stuff but was in love with him and so she'd done it too, night after night. In the early morning, she'd lie in bed, beside him but utterly alone, unable to move, her body a shell but her mind fluttering wretchedly, latching onto anxiety after anxiety, breeding them.

She'd done all she could, hadn't she? Confronted Paco. Confronted Simón. Talked to the Africans. Talked to the police. Hopefully, they were down on the beach right now. Inspecting the boat. Picking holes in his alibi. Seizing his phone. Breaking down his defences with expert questioning.

The church clock struck midday. Faint, genial chatter floated up from the square as worshippers emerged. It should have been a relaxing sound, but only served to exacerbate her unease. Did the whole town know about Paco's other trade? She had the sense that not just Paco and Simón, but Marea itself had surrounded her, backing her into this apartment, onto this chair. She rubbed her cheek against the coarse linen, the pattern of pink and blue hills and exotic birds and foliage, as if it could transport her into its fantastical land.

She fell asleep for a few minutes, and jerked awake. The square was quiet again; the light had shifted. She looked around her, at the apartment. Unlovely to begin with, the place was now moribund. Clothes had been hanging on the dryer for a week; empty milk cartons and cheese wrappers left on the side; piles of papers, important ones mixed with flyers and old receipts, banked against the skirting board. In the corners of the room, the dust was so thick it looked as if a rabbit had moulted.

If she died today, this is how she would be remembered. She inspected the room through the eyes of an official: the policeman with the deceptively cherubic face, maybe, or the woman who had answered the phone about Paco. They would give a cursory look around and think this is how she lived. This is who she was. Photos would be taken. This scene would be the last word on her.

Galvanized by disgust, she sprang up and fetched some bin liners from the kitchen. Moving through the rooms, clearing surfaces, she felt strangely weightless, and her head emptied of thoughts beyond her immediate task. Despite her meagre existence in the apartment, she'd accumulated a lot of clutter. By the time she reached the bedroom she'd filled several bin bags, and she wasn't even half finished. Out of her clothes, she spared two tops, two skirts, two jumpers, two pairs of jeans: everything else was out. She thought of the Senegalese men clambering onto the boat, all their possessions reduced to one double-wrapped plastic bag, and felt a compulsion to strip all the fat from her life.

Maybe she should take the stuff to the car boot sale. The prospect of joining those desperate Brits at their trestle tables was hardly appealing, but she might have to.

She tackled the pile of papers by the skirting board. Bills, flyers, receipts, old newspapers. And, underneath, a thick cardboard folder, bearing the label: *Sun, Smiles and Sangria: Our Spanish Adventure!*

Karen's manuscript. Anna put it aside, to remember to give it back.

After the declutter came the cleaning and then,

several hours later, the flat was spotless. She had even removed and scoured the fridge compartments. Plump bin bags lined the living room wall and the clashing scents of cleaning products hung in the air. The newly washed windows were lit with late-afternoon sun. The whole place looked anonymous and denuded, as if she was at the end of a week's self-catering holiday and was now waiting for the taxi to the airport.

Except, this *was* her home. Or the nearest thing to it, right now.

She retreated back to the Frank chair. It was only six. She couldn't go to bed. She couldn't open the bar. She was unwilling – unable – to leave the apartment, to re-enter the world of Paco and Simón. A box set? No; she felt incapable of suspension of disbelief. She had the desire for a chat; a breezy, inconsequential, distracting chat with someone who wouldn't ask questions, whose life was as messed-up as hers. Her father. She dialled Derek's number, but he didn't pick up, and hadn't activated his voicemail.

Replacing her phone on the table, Anna saw Karen's folder. She reached over and pulled out the manuscript. It was bound, with a copyright symbol prominent on the title page. She turned to the first page, titled *New Beginnings!*

> So why did we choose to move to Marea, I hear you ask? Well, our dearest friends from Hampshire, Janice and Ray, had a place out there and we had enjoyed many happy holidays with them relaxing in the sun. When Tommy and I were considering

early retirement, we thought it would be nice to move out to the same place. Unfortunately, Ray had a heart attack not long after our decision, but by then our minds were made up. Marea it was!

She turned to another page.

The Spanish love their fiestas! Part of the reason we came to Spain was to absorb the local colour and traditions, so we always make an effort to attend these events when possible. Fireworks explode in the sky, locals wear bright outfits and curious masks. In some towns, fiestas can be messy affairs – I hear there is a place where they throw tomatoes at each other!! There is also a festival where three men dress as the Three Kings, and one of them wears dark face paint to look black. Such a gesture might raise eyebrows in the UK, but as a visitor one must respect cultural differences. It is a tradition, and they do not mean any harm. In any case, the Spanish certainly like to live life to the full!

Anna's eyes drooped. As she replaced the manuscript, she noticed a loose piece of paper in the folder. It was a handwritten letter, and it was addressed to her.

Dear Anna,

I know about you and Tommy, and I have done so for a while now. I am not a fool. I am also realistic. It hurts my heart to know he is meeting you, but I know you can offer him things I cannot, and I do not blame him for wanting those things. Men are simple creatures who like familiarity in some areas and novelty in others, and you are not the first to catch his eye. However, I have my limits. I believe your affair started sometime in May, and I've noticed that you two are meeting more frequently than ever. So I want to say this. God willing, we will soon be moving back to the UK. By and large, Spain has been a happy chapter in our lives and we do not have many afternoons left here. I do not want to be spending them alone whilst you are being intimate with my husband. So I ask you now to find yourself a new taxi service, give me back my husband, and we shall say no more about it.

The letter was dated the end of December; just before Karen gave Anna the manuscript. As she reread it in astonishment, Anna wondered what she would have felt if she had received it then, at the time she was supposed to. Would it have sent her into a tailspin? Would she have given up Tommy immediately, or would she have clung on, relishing the drama? Now, with everything that had happened since New Year's Eve – everything that had happened that *day* – the letter seemed an artefact from a different era. She couldn't help but feel a certain respect for Karen, and her discreet chutzpah. What must she have been thinking these past weeks? She'd have presumed Anna had seen the letter; yet Anna had continued texting Tommy, asking for lifts. Did Karen think that Anna was wilfully ignoring her plea to leave him alone?

Questions for another day. Tiredness clubbed her,

and she laid her head on the chair arm, letting the letter drop to the floor.

She woke, ravenous. After her ruthless clear-out of the apartment, there was nothing perishable in her kitchen, so she went out to the shop. As she stepped onto the street and closed the front door behind her, she noticed a pensioner standing in front of the bar, staring at its facade. He turned his gaze to her, before lowering his eyes and shuffling off.

Even before she had turned to see what the man had been looking at, Anna sensed there was something different about the bar's facade. A new colour, so strong it seemed to tint the air around it.

She turned to see that the shutters on the front of the bar were now covered with graffiti. Or rather, just one piece of graffiti, a single vast word – but the background had been painted in too, so that not one inch of the shutter remained in its original grey metal state. The background was a psychedelic swirl of purples and pinks – almost exactly matching the bougainvillea nearby, presumably by accident – and the curly script typeface in yellow, so large that Anna had to step back to read it.

PUTA

The girlish prettiness of the colours and design, and the effort that had gone into the job, were so at odds with the word that at first Anna thought she must have read it wrong. But no, there was no doubt. *PUTA*.

Even the most linguistically challenged expats knew that meant 'whore'. But the word had another meaning too, Anna remembered. During her months spent around builders, waiting in masonry yards and garages and cash and carries, she'd heard it used as a general swear word, similar to 'fuck'.

So, read one way, this graffiti was a direct attack on her. A public shaming. Read the other, it was just a swear word, an elaborately rendered howl of frustration from some disenfranchised youth, and her bar's shutters merely a convenient canvas.

Judging by the looks she was getting from British passers-by, it was clear which way they were reading it.

Anna had a sudden image of Karen, out here at 2am with her spray cans, a bandana around her mouth. The Banksy of Marea. If only.

Acid corroded her stomach. She wanted to move but felt bolted to the spot, as if she were in the stocks. Passers-by continued to stare at the graffiti and then at her, some stopping in their tracks; the less brazen glancing and moving on.

After a few moments Anna forced herself to move and started to walk across the square, past the mini-mart, and into the town.

As she knocked on Jaime's door, it occurred to her that he might still be in bed – what did he have to get up for on a Monday morning? But he answered himself, fully dressed. His hair was scraped back in a bun and when he saw her he instinctively pulled it out of its band. Despite her agitation she registered a flicker of pleasure at the gesture.

Anna explained that someone had graffitied her bar and Jaime agreed to come and take a look, to see if he recognized the style. They walked up the street together, close, in silence.

'Found any good bits of scrap, recently?' she said, finally.

'Yeah, a great big copper pipe, as thick as this,' he replied, holding out his forearm. 'Served any nice customers recently?'

'No,' she replied. 'Not one. And this isn't going to help.'

They had just entered the square. Anna pointed towards the bar. Even from this distance, the graffiti was startling. Jaime whistled.

'Wow.'

'Quite a lot of effort, no?' said Anna, as they walked towards the shutters, cautiously, as if they were ablaze. 'Do you recognize the style?'

Jaime shook his head.

'No one I know would do something like this, just for the hell of it. They couldn't afford it. Look at how much paint they've used. That would cost, like, one hundred euros.'

They stood and looked at it together for a few moments. Anna stared without blinking, so her eyes filmed and the colours and shapes abstracted into a harmless decoration.

'Why would someone do this?' Jaime said, as if to himself.

His voice had a circumspect tone she hadn't heard before, and she felt touched that he was taking the matter seriously. Should she tell him about Paco and Simón? No. It was too long and complicated and she didn't feel confident of his reaction. At the moment, his concern was pure and straightforward: that's what she needed.

She shrugged.

'Maybe I poured someone a flat beer,' she said, lightly.

Jaime didn't smile, but looked down at her, with his long, half-handsome face. Then, to her surprise, he reached over and stroked her hair, just once, before promising to make some enquiries.

Anna watched Jaime lope across the square and resisted the urge to run after him and clutch his arm. She wanted to go with him, back to that safe little apartment of his, to stroke his cat and have his doe-eyed mother cook her green beans for dinner. As he disappeared down a side street, the calming effects of his presence dissipated, and she felt jangly and unnerved again. The square looked as placid and innocent as ever in the weak sunshine; and then there were the shutters, as jarring as a streak of blood on a white towel.

Anna knew she should paint over the graffiti, but she didn't have one hundred euros. Not nearly. She thought of the finca, that pyramid of casually discarded, half-empty paint pots piled up in the shed.

For now, she'd just raise the shutters. The health warning sticker on the window would blare out, but right now that seemed the lesser of the two slurs. She crouched to grab the handles and then . . .

'*Olé!*' called someone, from behind her. It was a familiar British voice, but she couldn't place it. Still crouching, she turned to see her father stepping up onto the terrace, hands waggling in a showman's pose.

'My girl!'

11

Anna stared at her father. He was wearing pale, too-tight jeans, with a heavy-buckled belt. He had worn that belt for as long as she could remember, and prided himself on never having to get another hole punched in it. He was carrying a plastic shopping bag and looked extremely pleased with himself.

'Aaah!' he said, laughing, as he saw her expression. 'I knew that Timmy was a good bloke. Said he'd keep the secret.'

Anna stood up from where she was crouched, wincing with the effort, as slowly as if she was under instruction from a yoga teacher. By the time she was fully upright, she had seen the whole story, and understood exactly how her father had come to be standing here on her terrace. It was so dreadfully obvious; a fait accompli. She heard herself gushing to him about the wonders of Spain; his questions about the cost of living. This was the price for her posturing! He had run out of people to look after him in the UK; his charm had worn too thin to get another wife and Marie-Anne's tolerance of him was limited. Now he had only his divorce payoff from Elsbeth to see him out. Not enough to buy anywhere proper in the UK, but enough for a knock-down place in Spain, where he could baste in the sun, under the care of his dear daughter. The one who liked a drink and wasn't uptight – a chip off the old block. Who was single and still had time for him. He hadn't been the best father, he'd admit that, but now they could make up for lost time, eh?

'You're wearing flip-flops,' she said to him now.

'I bought them myself. From a shop!' he said, proudly. He held out the bag and, through the thin plastic, she saw the shape of his pointy shoes. 'Haven't worn them since Bali. Rubbing to buggery.'

He opened his arms and she stepped forward to hug him. It had been a long time since they'd had physical contact. He smelled, faintly, of meat – she imagined him having a sausage sandwich for breakfast. The slightness of his torso surprised her; he wasn't much bigger than her. They were of the same stock. Unexpectedly, she flooded with warmth. Here was her *father*. He meant her no harm.

'How did you get here?' she said.

Derek took this more literally than she intended.

'I walked from my apartment,' he said, proudly. 'Timmy told me where you lived.'

'Tommy,' said Anna.

Derek explained that he found Marea Moves on the Internet, and a nice woman called Karen had arranged his trip. He was being put up in an empty holiday let on the urbanization, and later that day he was going to be shown a few places he might be interested in buying. Tommy and Karen's own villa sounded like it might be just the ticket.

'So, this is where you've been hiding,' he said, looking around the square. He had planted his hands on his hips in an oddly self-conscious gesture, and it occurred to Anna that he might be feeling nervous.

'Hardly hiding,' she said, weakly.

'That the name of your bar, then?' he said, pointing at the *PUTA*. 'Doesn't that mean . . . ?'

Without answering, Anna noisily hauled up the shutters.

'Would you like a drink?' she said, turning back to him.

Derek pursed his lips in mock-consideration.

'Oooh, go on then.'

He followed her into the bar.

'So I was on the plane and had a cup of tea and was talking to the girl, the stewardess,' he said, as Anna ducked behind the counter, 'and after a minute she said, "Sir – did you pre-purchase a chat-up voucher? Otherwise I'm going to have to stop you there."'

Anna smiled obliging as she stood up with the wine.

'And since when did seats not recline back?' he said.

'You sound like you haven't been on a plane for fifteen years,' she said. 'I thought you and Elsbeth were always zooming around Europe.'

'She liked going on trains,' he said. 'Thought it was romantic. Her idea of romance – being woken up by a Belgian bloke demanding our passports.'

Anna laughed. She was surprised at how pleased

she was to see him. And Derek, always happy when women responded well to him, was pleased too.

'You look very pretty,' he said, as he leaned over the counter to reach the glasses above the bar, in a nimble, practised move. 'Something's different about you.'

They brought two chairs out onto the terrace. The wine was corked – it tasted disgusting, actually – but Derek didn't seem to notice, or care. Reclining in his white plastic chair, glass in hand, squinting up at the sun, he was in his element. From her upright position of power, Anna appraised him. His oiled grey curls glistened in the sun and his ankles were shiny and swollen. The veins on his hands were like blue pencils. He had rolled his T-shirt up to his shoulders, like a superannuated heart-throb.

'So, what the hell are you doing here?' she said. 'You're not really coming to join the migrants?'

'Well, you did,' he said.

'Yes, but . . . that was different.'

'You said I should come!'

'No I didn't!' she said, frowning. 'When did I say that?'

'Everyone wants to come here, don't they,' he continued. '"Living the dream".' He did quotation marks with his fingers around the last phrase.

The gesture irritated Anna.

'Actually, lots of people are desperate to leave,' she said, tartly. 'They're spending their weekends sitting in car parks trying to sell their old sandwich toasters.'

'All the better for a good deal!' he said. 'That bloke Tommy reckons I can get a place for a song.'

If his eyes weren't already closed Anna was sure he'd have winked. Her affection for him started to wane.

'It's not like Bali,' she said.

'Ah, Bali,' he sighed. 'The beaches there were like talcum powder.'

'I know,' she said. 'I went there too. Remember?'

He frowned.

'When?'

'In my year off,' she said. 'You said you'd come and meet me there. Show me your old stamping ground.'

'Did I?'

'Yes, you did.'

'Oh, good.'

'I mean,' she continued, lightly, 'yes, you did say that. But you didn't come.'

'Oh, God,' he said, glancing across at her. 'Forgive me. I was such a hopeless bastard.' He closed his eyes again.

'Hey, guess who I saw at the airport?' he continued. 'Ruby.'

'Which one was she?'

'Little redhead. Actress. Liked evaporated milk in her tea. Teddies on the bed.'

Anna did remember Ruby: she was the first of Derek's girlfriends Anna had met after he'd decided to reacquaint himself with his daughters. Anna and Marie-Anne had been in their late teens. Derek had had a tiny part in a play at a pub in Fulham, and suggested that the two of them come to see it and then he'd take them out for dinner afterwards. Ruby was his fellow actress, narrow-faced and superior, and as Anna and Marie-Anne hung around awkwardly in the dressing room before the performance, she'd suggested that the girls tidy the make-up on her dressing table whilst she and Derek were on stage. Quite an extraordinary ask, in retrospect. But Anna had done as Ruby asked, carefully wiping the powder pots and arranging the brushes in height order. Marie-Anne had refused to participate, watching Anna, arms crossed and mouth open, a caricature of disgust.

'Why would you do that?' she'd asked Anna.

Now, the memory bothered her. Why had Derek allowed Ruby to boss her around like that? And why *had* she gone along with it?

'She was looking so old,' Derek continued. 'Hair like a horse's mane. Practically had a stoop.'

'I'm sure she was thinking exactly the same about you,' said Anna.

'I'm sure she was,' said Derek, amiably.

There was a pause. Anna moved to take another sip of the corked wine, but put it aside.

'So, what would you do out here?' she said. 'You know there are no jobs?'

Derek shrugged.

'I don't need much to live on, if a place is cheap. Got my piddly pension,' he said. And then, as if the thought had just occurred to him, he opened his eyes and looked over at her. 'Hey, maybe I could help you run this place? Be a little team?'

'Better late than never, eh,' she said. She didn't bother to keep the edge out of her voice this time.

He frowned. Derek could stand being gently ribbed, but actual criticism was a different matter. She hadn't said anything even vaguely challenging to him for years.

To her surprise, Derek didn't go on the defensive.

'Your mum wouldn't let me see you,' he said, looking over to her. 'I was desperate to see you, babe. The hours I spent on the phone to Janet, begging her. She always said you were busy doing some class.'

He squeezed his eyes shut, as if in pain.

'It's the great sadness of my life.'

Anna knew this wasn't true. But, looking across at her father reclining in his chair – wrinkles radiating from his screwed-up eyes, his small bones just like hers, swollen ankles exposed – she was hit by a wave of empathy. We're all a mess, we all make mistakes, she thought. Maybe it wouldn't be so bad having him here. She might barely know him but he was her father, and he probably did love her, in his way. That counted for something, didn't it?

'Dad,' she said, finally. 'I know it looks really nice here. And it is, in some ways. But there are some people around who I've annoyed. They don't want me to be here. They're after me.'

'Oo-er,' said Derek, and he half-rose from his chair, as if to scarper. Settling back in his seat, he smiled to himself at the joke, and then leaned forward to refill his glass with the off wine. Anna waited but there was no follow-up. The conversation ended at his gag.

She looked away from him, out into the square, punctured and embarrassed. She thought of Jaime's reaction when he saw the graffiti; his promise to find out who'd done it. Some twenty-five-year-old kid she barely knew showed her more concern than her own father. Yet here he was now, expecting her to look after him!

'Dad, if you come here, you're on your own,' she said, stiff with anger. Before Derek could respond, a sing-song voice floated towards them.

'*Hola, chica!*'

Derek glanced over Anna's shoulder, and she saw his face brighten. She turned to see Mattie, wearing her white tennis dress and that vast black sun hat. Derek pulled himself upright.

'*Hola!*' called Derek, with such warmth that Anna wondered whether the two had met before, earlier that morning.

But no.

'Who's that?' he asked Anna.

She didn't reply, distracted by a figure trailing behind Mattie, hobbling on crutches. As the person drew nearer, she realized it was Richard. His right leg was in a brace.

'Poor, poor Richard!' said Mattie, breathily, as she stepped up onto the terrace. 'Those mopeds should be banned!'

Derek had already stood up to offer Mattie his chair.

'I quite agree,' he said, as if they were in the middle of a conversation. 'I once fell off one on Westminster Bridge at forty miles an hour. Still got the dent, see.'

He lowered his head towards Mattie and pointed at

a spot on his skull. She giggled and leaned forward to touch it. Anna turned back towards Richard, who was awkwardly catching up. One leg of his suit had been cut to accommodate the brace. His hair was flat and unstyled, and she could see he was trying not to show pain, to act insouciant.

'What happened?' she asked in a low voice, as she moved alongside him.

'Oh, stupid accident,' he said, not looking at her. He seemed a lot older, his face bare and blanched. 'Got in the way of a scooter.'

'It wasn't an accident, though, was it,' said Anna, even lower. Richard glanced at her, but said nothing,

'Was it to do with the DVDs?' she went on. 'Supplying them to the men on the beach? What happened?'

After a pause, he started to speak, so quietly that Anna had to lean close to hear. He described how he had been walking home the previous night when he was attacked just outside the gates of the urbanization. A man approached him from behind and warned him to keep out of his business, then produced a length of metal piping and smashed him on the shin.

Unbidden, Anna had a flashback to Jaime, that morning. *'A great big copper pipe!'*

'Was he Spanish? African?' she said.

'He spoke Spanish,' said Richard. 'He may have been black. I don't know. It was dark.'

'But surely you could tell if he was a native Spanish speaker.'

'I don't know,' he hissed, irritated.

They had reached the terrace. Richard rearranged

his expression for the benefit of Mattie and Derek and said, brightly, 'Got here eventually!'

Derek jumped up, making a song and dance about getting a chair and settling him in, before proprietorially going into the bar and fetching another bottle of white and two more glasses. Sitting back down, Derek continued to focus on Mattie, but Richard strained forward to join in, smile fixed on his face, laughing at half-heard jokes.

Anna stood a few feet away, staring blankly into the square as she digested what Richard had said. She felt as if she was jumping to conclusions, but what were they? She had no idea.

Then, there was a presence at her side and she turned to see a policeman. She hadn't noticed him approach; he must have come up the side street behind the bar.

'This bar has been closed,' he said, indicating the sticker on the window. 'You can not have customers.'

'This is a private gathering,' said Anna, 'I'm not open for business.'

'There can be no use of the terrace. And you must pull down your shutters.'

He stood there, rubbing one hand with the other, his eyes invisible behind his dark glasses. Anna drew breath to protest, but then realized this meant she could get rid of the trio on her terrace.

'I've got to close up now,' she called out to them.

'Awww,' said Derek, pulling a cartoon sad face. He didn't ask why.

'You can go over there.' Anna pointed across to Sweeney's.

Derek helped Richard to his crutches before taking Mattie's arm and continuing their conversation as they shuffled over.

The policeman still stood there, waiting. Now the others had gone, Anna felt mulish again, and gracelessly took in the chairs and glasses, thumping them down inside, before locking the bar door and wrenching down the shutters. *PUTA*. The word seemed even bigger and more lurid, as if the curly letters were a fast-growing plant. She looked at the policeman, but if he had a reaction, she couldn't see it through his glasses. He turned and walked away, across the square into town.

Anna shivered. Over at Sweeney's terrace, Derek, Mattie and Richard were ensconced, a new bottle on the table. None of them glanced over at her. Maybe they thought she was going to join them. She felt exposed and hyper-vigilant, her gaze flitting between the entrances to the square. Each one had its dangers. From the south, the sea side, she kept expecting to see Paco. He would slowly emerge from the beach steps: first that shiny bald head, then the triangle of hard brown flesh of his neck and shoulders. His hands balled with anger as he walked towards her. From the north, the town side, the police. And then Simón, who could appear from anywhere.

'Psst!'

It was an insistent hiss, the sort you might give a cat who was tearing into your rubbish bag. Anna panned around the square, past the stiff, ambling couples, the waiting birds, the ice-cream shop, until she reached the woman in the You Chic shop doorway.

'Psst!' the woman said again, and she beckoned to Anna with one quick hand gesture. Then she stepped back into the shop.

She must want to complain about the graffiti. Resigned, Anna walked over and ducked inside. She'd never actually been in the shop before. It was low-lit, as if the shelves held ancient, priceless artefacts rather than glass paperweights and beaded lizards, novelty fans and shell ornaments. Flammable, child-sized flamenco dresses hung from the wall and brushed Anna's cheek as she passed. She saw that the objects were all dusted and regimented, and furniture polish hung in the air.

The woman was standing in the gloom at the back, stationed behind the till, as if Anna was coming in to buy a pair of miniature castanets. Despite seeing the woman every day, Anna had never been this close to her, and she was younger than Anna thought: in her early thirties, maybe, with drawn features and a growing-out perm. A feather duster lay on the counter.

'Look, I'm so sorry about the graffiti,' Anna said, in Spanish.

'I saw him,' said the woman in reply.

'Who?'

'Shouting at you the other day,' the woman said.

She spoke furtively, as if they might be overheard, even back here.

'You mean Mr Ruiz?' Anna said, finally understanding. 'The little guy?'

'*Sí, sí,* Mr Ruiz,' said the woman. 'And now, the painting.'

'What?' said Anna. 'You saw him do it? The graffiti?'

The woman waved her hands at this preposterous thought.

'You think he asked someone else to do it?' said Anna.

The woman nodded.

'And I saw you,' she continued. 'And the English man. In the Plaza del Sol.'

Anna stared at her. The woman looked pained, but kept her gaze. Anna had the feeling she had steeled herself for this encounter, and was determined to see it through.

'I live there,' the woman said. 'And I saw you.'

'You live there?' said Anna, very confused now. 'But it's empty.'

'It's not empty,' said the woman.

Anna had an image of the woman squatting in one of those half-built buildings, watching silently from the window cavity at Tommy and Anna in the car. Observing in the same furtive, unsmiling way that she peered out from under her display of T-shirts.

'You mean you live there permanently?' said Anna. 'But there's no electricity or water or anything, is there?'

The woman shook her head impatiently. This

wasn't what she wanted to talk about. She leaned in close to Anna.

'The man, Mr Ruiz, he also goes there,' the woman said, head bent, almost at a whisper. 'He goes there, after work. Around six. You should go there then, too.'

'Wait, what?' said Anna, reaching out to take her arm. 'I don't understand. Why are you telling me this?'

The woman hesitated and frowned, as if trying to decide how much to say.

'He is *hipócrita*.'

And with that, she picked up the feather duster and turned away back to her shelves.

As Anna emerged from the shop, she glanced up at the church clock. Just past four. Crossing over to Sweeney's, she told Derek that she was nipping up to the cash and carry.

'Don't worry, you stay here,' she added, superfluously.

He smiled up at her, beatific, his arm draped over the back of Mattie's chair.

'Your man Tommy is going to show me his villa later,' he said. 'I'll give you a call.'

Anna got into her car and drove away. She was too early for the Plaza del Sol and so stopped at the edge of town, went into a random empty restaurant and ordered an omelette and chips. She sat at the window. Opposite the restaurant was a Spanish tapas bar, and she watched as the owner came out and sprinkled a handful of toothpick wrappers and crumpled serviettes on the pavement around his outdoor tables. An old trick, she knew, to give the impression of popularity.

Her food arrived and as she ate she went over the bizarre conversation in the shop. The woman had seen Tommy and Anna's secret trysts in the car. She'd seen Simón shouting at Anna in the square. And she suspected Simón of ordering the *PUTA* on Anna's shutters. Did she think that Anna and Simón were together, and Anna was betraying Simón with Tommy, and Simón had found out?

It was the only theory that made any sense; all this time, the woman had been watching her and constructing a false narrative. But in that case, why would she send Anna to the Plaza del Sol?

'He is a hypocrite,' the woman had said. So Simón must be up to no good, too.

After paying up, Anna still had some time to kill. She wandered aimlessly around a nearby minimart, finding herself faintly repulsed by the amount of booze on offer; half of the aisles were devoted to bottles. Finally, it was almost six, and Anna got back in the car and drove towards the Plaza del Sol. She passed the steep road that led to the urbanization where Tommy and Karen lived. Derek was going up there later, to check out their villa. He might even be up there now. She still hadn't fully absorbed the fact that he was here.

The coast road was relatively busy. The driver in front of Anna activated their windscreen washers instead of indicating: the classic tic of the freshly arrived tourist in an unfamiliar hire car. Anna overtook the spray with the impatience of a local, only to be trapped behind a vast, fume-belching truck loaded with a jumble of red and green plastic chemical containers. She'd been stuck in a similar position many times before, but now Anna looked at the truck properly and saw there were workers in the back, too. Several pairs of arms were visible, gripping the side for balance.

Eventually the truck turned off, heading towards an unseen greenhouse. A minute later, Anna reached the entrance to the Plaza del Sol.

As she passed by the rust-stained girder and entered the colonnade of immature trees leading to the complex, it occurred to Anna that she didn't know where she should be heading; she hadn't asked where the woman lived. But – of course – if the woman had also seen Tommy and Anna from her window, Simón must be using the same spot.

Anna parked up on an unobtrusive side street near the cul de sac, and sat in the car for a moment before slowly getting out and easing the door shut. She'd never been here alone before. The complex appeared as eerily barren as ever, its aborted buildings and shuttered shops as dead as its neat squares of brown lawn and dry water features.

But today, after her conversation with the gift shop woman, the place had a silent charge. As she walked slowly up and down the pavement, she felt observed by ghosts living in the shadows of the buildings. Before, those dark window cavities had seemed to her like open mouths, caught in rictus alarm at their eternal incompletion. Now, they felt like eyes.

She fought the urge to jump back into her car and flee. To distract herself she thought about Jaime, about how he helped to build the Plaza del Sol in its glory days, when the place was alive and full of potential. Before they knew they were building a ghost city. She imagined him here, surrounded by cranes – 'the national bird of Spain'. Lowering breeze blocks into place. Switching on the cement mixer. Carrying one end of a clutch of reinforcing steel rods, the same ones that now protruded guilelessly from the tops of the least-finished buildings, reminding Anna of Sherbet Fountains. Cracking jokes with his work mates and then, on his lunch break, getting out his phone, making plans to meet his friends at the bar that evening to spend those 500-euro notes.

She stopped pacing and sat down, leaning her back against the wall. To her right she had a direct view of the parking spot but there was still no sign of Simón, nor anyone else. The ever-present wind sent bits of rubbish skittering down the pavement.

Opposite her was a wall of graffiti: a riot of tags and phrases and drawings, twisted and colourful, in striking contrast to the plain concrete and straight lines around them. Some of the writing was well-designed, uniform. Once, in her old life, she'd known hundreds of typefaces by sight.

Her gaze rested on one particular word, *Ojo!* This, she knew, meant, 'watch out!' But it was more the design that caught her eye. The pink and red script was almost identical to that used on her shutters.

It was 6.10pm. The wind had died down and the streets were deafeningly quiet. It seemed impossible that anyone else would turn up, that this silence would ever be broken. Ten more minutes, she thought, and she'd leave.

Then – the sound of a car. A low, expensive purr – but in those bald boulevards, it was impossible to be discreet. Anna pressed herself against the wall as a BMW pulled up, one bay along from where she and Tommy used to park. From her crouched position, she could see into the back windscreen.

The driver's window was open and she saw a short, tanned forearm, with a prominent watch, resting on the side of the car. He turned to speak to his passenger and she saw Simón's profile in the gap between the seats. Even from a distance she could see that he was smiling. Properly smiling, his teeth exposed – not the means-to-an-end stretch of lips displayed when she first met him, when he wanted the finca. He laughed at something, and then leaned forward towards his passenger. They kissed.

The passenger was tall; it looked awkward. Anna squinted and looked harder, curiosity struggling with her embarrassment at the prurience. It was hard to make out any identifying features. Then, the two profiles broke off from kissing and the passenger's own arm emerged from the window.

A black, male arm.

The passenger lifted his hand to touch Simón's

face. The men laughed again and then started to kiss properly, and Anna's discomfort became unbearable. She got clumsily to her feet and ran down the street, away from the BMW, sticking close to the wall, although there was no real need. She drove out of the complex, adding her own tyre marks to those of the joyriders.

Safely out on the coast road she slowed, her head a whirr. The fact that Simón was gay was not that shocking in itself. Yes, he had mentioned a family – and there had been that picture of him and his wife online – but since when did that ever stop anyone? But – was the man Simón's employee? Was he spending his days bent double in the greenhouses, sodden with sweat, earning a couple of euros an hour, before sneaking off in his boss's air-conditioned car for a secret rendezvous? She thought of Mattie telling her that the men would do anything for a work permit.

But the pair had looked relaxed and happy. In the admittedly short time Anna had watched them, she hadn't seen any sign of coercion.

Maybe the man wasn't an employee. Maybe he and Simón had met in a club in Barcelona, or on a website. Maybe he was a high-powered businessman, too. Was she being racist, assuming that the black man was poor, and that a relationship between a white man and a black one had to be exploitative?

One thing Anna felt sure of, though, was the fact that Simón would not want this affair to be public knowledge.

A horn blast made her jump, and the car behind aggressively overtook. Anna realized she was driving far too slowly and pulled into the verge. It was then, when the engine was off and she was still, that she realized how she could use this information. The woman in the gift shop thought she was helping Anna by revealing Simón's secret, and she was – just not in the way she thought.

Anna took out her phone and composed a text.

I saw you with that man, she began – and the phrase triggered the memory of her altercation with Simón in front of the bar. *I know what you did with that man,* she'd told him, meaning the body on the rocks. And Simón had stiffened, briefly, before relaxing again as she explained.

She continued – *in the Plaza del Sol, and I have photographs. Unless you leave my property immediately, I'll send them to your wife and display them all around town.*

She moved to 'send', then hesitated. The image came to her of Simón with his boyfriend in the car. Hearing his phone buzz, untangling himself to check it. Then his smile dropping as he stared incredulously at the message. For a second, her desire not to spoil the moment overcame her loathing of Simón. She thought of the fact he didn't spray pesticide in the faces of his workers; what counted as being a good employer out here. Then, she thought of his lies to get the finca. His arrogance about gouging out her land without permission. And what *if* the man didn't want to be in his car? She pressed 'send'.

Her system flooded with nauseating adrenaline. To distract herself, she called Derek. He told her he was up at Tommy and Karen's. They'd just shown him around the villa, and now Karen was making some tapas.

'Where are you?' said Derek. 'Come over!'

'OK,' she said. 'Are you sure they won't mind?'

'You don't mind if my dear daughter drops by, do you, Karen?' she heard Derek say.

Anna couldn't hear Karen's reply, and imagined her tight smile of assent.

'Yes, come over!' said Derek, back on the phone. 'What number is this, mate?' Anna heard Tommy say something.

Anna said she'd see him in a minute and hung up. As she started the engine and headed towards the urbanization, she felt pretty sure that this was a terrible idea, but she couldn't bear to spend another moment alone.

12

She swung the car up the steep road to the urbanization, passing under an arch with peeling paint and a security booth that Tommy had told her was now permanently unmanned, acting like a decoy owl. A colonnade brought her to a fan of roads lined with identical white and yellow villas; beyond them was a cluster of taller apartment buildings in the same colours. A sign directed her towards the pool, the doctor's, the minimart, the cafe bar. Coming straight from the Plaza del Sol was surreal, like seeing a skeleton fleshed out. This is what the other place was supposed to be: only by an accident of birth had this one survived.

But it was only just surviving. Anna had been here only once before, at the beginning of her time in Marea. Then, her visit was soundtracked by lawnmowers and leaf blowers and sprinklers, the shrieks of children in unseen pools. 'Thriving' was perhaps too strong a word – many of the properties were holiday rentals and lying empty, with overgrown gardens and dusty ironwork – but there had been life here. Now, there was no noise from children, no trikes in the yards. This place had the air of a retirement village that, unlike the caravan park, wasn't replacing its residents when they died.

That first visit, Anna had come for dinner at a couple's villa – this was back in the day when such invitations were routine, and she accepted them. Before she started seeing Tommy. Her memories of that evening were of an unseasoned chicken chasseur and gossip about the power-drunk 'urb' president, who had introduced a load of new rules. Cars had to be moved every week so that the road underneath them could be cleaned, and those not complying would be towed at the owner's expense. Children were forbidden to splash in the communal pool. All awnings had to be white, and no washing could be visible from the street.

Listening to this, Anna had wondered why they'd all chosen such a restrictive, homogenous existence. She hadn't understood then that, despite their bitching, equality was the attraction here. Life was on a level playing field; the old class system was irrelevant. No one at the dinner had seemed particularly interested in what Anna had done before moving to Marea. During a break in the conversation, she'd found herself offering up an unsolicited autobiography: something she'd never done before, not even with Michael's maddeningly indifferent friends. She name-dropped that she'd gone to the RCA, had once (briefly) worked for Saatchi and Saatchi, and that she'd lived in central London. People listened politely enough, but didn't follow up anything she said, and soon she fell silent.

Later, as they 'sat soft', the female half of the couple had said to Anna, quite kindly, 'In Marea, it's about what you are, not what you were.'

That couple were long gone, back to the UK. Anna couldn't even think of their names. She remembered their villa, though, and how it looked identical to 108, where she'd now arrived. High gates; two storeys; white stucco trimmed with mustard yellow; doors and windows lined with black security grilles. In the front yard, Tommy's Rover was parked next to an impeccably clean built-in barbecue.

She gave herself just a moment to speculate on what must be going through Karen and Tommy's respective heads at the prospect of her arrival, before ringing the bell. Tommy answered, almost instantly.

'Well, hello!' he said, loud and avuncular. He was wearing a chunky blue V-neck jumper she didn't recognize – a hand-knitted job. He gave her the briefest air kiss before turning back inside.

'Hungry?' he said brightly, over his shoulder. 'Karen made tapas.'

He led her through into the kitchen diner, a room familiar to Anna from photos on the website. Large and well-equipped and neutrally decorated, it was one of the property's selling points. Karen and Derek were sitting at the table. Derek leaped to his feet and gave her a kiss. Karen was in pastels. She smiled in Anna's direction, but didn't get up.

'Would you like something, Anna?' she said evenly. 'There should be enough.'

'Oh no, no,' said Anna. 'Thank you.' She sat down

at the table, wondering again what the hell she was doing here. On the table was a small leg of *jamón*, clamped for carving on a stand, alongside a gingham-lined basket of bread and a platter of machine-sliced cheese. There were napkins and crystal glasses and place mats and coasters, even though the glass table meant there was no need for them. Soft classical music played from a little square stereo on the sideboard.

A *jamón* leg like that must have cost thirty euros and no one really used those stands here – they were the equivalent of a tureen or a decanter, brought out only at special occasions. Derek might not realize that, but Anna did, and Tommy and Karen knew she did. Anna felt embarrassed at the sight of it, to be witnessing such a naked attempt to impress. God, don't go to all this effort for him! she wanted to say. The bottle of rosé at his elbow is more than enough.

Karen was looking at Anna, her fingers rubbing the stem of her glass, and what she was thinking could only have been clearer if she had stood on her chair and bellowed it: was Anna here to scupper their sale, or to claim her husband?

'What a gorgeous house,' said Anna, attempting to allay one of those fears. 'Stunning.'

Karen blinked. Derek poured Anna a glass, oblivious to the tension around the table.

'I'm hearing about the wonders of golf,' said Derek. 'Your man here has been quite lyrical.'

'And I was just telling your father how we're going to put in a borehole, to water the grass,' said Karen.

'Tommy found someone who says he might be able to help. He's putting it to the urb committee next week.'

Tommy was standing by the fridge, and ostentatiously avoided Anna's glance. So that's why he had been so keen to get Simón's number: not to help her out, but to pick Simón's brains on irrigation methods. She looked at the bulky, sandy-haired bloke fiddling with the ice-cube machine, and saw a total stranger. A novelty magnet on the fridge beside him read: *Golf diet: Stay on Greens.*

'You know, I've never been here before,' she heard herself saying. 'I'd love a little tour.'

'I'll show you,' said Tommy quickly, moving towards the door. Anna didn't dare look at Karen.

He led her into the hallway.

'Guest bathroom,' he said, gesturing towards an open door. Anna peered in obediently, playing the role she had given herself. Corner bath. Vanity unit. A line of flowery tiles. She followed him into the living room. Two neat leather sofas, three angled cushions apiece. A bookshelf with a short row of Patrick O'Brian novels. A bowl of golf balls sat on the glass coffee table. Anna remembered hearing about Tommy and Karen's evening strolls around the course, collecting stray balls to sell back to the club. The walls were dominated by several large studio portraits of their daughter and grandchildren. Dozens more framed family photos lined the cabinets.

'Lovely,' said Anna. Tommy, stiff with nerves, said nothing, and led her through the folding doors and onto the back terrace, out of range of the kitchen.

They stood a few feet apart, looking out over the golf course. The light was waning, the sky peachy. A lone couple in their whites were picking their way around the dun-coloured grass.

'Looks pretty bad,' she said, gesturing at the course. 'I can see why you'd want a borehole. How much is Simón charging you for it?'

Tommy looked at her for a moment. His cheek twitched.

'I did ask him about your place, of course,' he said, 'but he said there was nothing he could do. I tried, darling, I really did. And then I thought, whilst I was there . . .'

Anna watched him bluster, his desperation not to be seen as a bad guy making him stumble over his words.

'There's no need for this,' she said, cutting him off, and then turned back inside, not waiting for him. Back in the kitchen, Derek and Karen still sat at the table, Derek upending the last dribble of wine into Karen's glass, even though it sat untouched.

'How exciting to be an actor,' Karen was saying politely, hands clasped on her lap. Anna guessed Derek had been telling her his Diana Rigg story.

'Listen, I've got to go,' said Anna. 'Dad, call me later.'

She turned to Karen.

'It's a lovely house, Karen. And, by the way, I read your memoir. Every single page. I think it's really good. Really informative.'

Karen looked up at her, and Anna saw the tension seep out of her face. Then she nodded and gave Anna a hint of a smile.

Anna drove back and parked beside the bar. It was coming up to 9pm, but the square was deserted. No one sitting on Sweeney's terrace. No teenagers at the fountain. Even the little permanent flashing train outside the gift shop was powered off. Where was everybody? The thought of the text she had sent Simón resurfaced, and she felt her ribcage contract with apprehension. How had he reacted? Was he up there now, smashing up the finca? Was he waiting for her in one of those silent side streets, his engine turned off?

Her throat felt as if she had swallowed clots of dry turf from Tommy's golf course; she was in dire need of a drink. Lifting the bar's shutters halfway, she unlocked the front door and went inside. The room smelled funky, like blocked drains. Maybe the Environmental people were right to close her.

She tried the light switch but it just clicked fruitlessly. The dishwasher and TV lights were off, too. A fuse must have gone. Or had she been cut off?

Never mind; there was enough light to see the bottles. She needed something to soothe her throat. She grabbed three mixer bottles of juice from the shelf, prised the lids off and downed them one after the other, the warm, thick, over-sweetened liquid providing some relief. She was just reaching down for another when there was a hideous jarring noise and the room started to darken.

It took her a moment to realize what was happening: someone was wrenching down the shutters from the outside. It was all over in a couple of seconds. Looking across to the door, mouth fallen open, she glimpsed a pair of dark trousers before the shutter smashed against the ground and the room was plunged into blackness.

'No!' Anna shouted, and then, panic rising, 'No, no, no, no!'

She lurched for the wall, knocking over a stool. When her hand touched the stucco surface she groped around for the light switch, gasping with relief when she found it: in that moment of terror she'd already forgotten it didn't work. She pressed it again and again, desperately, and then stood still for a moment, squeezing her eyes shut as she willed herself to calm down. After several deep breaths, she placed both hands on the wall and started to inch her way towards the door. Her fingertips ran over obstacles – the dartboard; the small, greasy shades of the useless wall lamps – until she touched glass and, finally, the open door. Steadying herself on the door frame with one hand, she reached out with the other to find the shutter. Then, when she had her bearings, she bent down and grasped the bottom of the shutter with both hands. There was no indoor handle, and only her fingertips could get a weak purchase on the ridge of corrugated metal. She tried to heave it up, but it didn't budge.

After a few more attempts she started hammering on the shutters with her fists.

The metal reverberated as she hit it again and again, its ridges bruising her knuckles. Then, after what felt like hours, she heard a sound from the other side and froze, fists in the air.

'What's that?' said the voice.

'Open the shutter, I'm locked in!' Anna shouted.

After a lengthy pause the shutter started to rise laboriously, accompanied by heavy sighs. As they inched up, the darkness started to leaven, and looking down Anna could see first a bunch of spindly, furry legs, and then some stout, pale human ones clad in walking sandals. Then, some narrow doggy faces, dark eyes gleaming, tongues hanging out. Then a green corduroy skirt and an oversized blouson-type jacket, arms straining with the effort of lifting the metal.

'The whole square could hear you,' said Caz, panting, as she and Anna came face to face.

'Someone locked me in,' said Anna. Shock had made her as short of breath as Caz.

'Why would they do that?'

'Did you see anyone?' said Anna.

Caz pursed her lips.

'Maybe it fell down by mistake,' she said. 'Or one of the local lads did it for fun. They get bored, you know. My bin was stolen last week.'

Anna nodded distractedly, looking over Caz's shoulder, eyes darting around the dark square as if the culprit might still be lurking. A boy had appeared, doing skateboard tricks against the side of the fountain. The sound jarred.

Then, the delayed shock of being trapped in the bar, those few minutes of panic in the blackness, overwhelmed her. Faced with Caz's doughy lack of sympathy, she sat down heavily on the terrace.

One of the dogs started to lick her fingers, and she turned her palm to its raspy tongue. She felt movement at her side, and looked up to see that Caz had sat down beside her, bare legs planted apart.

'Are you having a breakdown?' Caz said.

Her voice was flat: she could as well be asking Anna for a straw for her red wine and lemonade.

Anna looked over at Caz. Her head was slightly bowed, and Anna saw the parting in her hennaed hair was sunburnt, like a scar. The dogs had settled on the ground around her, one with its paws primly crossed.

'With what happened before,' Caz added, still not looking at her. 'That *iss*-ue.'

Anna stared at Caz, astonished, as it came to her that on one afternoon, a long time ago, she'd sat in this woman's front room, fumbling to open the box of tissues on the coffee table, and told her things she'd told no one else.

'You were called Caroline,' said Anna, more to herself. 'And your hair's different.'

Caz shrugged *yes*.

'You never said so,' said Anna. 'All this year.'

'The guidelines state that when therapist and client meet outside the therapy room, the therapist takes their cue from the client,' said Caz, atonally.

Anna couldn't think of what to say. The two women sat together in silence, looking out over the square. A paper napkin escaped from the ice-cream parlour skirted about in the breeze. Caz's hands rested in her lap, and Anna noticed the little gold watch on her wrist, at odds with her eccentric hiking attire. She wondered whether Caz had bought it for herself, or if it was a gift from an old lover – a relic from a happier, richer life pre-Marea, as were the laughter lines like receding ripples across her cheeks. Anna scratched the coat of the mangy little dog, digging her nails under its fur.

'He came to see me too,' said Caz, after a pause.

Anna looked up.

'What?'

'Your boyfriend. He came to see me too.'

Surely not. Michael and Caz inhabited different universes. The thought of them sharing the same room was impossible to imagine, let alone Michael confiding in Caz; paying for her advice.

'When?' asked Anna.

'About the same time as you did.'

'Before or after me?'

'Before,' said Caz. 'And after. He came . . .' She paused, to count in her head. 'Four times.'

Anna stared blankly at the ground in front of her, sifting through memories. When had he gone? When he said he was going to the neighbouring valley to catch the light? When he said he needed to drive to the big town to find a particular kind of size 4 paintbrush, and that he might be some time? When he professed a new interest in football, and went down to the bar by himself to watch it? Was he really going to sit in Caz's apartment, on that hard vinyl two-seater sofa, in front of that thoughtlessly shrink-wrapped box of tissues?

'What did he say?' she asked.

Caz remained silent, as if bound by the ethics of the profession she was entirely unqualified for.

'Oh, come on,' wheedled Anna, nudging her with sudden familiarity.

'He was upset,' said Caz, finally.

Anna realized that she was gripping her own wrist so tight that white bones glowed under her bruised knuckles.

'He didn't actually talk about you that much,' continued Caz. Anna snorted. Even from a distance, Michael could still squelch her. 'It was more about him. His issues.'

'And what were his issues?' asked Anna, conscious of how pathetic it was that she had to ask.

'Relationships and that,' said Caz, who appeared to have overcome her reluctance to divulge. 'He said they always have a good start and then it all goes pear-shaped. He starts hating the woman for the same reasons he liked them at first. No – contempt was the word he used. He says it happens every time. With you it lasted longer than with the others.'

Anna stared at a discarded fag butt squashed between the tiles. So she, Anna, could have been anyone. Maybe the pattern was repeating itself right now, and, a thousand miles away, Satine was staring numbly at the exposed brick wall of her Hackney flat, trying to work out what she'd done wrong.

'He said he found it unbearable to be perpetually exposed to another person,' Caz said, eyes narrowed in recall. 'And that love couldn't survive that.'

It did sound like the kind of thing Michael would say.

'He couldn't sit down, kept pacing around the room,' Caz continued. 'The man downstairs complained about the noise.'

'Did he say anything about me?' asked Anna.

Caz glanced at her, with what could have been pity.

'He said you were nice,' she said. 'He said it wasn't really about you.'

They sat in silence for a bit longer. Anna wondered why she didn't feel more affected by the news.

'Caz, why did you become a counsellor?' said Anna, finally. 'I mean, you're not qualified or anything, are you?'

'No,' admitted Caz. 'But I had a . . .'

She stopped, and, for the first time since Anna met her, she seemed vulnerable and hesitant. '. . . An issue when I was young. Your age. Talking to someone helped me.'

'I'm sorry about that,' said Anna. 'Your bad time, I mean.'

'Why are you apologizing?' said Caz. 'It wasn't your fault.'

'It's . . . just a turn of phrase,' said Anna, suddenly tired. 'I'm sympathetic, I mean.'

Caz stood up. Their moment of unlikely connection was clearly over. The dogs scrabbled to their feet. Still sitting, Anna looked up at her. Caz's forehead creased as she looked around the square.

'This place,' she said, as if to herself. 'I should have gone to Dubai.'

She set off across the square, the dogs clustered around her. Anna watched her until she disappeared down a side road. Whilst they'd been talking, the boy on the skateboard had gone, and the square was again deserted. The streetlamps barely punctured the darkness and, on the sea side, the palm trees cast unfamiliar man-sized shadows. Beyond them, in the blackness, the murmur of the waves sounded alien and sinister.

Her phone buzzed, making her jump. She opened her texts with an unsteady finger.

Not Simón. It was her dad.

Agreed on Tommy villa! Got good deal. And staying another 3 days. Karen changed flight for me. Viva Espana!!

Anna scrambled to her feet and ran up to her denuded apartment. Locked in, she climbed into the Frank chair and bunched up tight. For once, she saw the point of the grilles on the window. Breathing deeply, she tried to clear her mind, in what she hoped was an approximation of meditation. After some minutes, when her heartbeat had slowed to a tenable rate, she relaxed her grip on her knees. She tried to absorb the events of the last few days but her mind buckled under the weight. Instead, in her head a parade of men encircled her – Paco, Simón, Derek, Tommy, Michael, Jaime, Almamy, moving faster and faster, until it was as if she was at the centre of a zoetrope.

Her slide into unconsciousness was interrupted by a buzz from her mobile, and with a start she was upright, all her senses alive again.

She didn't recognize the number. The text read: *We are gone.*

Then, as she was staring at it, another came through, from the same number.

We are sorry.

13

She woke just after noon, with a start, and within three minutes was out of the apartment, car keys in hand. As she leaned down to unlock the car, she glanced back at the bar and stopped, her key in the door. The *PUTA* had been obscured by a neat, long rectangle of black paint, large enough to censor the word but not quite covering the tops and bottoms of the letters.

Anna looked at it for a moment and then smiled, before getting in. Jaime; it must be. She detected his hand in the judicious use of expensive paint, and his attempt to make the cover-up as neat as possible. As she edged through town, she thought of him, a near stranger out there in the darkness, spray can in hand, bandana over his mouth, and decided that this was the nicest thing anyone had done for her. Never mind Michael's sheaves of delicate little love notes, sketched over rye toast and espresso: they were no match for a blob of industrial black paint, hurriedly applied in the dead of night.

Stopped at the traffic lights, Anna took out her phone to text Jaime her thanks before realizing she didn't have his number. She drove on, up the coast road and through the greenhouses. Lorries were parked outside, having delivered the day's workers. As ever, the opaque walls of the structures gave little hint as to the industry within. Now, though, she noticed the little shacks and lean-tos dotted around, limpeted onto the greenhouses. Mickey lived somewhere like that. And it struck Anna that if Almamy and the others had abandoned the finca, they would be spending tonight in one, too.

'We are sorry,' the text had read. As she drove past the greenhouses, Anna shouted in their direction: 'It's not your fault!'

She wound up the mountain road; passing through the tree tunnel, the light in the car dimmed and goosebumps sprang up on her bare arms. She opened her window to breathe in the fresh scent. Approaching the finca, she passed the unmarked entrances to properties; dogs alerted their never-seen owners to her presence. These people knew her comings and goings with the precision of a factory timesheet but, apart from Alfonso, she'd never fraternized with them, and now she never would. They didn't care who they shared their mountain with, as long as there was no intrusion on their lives.

But hadn't they felt the same, she and Michael, when they'd first arrived? To live up here was to choose to become an island; to clearly signal that all you needed was some land, a view and each other. If you craved community, you'd live down in the urbanization. But how could any relationship survive such isolation? She thought about what Caz had told her, about how her familiarity bred Michael's contempt. If she hadn't been so unhealthily in thrall to him, she might have felt the same way. These unknown couples, who lived down those unmarked turnings – maybe they secretly hated each other too. Or perhaps they just had realistic expectations. Never mind nourishing each other's souls – perhaps it was enough if your partner replenished the wood shed without having to be asked.

At the finca, she parked up on the verge. During the drive, she'd done a fair job of keeping trepidation at bay but now she had turned off the engine, it flooded her system, threatened to undo her. She forced herself out of the car, and walked over to the gate. It was ajar, the padlock on the ground. The sign with her phone number on it was propped back up; that must have been how Almamy had got her number – if, indeed, the text had come from him.

The space beyond the gate was empty. No BMW. No pick-up truck.

She stood still for a few moments, listening to her breathing. It was the only sound around. The light was pellucid today, and, above the house, the horseshoe mountain looked particularly arid and inhospitable. The sky was vast, cloudless and empty; no eagles circled on the currents. The weeds in the front garden had turned yellow; the rosemary bush looked even larger. She imagined it encompassing the house, like the innermost circle of a maze.

The house shutters were closed. Anna started down the path, hearing the gravel crunch underfoot. The washing line now sagged empty. As she crossed the path down to the terrace, she looked towards the almond grove, and stopped at the sight. The trees, so impoverished a week ago, were now topped with a froth of white and pink blossom. It was a magical spectacle that lasted only a brief few weeks at the start of spring, and made the valley look as if it had been scattered with candy floss. The traffic on the road increased markedly during the blossom season, due to day-trippers from the coast. After a couple of weeks the flowers would be replaced by green shoots, signalling the start of spring.

On the drive up, Anna had wondered whether she should go and look at the borehole. Now, gazing over the blossom, she decided she wouldn't. A delicate curtain had been drawn over the sight.

She carried on, to the front door, and stopped. Dead quiet. She turned the key in the lock, pushed it open and turned on the light. The sitting room was intact. The furniture had even been moved back to an approximation of its original position. She stepped into the centre of the room. The men's belongings had all gone but the place hadn't been cleaned; the floor was gritty, surfaces unwiped, rugs pulled roughly back into place. Bits of paper and empty packaging sat on the table and shelves. It was, she thought, in the same condition you would leave a hotel room in if you were madly late for your plane.

A valve opened, and tension seeped from her. She looked at her possessions: the books, the lamps, the paintings in their artful little clusters on the walls;

the pile of Michael's sketches on the sideboard, now as curled and discoloured as autumn leaves. At last, she had got her house back. But the place had lost its potency. Glancing around the room, she felt as unmoved as she had when looking at Michael's photo on his website. She saw it through a stranger's eyes: it was no longer her home, just a house full of objects. The table was just a table, rather than the delivery device for that fateful letter; the sofas were just sofas. Either her tenants, or time, had leached the place of its associations.

She walked into her bedroom. The duvet had been pulled roughly over the bed and its innards poked out of the bottom of the cover, which hadn't been closed properly. She couldn't blame her departed guest for not bothering; the cover was fastened with tiny, affected mother of pearl buttons rather than poppers.

In the bathroom, an empty bottle of shower gel lay in the bottom of the bath. The grouting between the smashed tiles was grimy. The bin hadn't been emptied; inside were scrunched-up tissues and the intimate detritus of five strangers. Someone had, finally, thrown away that long-dead bunch of wild flowers on the sill.

There was something different about the room, and it took her a few seconds to work out what. There was more white than usual. Then, she saw: the square mahogany lavatory seat had gone. She stared at the bare bowl.

She heard a vehicle crunching across the gravel of the driveway. She snapped out of her reverie and shot through the sitting room and out of the open door like a rabbit, towards the almond grove. She'd almost reached the protection of its blossom clouds when she glanced over her shoulder and saw it was only Alfonso. He was standing beside his truck, looking in her direction.

She came to a halt, turned and trudged back towards the house. Alfonso watched her, bemused, but she didn't have the energy to make up an excuse as to why she had fled.

'*Hola*,' he said, as she reached him. He had grown fatter since she'd last seen him; braces were holding up his stained work trousers.

'When did they go?' asked Anna, out of breath. 'The men who were here?'

'Last night,' he said. 'Made some noise about it.'

'And Mr Ruiz?' she said.

Alfonso nodded. 'Gone, gone.'

He changed the subject, to a motorbike race that had passed through the mountains the previous weekend, terrifying his animals. Anna listened politely for a few minutes before excusing herself, saying she had to get back to town.

'You coming back to live here now?' he asked.

'No,' said Anna. 'I don't think so.'

She surprised him – and herself – by giving him a kiss on the cheek.

When he had gone, she locked up the house, leaving the key under a plant pot, and left the gate open. Then, before getting back into the car, she picked up the For Sale sign by the gate and flung it into the bushes.

As she drove away, she thought again about the lavatory seat. Almamy's 'We are sorry' text – perhaps it referred to them taking it. Where would it end up? Being flogged in the flea market for a couple of euros, or in an antiques shop in Madrid, hugely marked up, to be bought by another couple like her and Michael?

Or maybe they didn't take it to sell, but to use. She remembered what Mickey had said, about how cruddy the toilets at the greenhouses were; how luxuries such as paper and soap appeared only when the owners knew the inspectors from the supermarkets were coming, and were removed immediately after. The men knew what they were going back to when they left the finca; maybe the seat was an impulse steal, something they could bring back with them that would make a material difference to their everyday lives. Or perhaps it was a joke, to make their roommates laugh: a souvenir of their weird luxury hiatus.

She carried on down the mountain road. Alfonso turning up like that had relieved her of the opportunity to say goodbye to the finca ceremoniously. But what would she have done? Appreciate the valley one last time, savouring the restless shift of light and cloud, the way that strata on the rocks twenty kilometres away would in a blink be obscured – everything shrouded but the finca's own land, making it feel like a castle in the clouds? Gaze poignantly at the wisteria planted by the front door, still in its infancy, that she'd now never see smothering the front of the house? Run her fingers over the finca's shelves and mantelpieces, caressing their nicks and dings, the evidence of her ancestors that had made the wood so valuable to her?

Or should she have walked through the almond grove, brushing past the blossom, and stood in front of the borehole, unceremoniously gouged out of her land? Then followed its piping snaking over the hill to the vast plastic ocean it was feeding, which was in turn the lifeblood for thousands of men who risked death to work in the greenhouses, growing the lettuce to fill those puffed-up bags in Tesco Metro.

A memory came to her, of that awful weekend with Farah and Kurt, just before Michael left. They'd gone for a walk, Michael had ignored her, and Kurt had lectured them about the ingenious ancient irrigation system in the mountains established by the Moors from North Africa. 'Of course, water is an Islamic symbol of paradise,' he'd said.

As she mindlessly manoeuvred down the hairpin bends, Anna thought about her past, present and future homes – the finca, the bar, London – and what she would do now. By the time she hit the coast road, she knew.

'OK, I've got a plan,' she said.

She was circling the fountain in the square, on the phone to Derek. He was having lunch with Mattie; from his description she guessed they were at the fancy restaurant in town, the one with the terrace where she and Michael had eaten bisque to celebrate buying the finca. Mattie must have suggested it. Anna admired her audacity. She imagined Derek looking down the menu, doing slow calculations in his head as he recalled the euro exchange rate he'd seen at the airport, and trying not to wince.

'You've got one hundred and fifty thousand pounds – that's right, isn't it?' Anna continued on the phone, buzzing. 'Forget Tommy's villa; you can have the bar *and* the finca. You wanted a bargain – this is the deal of the century. Seriously. And no estate agent's fees or anything. And I'll go back to London with the money.'

She thought he might say, for form's sake at least, that he didn't want to live here without her; that spending time with his daughter was one of the attractions of coming to Spain. But he didn't.

Instead, he said, after a pause, 'Yeah, a hundred and fifty thousand pounds. That's what the estate agent said.'

'What?' said Anna. 'Your studio in Manchester – you haven't actually sold it?'

'No, not yet. Wait a sec.' She heard him say to the waiter, 'So it's still twitching on the plate' before he came back onto the line.

'Yeah, so . . .'

'Why did you come over here to look at properties if you haven't sold your place?' she interrupted. 'Karen and Tommy think you have the money.'

'Well, I've put the flat up for sale,' he said, huffily. 'The bloke reckons it'll be snapped up.'

'Dad,' said Anna, actually stamping a foot. 'You do realize that property isn't selling anywhere? You know what's going on? And even if you were lucky enough to get an offer, these things take months and months to go through?'

'Yes, course. I'm not thick.' He gave a dry little laugh; trying to keep his tone light in front of Mattie.

After a strained pause, Anna said, 'Look, never mind. I'll leave you to your lunch.'

She hung up and pressed the heels of her hands against her eyes, trying to block out the disappointment. She felt like a mole scrabbling towards the surface after months underground, and discovering the earth had been paved over. She sat, slumped, as if she were already a pensioner, fit to join those pottering about around her, lending the place its slow metabolism.

She spotted Rose amongst them, and raised her hand in greeting. Rose made her way over and sat beside Anna at the fountain, giving a small *oof* of relief as the weight came off her feet.

Rose was always nicely turned out but especially so today, with an old-fashioned ruby brooch on her camel coat, and hair newly set.

'Where's David?' said Anna. 'Inside making you lunch, I hope.'

Rose glanced at her.

'Oh no, my dear,' she said, with kindness. 'He's gone.'

For a brief, stupid moment Anna thought Rose meant her husband had bailed out, followed the exodus of Brits back to the UK. But then she realized.

'God,' she said. 'I'm so sorry.'

Anna held Rose's arm and listened to her explain

that David had had a fatal stroke in bed a fortnight earlier, and Rose had woken up next to his body. He was cremated shortly after. They'd both agreed they wouldn't have a burial or be repatriated: mortuary costs were so expensive here.

'I wish I'd known,' said Anna.

'Oh, I didn't want to bother you,' said Rose. 'Every time I saw you, you looked so busy, rushing around. Besides, it was going to happen soon enough. To one of us. I just wish it had been me.'

There wasn't a hint of self-pity in her tone. Anna looked at her, smiling faintly as she looked out towards the promenade. She'd been in Rose and David's apartment; it was as uninspiring and sparsely furnished as hers. Not a place to live alone.

'What are you going to do now? Will you go back?' said Anna.

'Oh, no,' Rose said, surprised. 'I'll stay here.'

'Why?' said Anna, bluntly.

'It's nice to have the sun.'

And the way she said it, it made sense.

They sat in silence, feeling the warmth on their faces, hearing the gentle circulation of people around them. Then, Anna noticed something and stiffened. A figure crossing the square at a different tempo, striding with a sense of purpose and shouldering a large sack as if it weighed nothing.

Paco. Anna shrank behind Rose, nose grazing the fabric of her coat. He was coming down the west side of the square; she couldn't bolt to her apartment without crossing his path. After half a minute, she glanced up.

He was nearly at the other end of the square. From the back, the red writing on the sack was visible: *arroz.* She watched as he reached the promenade and disappeared down the beach steps.

Arroz. Rice, for his paella. He was still in business. The police hadn't arrested him after her tip-off. Or, if they had, it hadn't gone any further.

'I have to go,' said Anna to Rose. 'Please do let me know if you need any help,' she added, uselessly.

She gave Rose an awkward hug and set off in the direction of the police station, her anger at the sight of Paco rising to full boil within a few strides. But, before she reached the end of the square, she had slowed down. She couldn't go to the police and demand to know why they hadn't arrested Paco. Her tip-off had been anonymous, and a strong instinct told her that she should not unmask herself as his accuser. The man had power: that was clear. She thought of Richard being beaten up after trying to muscle in on the beach hawkers. The attacks on her bar. The sense that anyone who interfered with the Africans was warned off.

And then she thought of something else, something she had never properly investigated, and changed her course to Jaime's flat.

He was in his car, looking at something on his phone. Anna tapped softly on the window. He jumped, and opened the door to speak to her. Instead, she went round to the passenger seat and got in beside him.

'Hey, so I've been asking around about the graffiti but no luck,' he said. 'No one knows who did it. But it looks a bit better now, no?'

'*Muchas gracias*,' she said. 'It was the nicest thing anyone has ever done for me.'

Jaime smiled quizzically, and Anna remembered that some thoughts were best left unspoken.

'All good with you?' she said, awkward now. She looked away from his face, down towards his shoeless feet. His socks were bright white, and shone in the dim footwell.

'Pretty good,' he said.

'Listen, there's something I wanted to ask,' she said. 'What do you know about Paco?'

'How do you mean?'

'I mean – you told me that everyone knew Paco. Do you know what he does? Apart from sell paella?'

'You mean the Internet cafe?' said Jaime.

'Not that,' said Anna. 'I mean . . .' She didn't want to mention the migrants, not yet. 'Does he have a connection to Simón Ruiz? Does he work for him? Or the other way round?'

'Well, yeah, they're connected,' said Jaime, after a pause. 'Paco's his uncle.'

El Tio. Boss. Uncle.

Astonished, Anna looked at him. 'That true?'

Jaime nodded.

'Why do you ask?'

Anna looked away from his long, unknowable face.

An air freshener in the shape of pine tree dangled from the rear-view mirror. He hadn't divulged whether Simón and Paco had a business relationship. Was that intentional? Was it an open secret in town that Paco helped to supply the men who worked in Simón's greenhouses?

She opened her mouth to ask and then stopped. She was afraid of the answer: that he might shrug insouciantly, or get defensive and close ranks. He might tell her that she was an outsider with no idea of how things were done here. That the men were necessary for the economy, and did work no Spanish were prepared to do. The Africans wanted to be here; Paco got them across; Simón gave them work. What was wrong with that? And if he said any of those things then she would think differently of him, and what was clear-cut would be muddied.

So, instead, she said, 'Listen, Jaime, I'm going home. To the UK.'

His face shifted.

'Not because of some fucking graffiti?'

'No, not because of that. Other things. I just need to go back. But, um, thank you for your help, and – everything.'

She felt suddenly bashful.

'When are you going?'

'I'm not sure yet. Soon.' The question deflated her, reminding her of the practicalities. 'I have to work out what to do with the bar, and now my bloody dad has turned up and wants to live here.'

'If he wants to live here, can't he buy it off you?' said Jaime.

'Tried that,' she said. 'He doesn't actually have any money.'

'Maybe you should just swap,' said Jaime. 'You want to be there, he wants to be here.'

'Yeah,' said Anna, thoughtfully. Then, after a pause, she repeated herself, emphatic now. 'Yeah. Yes!'

She reached to open the passenger door. 'I have to go. But if I don't see you again then thanks, and good luck with it all. With the business and everything.'

'Yeah, well, you too.'

They hugged across the gear stick, and Anna got out. As she closed the car door, a thought came to her, and she stood still for a moment, digesting it. She smiled to herself, and then took her phone from her pocket and leaned down to the window.

'You know, I haven't got your number,' she said. 'Just in case.' He told her and she typed it in. Then she said goodbye and started walking, then running, down the street.

Walking through to the restaurant's terrace, Anna was irrationally pleased to see that even though the place was near empty, Derek and Mattie had not been seated at the prime corner table, but squeezed onto a small one near the back, next to an empty lobster tank that was still backlit and bubbling with oxygen, as if that would disguise the lack of actual crustacean.

Not that they looked as if they cared in the slightest. Mattie was indelicately attacking a pile of profiteroles, her long hair grazing the chocolate sauce, whilst Derek sucked on a pint and watched her admiringly. He was still wearing those jeans, Anna noticed, but now with the addition of socks under his loafers, presumably to conceal his alarming ankles from Mattie; like putting up a poster to hide a patch of damp.

Mattie began one of her voluble greetings and Anna smiled briskly in return. On the way over she'd planned to ask Derek for a word in private, but now realized that it might actually help her to do it in front of Mattie. She crouched down beside her father.

'Listen, Dad, I've got it,' she said. 'You give me the key to the Manchester flat. I'll give you the keys to the bar and the apartment. And that's it. We'll just swap.'

'Oh, I love it!' said Mattie. 'So neat!'

Derek looked sideways at Anna.

'She's right, Dad, it's completely neat,' said Anna. 'I don't know why we didn't think of it before.'

She could see Derek struggling to work out what was happening, and whether he was being offered a good deal, without saying anything that might harm his chances with Mattie.

'Look, come with me a sec,' Anna said. 'Excuse us, Mattie.'

Derek reluctantly stood up, taking his pint, and she led him out to the front of the restaurant. They stood beside one of the pair of cracked plaster lions that guarded the entrance.

'This is all a bit sudden,' he said.

'I know,' said Anna impatiently. 'But what do you think?'

'But what's your place valued at?' he said. 'The estate agent said I could get . . .'

'Never mind all that,' she said. 'This is the best way.'

'I need to think about this.'

'No, you don't,' she said, desperately. 'You want to be here, I want to be there. I get an apartment, you get an apartment. Plus a bar thrown in, too.'

He was uncharacteristically quiet. His skin was already the colour of tea, after only a few days here.

'You mentioned your house too, before . . .'

'No,' she said. 'Not the finca. The bar and the apartment. It's a good deal. A great deal.'

'Just do this for me,' she said. 'Please. We can sort out the legal stuff later.'

He glanced back at the restaurant, towards Mattie.

Anna looked at this ageing man who just happened to share her genes, who had given her so little, beyond her bone structure.

'Actually,' she said, quietly, 'it's the least you can do.'

She paused, and then found herself continuing, saying more than she had planned.

'It had an effect, you know. You not being there. Not being interested. It's happened now, and I'm a grown-up and I know we're all imperfect and make mistakes. I'm not trying to make you feel bad and beg for my forgiveness, but I want you to know that. That it had an effect.'

Derek met her eyes briefly before looking away, towards the traffic-clogged coast road.

'You know the Manchester flat is titchy, don't you?' he said, finally. 'One room, really.'

'I don't care.'

They stood there in silence, for a moment.

'And the bar? What do I do with that?'

'You'll work it out,' she said. 'It's easy. You'll like it. All the paperwork is there, under the bar. You can ask Sweeney if you need help. I'll leave the keys for you in the shop opposite.'

'You're going now?' he said, alarmed.

'Not right now. But soon,' she said. 'Tomorrow.'

She gave him a kiss on the cheek, both sides, and then once more, continental-style. He smelled of shower gel and lager.

'Come and visit, yeah?' He clutched her arm. 'Even though I'm a hopeless old fucker?'

'Yeah, course,' she said.

She smiled at him, for quite possibly the last time, and then he turned and went back in to Mattie.

Back at the apartment, Anna looked at the bulging bin bags slumped against the walls; the scoured bare surfaces. She was basically packed up already. On the way back from the restaurant, she had called Marie-Anne and asked her to book a one-way ticket back to Gatwick the following morning, on the earliest available flight.

'No, sorry. Not Gatwick. Manchester,' she corrected. She heard Marie-Anne draw breath to begin interrogating, and cut her off. 'I'll explain everything when I get back, promise. I'm in such a rush.'

The bag she was taking was small enough to carry on. As for the rest of the stuff in the flat: the rubbish she would chuck, but what about the clothes and clutter? She found a piece of paper and wrote a note.

Dad, here are a load of old clothes and things that might fetch something. Ask Mattie if she wants to sell them at the car boot sale.

All that remained was the Josef Frank chair: the only relic from her old life. She looked sentimentally at its riot of flowers and jewel-coloured fruit. It would be wasted on her dad. It was certainly not going to the car boot sale, to be prodded and joylessly haggled over.

She wrote another note.

This chair is for Rose, the elderly woman in the apartment next door. Could you take it over to her and say it's a gift from me?

She tucked the note in the side of the chair and sat down to wait.

Her alarm went off at 3am, but Anna didn't need it: she was already lying awake in the dark, alive with nerves. She sprang up, and in a few minutes was washed and dressed. The previous evening she'd prepared as much as she could for her departure; the only thing she'd forgotten was to strip the bed for Derek. Tearing off the sheets she hadn't slept in for weeks, she considered making it up for him, but no – she felt too on edge for such time-consuming niceties. She dumped a pile of clean bedding on the bare mattress. Then she grabbed her bag and turned off the lights. Audrey gazed down from the wall, hand on her chin; at last, here was some action to reward her patient fascination.

She stepped out onto the silent square. The clock on the church bell tower read 3.17am. The moon was nowhere to be seen, the darkness complete and uncompromising: only the fluorescent pink of the bougainvillea and the white marble fountain base glowed dimly. Leaving her bag beside the car, Anna crossed over to the You Chic shop and reached through the security grille to post her set of keys, with a note instructing the woman to give them to Derek.

She went back to the car and eased open the boot. She put in her bag, and took out a plastic can containing two and a half gallons of petrol, the one she'd kept there during the finca days, in case of emergencies. Finally, after checking her pockets to make sure she had everything she needed, she closed the boot as quietly as she could and set off towards the beach.

She knew her mission might fail. The boat might not be there. Maybe she'd be unlucky and Paco was at this moment dropping men off at the next bay, the one that wasn't overlooked by hotels, hitting them on their backs as they scurried up the sand to take shelter in the bushes until dawn. The boy had said that the crossings were only once a week at this time of year, so the odds were in her favour, but it was possible.

Reaching the steps, she looked down to the end of the beach. It was too dark to see whether the boat was there. She crept down the stairs, clutching the container with both arms, and started walking along the back of the beach towards where the boat should be. The sloshing of the petrol next to her chest sounded to her so loud, she felt the whole town must be able to hear it; it drowned out the waves lapping to her right.

As she neared the rocks, the shape of the boat started to emerge from the blackness, like a long-sunken ship being finally encountered in the murky depths. She felt a rush of exhilaration; simultaneously, the thought occurred to her that Paco might be sleeping in the boat. Although he wasn't the homeless bum he pretended to be – he probably had a nice three-bed villa somewhere in town, bought cheap off his nephew Simón – the old man seemed to have a genuine affinity with beach life. It wasn't impossible to imagine him occasionally bedding down in his boat, exhausted after a night ferrying.

Anna stopped a couple of metres away and listened for a few moments. There were no signs of life, but that didn't mean that Paco wasn't in there.

To get a proper look, she'd have to get closer and light a match. At the thought, the container felt unbearably heavy in her arms. She heard herself expelling air from her mouth, too loudly, and pressed her lips shut. Lighting a match was a risk. She imagined leaning in and scraping the match against the box; Paco's face suddenly illuminated, twisted in fury.

But she had no other option, except to wait here

until the clouds passed and the sun came up, and then it would be too late for anything.

She put the petrol can down on the sand and took two steps forward, until she felt the wooden ridges of the boat press against her thighs. She took the matches out of her pocket. Holding her hands above the void of the boat, she struck one, wincing at the rasping sound.

The match flared for a split-second before the flame shrank to a nub. Anna glimpsed a tarpaulin, neatly folded, at the bottom of the boat, and the empty paella dish. No Paco.

Her relief flared, as brief as the match flame. She must act fast. She reached back for the petrol container and fumbled with the safety lid, squeezing and twisting it hard in her fist, making several attempts before it came free. Then she lifted her arm and swung the contents of the container over the boat. She couldn't really see what she was doing, how much petrol was reaching its target and how much was getting lost on the sand, but she kept on swinging the container until it felt empty. Then she threw in the container too. The fierce petrol fumes filled her lungs and made her eyes water; she tried to breathe through her mouth.

She reached for the matches and paused, the tip of one pressed against the box. Before she could lose her nerve she struck it and flung the flame into the dark interior of the boat. And then she ran.

There was a surprisingly gentle *whoomp* behind her and she felt heat thump her back. She kept going, focusing only on her feet, refusing to let the sand slow her down, not letting herself turn around, feeling the air around her being sucked into the flames in her wake. It was only when she reached the beach steps that she allowed herself, finally, to turn and see what she had done.

The boat was in full blaze. The fire illuminated half of the beach, like an upstart rival to the sun as it prepared to emerge from beyond the horizon. She wondered whether the other captains of illegal boats, the other Pacos who silently ferried migrants across these waters, were seeing the flare, like a warning beacon.

Anna allowed herself only a moment to gaze at the sight before turning and scrambling up the stairs. At the square, she forced herself to slow down to a walk, in case anyone in the surrounding buildings was now awake and watching. She got in her car, started the engine with shaking hands and crawled through the deserted streets.

Past Jaime's flat. The caravan park. The police station. The road to Tommy's urbanization. Onto the coast road. The entrance to the Playa del Sol. As Marea fell away behind her, she felt a rush of triumph. Yes, Paco might get a new boat. And even if he didn't – if the blaze somehow aroused something buried deep in his conscience and he decided to jack in his nocturnal trade and concentrate solely on making paella for tourists – someone else might take his place as a night ferryman, for people thinking they were heading for a better life. But she'd done something; all she could. It would have an effect.

She reached the airport within fifteen minutes, and parked in the long-stay car park. As the engine cooled she sat motionless, in the perfect silence. Then she got out, leaving the keys in the glove compartment and the car unlocked.

The airport was nearly empty, run by a skeleton crew. Anna checked in and sat on a row of seats in the departure lounge. The man seated opposite was asleep, his head leaned back uncomfortably against the chair. From his sandals, yellow toenails and puce complexion he was almost certainly British. His arm was draped protectively over a large bag. Too large for carry on, Anna noticed. It occurred to her that maybe this was the mythical airport expat, the man she'd heard about, who, having lost his home in Spain, and burnt his bridges in Britain, had made his home at the airport, living in a permanent limbo.

Looking at him, Anna wondered whether he had made his peace with his situation; whether he had learned how to live somewhere between the life he wanted, and the one he had.

Her flight was called. She took out her phone; there were two texts to send before she left.

The first was to Tommy. *Hi, I've gone home. Derek is having my apartment. Sorry about the villa – but he wouldn't have been able to buy it, anyway. Good luck with it all. Anna.*

Then to Jaime. *I've left my car in the airport long stay car park. Registration ends 7XY. Door open, key in the glove box. It's for you, dismantle it as you wish! Anna.*

She and a handful of others, sleepless zombies, boarded the plane. Anna sat by the window, looking out at the mountains beyond the runway as the sky lightened behind them, and then realized she'd forgotten something. She took out her phone, and wrote again to Jaime.

Also, you remember how to get to my finca? Well, that's yours too. Live in it, strip it of materials, do whatever you want with it. Key under the paint pot to the right of the door. X PS thank you.

The flight took off. Anna watched Spain fall away below her as the plane rose into the tinted clouds. The greenhouses glinted like mosaic tiles under the sun. Someone in a row behind her unwrapped something meaty; the smell made her queasy and she closed her eyes. She was getting used to the nausea now.

Finally, there in her window seat, en route to a city famous for its rain, Anna could allow herself to consider what she had half-suspected for a fortnight, since that night with Jaime. What she really had to thank him for, and what he would never find out. If what her body was telling her was true, she was leaving Spain with something, after all; another life.

She leaned her cheek against the grainy moulded plastic of the plane wall, folded her hands over her stomach and smiled, as they were taken to their new home.

Acknowledgements

I am indescribably grateful to my editor, Francesca Main, my agent, Antony Topping, and my mother, Deborah Moggach. Without them, this book would not have been possible; or certainly not publishable.

I'm also indebted to the team at Picador – Paul Baggaley, Claire Gatzen, Saba Ahmed; Emma Bravo and Amy Lines; Susan Opie and Fraser Crichton; to everyone at Greene & Heaton, and to Matthew Bates at Sayle Screen.

Love and thanks to:

Tom Moggach, Larushka Ivan-Zadeh, Sathnam Sanghera, Susannah Price, Chris Atkins, Mark Williams, Alex O'Connell, Laura Yates, Flora Bathurst, Lucy Bathurst, Rebecca Rose, Vita Gottlieb, Caroline Maclean, Ben Markovits, Mark Watson, Daniel Pemberton, Leanne Shapton and Danielle Stevens. Also, to Malika and Drew McCosh for the wall in Istanbul; Sarah and Johnny Robinson for the view from Caserio del Mirador; and Joe Palmer, whom I met in Torremolinos and who knows how to live well. And, always, to my son Kit.